7/11

Advance Pra
Pride and Prejudice: H

"Thank God for Mitzi Szereto! Now the literary purists have someone new to go after with their pitchforks. Adding zombies to *Pride and Prejudice* was one thing, but SEX SEX SEX? It's sacrilege! Raunchy, hilarious, subversive sacrilege...which is the best kind, of course."

—Steve Hockensmith,
author of *Pride and Prejudice and Zombies: Dawn of the Dreadfuls*

"Mitzi Szereto's deliciously erotic retelling of *Pride and Prejudice* boldly turns Austen's classic on its pretty little head, knickers-side up. With keen wit (I laughed out loud many times), elegant prose, and a wicked imagination, Szereto exposes hidden lusts and truths, paying irreverent homage to Austen's romantic entanglements of yore while at the same time revealing a great deal about contemporary matters, sexual and otherwise."

—Janice Eidus, author of
The Last Jewish Virgin and *The War of the Rosens*

"Mitzi Szereto's *Pride and Prejudice: Hidden Lusts* is a luscious tribute to Jane Austen. This erotic version of the classic honors the wit, romance and sociological observation of the original. At the same time, it's as though Szereto knows the wicked thoughts that went through many of our minds went we first read *Pride and Prejudice*. Austen lovers will savor this hot Regency romance—perhaps even your aunt who worships the PBS versions. And those who don't love Austen can enjoy this entertaining, smart and sensual novel."

—Polly Frost, author of
Deep Inside: Extreme Erotic Fantasies and *Sex Scenes*

"Mitzi Szereto's adaptation of *Pride and Prejudice* is a mysterious and delightful uncovering of random sexual encounters among the landed gentry. You will have a ball!"

—Nick Belardes, author of
Random Obsessions and illustrator of *West of Here*

Pride and Prejudice

Pride and Prejudice

Hidden Lusts

Mitzi Szereto

CLEiS
PRESS

Published in the United States by Cleis Press, Inc., 2246 Sixth Street, Berkeley, California 94710.

Printed in the United States.
Cover design: Scott Idleman/Blink
Cover photograph: Christine Kessler
Text design: Frank Wiedemann
10 9 8 7 6 5 4 3 2 1

Trade paper ISBN: 978-1-57344-663-1
E-book ISBN: 978-1-57344-684-6

Library of Congress Cataloging-in-Publication Data

Szereto, Mitzi.
 Pride and prejudice : hidden lusts / Mitzi Szereto.
   p. cm.
 Summary: "In Pride and Prejudice: Hidden Lusts, Mr. Darcy has never been more devilish and the seemingly chaste Elizabeth never more turned on. The entire cast of characters from Austen's classic is here in this rewrite that goes all the way."-- Provided by publisher.
 ISBN 978-1-57344-663-1 (pbk.)
 1. Austen, Jane, 1775-1817--Parodies, imitations, etc. 2. Bennet, Elizabeth (Fictitious character)--Fiction. 3. Darcy, Fitzwilliam (Fictitious character)--Fiction. 4. Courtship--Fiction. 5. Social classes--England--Fiction. 6. England--Fiction. I. Austen, Jane, 1775-1817. Pride and prejudice. II. Title.
 PS3569.Z396P75 2011
 813'.54--dc22
                                        2011005325

With heartfelt appreciation to Miss Jane Austen
for her kind patronage (with some additional
encouragement courtesy of Mr. Colin Firth)

It is a truth universally acknowledged
that a single man in possession of a good fortune
must be in want of a wife.

—Jane Austen, *Pride and Prejudice*

Chapter One

When news reached Mrs. Bennet that Netherfield Park was to be let to a young gentleman in possession of a good fortune, she determined to make him a husband to one of her five daughters. "A single man of large fortune, four or five thousand a year. What a fine thing for our girls!"

"How so? How can it affect them?" asked her husband. "The gentleman of whom you hold so high an opinion, this Mr. Bingley, has not even alighted at Meryton as yet."

"My dear Mr. Bennet," replied his wife, "how can you be so tiresome! You must know that I am thinking of his marrying one of our girls."

Having to maintain five daughters and a wife on a modest income, Mr. Bennet was of a more practical disposition than Mrs. Bennet. "Is that his design in settling here?"

"Design! Nonsense, how can you talk so! But it is very likely that he *may* fall in love with one of them, and therefore you must visit him as soon as he comes." Mrs. Bennet's tone indicated that the matter was settled.

Mr. Bennet had no wish to visit Mr. Bingley or anyone

else. He wished only to retire to the sanctity of his library, where a small parcel recently arrived awaited him. "I see no occasion for that. You and the girls may go. I daresay Mr. Bingley will be very glad to see you, and I will send a few lines by you to assure him of my hearty consent to his marrying whichever he chooses of the girls, though I must throw in a good word for my little Lizzy."

"I desire you will do no such thing. Lizzy is not a bit better than the others, and I am sure she is not half so handsome as Jane, nor half so good-humored as Lydia. But you are always giving *her* the preference."

At the mention of his youngest daughter's name, Mr. Bennet shook his head. Although quite pretty, Lydia was a lively headstrong girl prone to a breathiness of speech and a most peculiar fondness for raising up the hems of her gowns to rub her lower half against objects and furnishings and, to the embarrassment of all parties concerned, young officers. Until recently she could be found sliding down banisters at all hours of the day and night, and only his threat of dispatching her to a nunnery finally broke her of the habit. He despaired of Lydia and for any man who would eventually take her as a wife. Neither did he maintain great hopes for the equally frivolous Catherine or the plain and pedantic Mary. That he was partial to his Elizabeth, he made no secret of. "Our daughters have none of them much to recommend them," replied Mr. Bennet. "They are all silly and ignorant like other girls, but Lizzy has something more of quickness than her sisters."

At this Mrs. Bennet launched into a tirade about her nerves, and Mr. Bennet, having been given sufficient of his wife's ceaseless chatter about Mr. Bingley's five thousand a year and which of his daughters should be the first to wed, departed without ceremony to his library.

Mr. Bennet settled himself before his escritoire on which rested a sealed portfolio that had arrived that morning by special post; fortunately, he had managed to collect it before Mrs. Bennet could inquire as to the nature of the dispatch. Breaking the wax seal, he removed a sheet of stiff paper, his breath quickening with anticipation as to what would shortly be revealed to him. He had secured it from a gentleman of his acquaintance in London, who consorted with the city's more unsavory residents. It was a drawing—indeed, the first of many such drawings due to arrive, providing his contact made good on his promise, and providing that Mr. Bennet likewise made good on his timely payment of the prohibitive fee demanded of him.

The drawing displayed a nubile young woman outfitted in the manner of a horse. Unadorned of attire save for the finely tooled saddle secured to her back, she had been positioned on her haunches, presenting a pleasing rear vista to the artist who had sketched her. What made this vista all the more appealing to Mr. Bennet, however, was the fact that the subject possessed the tail of a horse as well, which had been fitted most cleverly into her hindmost region. As he surveyed the drawing in the light coming through the window, a presence began to make itself known in his breeches. All thoughts of their new neighbor Mr. Bingley and his wife's determination to make him a son-in-law became a distant memory as Mr. Bennet unbuttoned the flap of his breeches and reached inside, his fingers encountering an object that rose up with a vigor the likes of which he had not experienced since his youth, and he grasped it firmly in his hand, eager to begin his long-neglected journey to pleasure.

How very distant those days now seemed when he had had access to any number of servants in the household, none of whom would dare to turn away the advances of a lusty young man, particularly when the young man was the son of their employer. Mr. Bennet would often begin his day by applying himself to the womanhood of the maid who had come to tidy his room, raising up her skirts as she bent forward to attend the bed linens and thrusting inside her before she even realized what was happening, his hands grabbing hold of the abundant flesh of her bosom, which he had freed from her stays, to keep himself steady. That his attentions were unwelcome was not the case, for his manhood always met with a generous wetness, followed by a most agreeable clenching of the maid's interior, serving to expedite his release, his pleasure discharging inside her just as she finished plumping up the pillows on his bed.

Mr. Bennet, in hoping to rekindle the halcyon days of his youth, had eagerly consented to the acquisition of drawings such as the one he now had before him. Although he was not the most accomplished rider in the county, the theme of the drawing provided him with sufficient inspiration to improve his equestrian skills. As he imagined himself riding his special horse-girl over the rolling green hills of Hertfordshire, his hand moved with increasing swiftness over his manhood, squeezing the tip with so much enthusiasm that he cried out with pain. His breathing began to grow quite labored, especially when he thought he heard movement outside the library door. He prayed that Mrs. Bennet would not endeavor to trespass in his private domain and inflict herself on him any more than she already had—or any of his frivolous daughters; although he was extremely fond of Lizzy, he found it most impolitic to reflect on her at this moment. Instead he returned his attention to the matter before him, imagining that it was his manhood rather than the false tail mounted inside the horse-girl from the drawing. Such a scenario afforded him with much in the way of delight, just as it had in his youth when he had found a surprising number of maids willing to oblige him in this highly unsanctioned manner, particularly the younger ones whose greatest fear was to be got with child. Mrs. Bennet had never taken kindly to the proposal herself. It had been near to the time when he first attempted such an endeavor on her that she began to suffer with her nerves. From that point onward, she took to ministering to herself with a number of curious medications obtained from gypsies passing through the town in her quest to seek relief. The pupils of his wife's eyes had never been the same since.

As the house filled with the sound of footsteps and the excited squeals of Lydia, Mr. Bennet proceeded to stroke his manhood with greater urgency, the pressure building in his loins indicating that it would soon require release. He knew he had to make haste before his pleasure was lost to him forever. Concentrating on the drawing, Mr. Bennet bounced up and down in his chair, launching the full length of himself into his phantom horse-girl's backside, the groans of the chair legs as they threatened to collapse beneath him rivaling those that sprang from his lips. He considered the model's shapely hindquarters most pleasingly rendered and wondered if the artist had engaged with his subject as Mr. Bennet now envisioned himself doing. That the folds of her womanhood were also most charmingly depicted was an added delight, her position offering a teasing hint of rosy pink beneath the tail. As he imagined his fingers occupying themselves within them, he cried out with joy, then agony, the release he sought finally arriving when a hot stream of liquid shot upward from his lap directly into his eye. Had he been fired upon by a gun, Mr. Bennet's misery could not have been more grievous.

The animated voice of Lydia was shortly joined by those of her mother and sisters, as it had come time for the family to gather at breakfast. Within all the feminine mayhem, Mr. Bennet could make out but a single word.

Bingley.

Chapter Two

"I AM SICK OF MR. BINGLEY!" CRIED MRS. BENNET THE following morning as their new neighbor continued to be the main topic of conversation in the Bennet household.

"I am sorry to hear that," replied Mr. Bennet. "If I had known as much this morning I certainly would not have called on him. It is very unlucky, but as I have actually paid the visit, we cannot escape the acquaintance now."

The astonishment of the ladies was just what he wished, and much discussion ensued as to the reported handsomeness of Mr. Bingley, followed by speculation as to who would be included in the large party he was expected to bring with him to the upcoming ball in Meryton. "If I can but see one of my daughters happily settled at Netherfield," said Mrs. Bennet to her husband, "and all the others equally well married, I shall have nothing more to wish for."

Mr. Bennet was not in a particularly good humor this morning. His eye continued to give him pain, the white of which had gone a bright red. "Then I expect, Mrs. Bennet, we shall hear no more on the subject for the rest of the day," he replied, returning to the haven of his library.

After some days had passed, Mr. Bingley returned Mr. Bennet's visit, calling on him in the library. He had heard much spoken of the beauty of the Bennet sisters, although, to his disappointment, none would make an appearance. The visit was brief, and Mr. Bennet found himself feeling that there was something not quite as it should be about their new neighbor. Though he was as handsome and agreeable as on their first meeting, thus corresponding with reports gained from their neighbors Sir William and Lady Lucas, Mr. Bennet was left with a sense of unease after Mr. Bingley's departure. That he possessed a very pleasing disposition and would make an excellent husband to one of his daughters there could be no doubt; but something in his manner, a fastidiousness that appeared overly feminine, gave Mr. Bennet pause. Rather than allowing it to plague him, he decided to console himself with his horse-girl, catching the results of his pleasure in a handkerchief rather than soiling his garments as he had done on prior occasions. He hoped the recent increase in laundering would not inspire the tongues of the servants to wag any more than they now did. Hill, the housekeeper, had already begun to look at him askance.

An invitation to dinner was afterward dispatched to Mr. Bingley, who was obliged to be in London and had to decline. A report soon followed that he was to bring twelve ladies and seven gentlemen with him to the ball. The girls grieved over such a number of ladies, but were comforted when, on the evening of the ball, Mr. Bingley arrived accompanied by his two sisters, the eldest's husband Mr. Hurst, and another young man, a Mr. Darcy. Miss Bingley and Mrs. Hurst were fine young ladies with an air of decided fashion, and they appeared to go to great pains to project a sense of importance, particularly Lady Caroline Bingley, who always made certain to keep her brother's handsome friend within close range, for it was this very gentleman who commanded the most attention.

Mr. Darcy stood tall and regal, with an air of aloofness that set him apart from the laughter and merriment of the other guests, and it quickly became apparent that he did not enjoy the fripperies the evening provided. Neither did he seem willing to engage in conversation with anyone save for members of the small party with whom he had arrived, though even this was sparsely provided. Other than Miss Jane Bennet, whom his friend insisted join their party, Mr. Darcy declined to be introduced to any other young ladies present.

Mr. Bingley spent much of his time in conversation or dancing with Jane, the eldest of the Bennet sisters. The two made a handsome couple, and Mrs. Bennet was beside herself with excitement that the eligible Mr. Bingley found her daughter's company so pleasing. He was an excellent dancer, and moved with a grace and lightness of step far superior to that of most men. As for his friend Mr. Darcy, not even talk of ten thousand a year and a large estate in Derbyshire could prevent the tide of popularity from turning against him. Mr. Darcy was soon discovered to be proud, above his company, and above being pleased, and everybody hoped that he would never come there again.

The presence of so many attractive and unattached young ladies in the room encouraged Lady Caroline to place herself as near to Mr. Darcy as was practicable. She had no intention of allowing anyone else to join their small party, particularly marriage-minded young ladies who might find the prospect of a handsome young man with ten thousand a year most appealing. Her elegant gown was cut immodestly low and fitted tightly in the bodice, and as she leaned to whisper in his ear, it looked as if she were offering him a platter of ripe fruit. "Mr. Darcy, might I persuade you to accompany me outside to enjoy a nice thrashing of your backside?" Miss Bingley spoke with the ease of one who has shared a long acquaintance, as indeed, she and Mr. Darcy had. "I am certain it shall be far more pleasurable than the company of these country peasants! I seem to recall a tree quite near to where we alighted from our coach, from which I may secure a branch suitable for a good birching."

Miss Bingley's words provoked an urgent stirring in Mr. Darcy's breeches and he coughed into his hand, more anxious that his friend's sister not be overheard by the other guests than for any reaction of his own to her flirtatious proposal. Though this was not the first instance of such overtures from that quarter, it nevertheless did not leave him entirely unmoved, and he shifted his stance, hoping to alleviate the pressure caused by the fabric as his manhood rubbed against it, dismayed when it seemed to grow stiffer yet.

"I shall very much enjoy drawing a quantity of red stripes upon your flesh," continued Miss Bingley. "I am told I am quite expert. If you go to your knees to please me, I promise not to make you bleed." She allowed her hand to brush against the flap of his breeches, and a smile formed on her lips when it encountered the rigidness beneath it. "Indeed, sir, I can promise that you will find my flavor most pleasing."

Mr. Darcy coughed again, this time to hide his groan of desire. Lady Caroline was, without doubt, a handsome young woman and one worthy of reckoning; few men in his society had the power to resist her. In fact, he knew of several who had relinquished their backsides to her birch in exchange for servicing her with their tongues. That they had spoken so openly astonished him, for much mention was made as to her affection for seating herself upon a gentleman's face until she had received several bouts of pleasure from their tongues. Darcy had even heard that one such gentleman had died of suffocation, though he questioned the veracity of the report. The close fit of his breeches did little to conceal his reaction to Miss Bingley's words, thereby making it impossible to go unnoticed had anyone glanced in his direction. Indeed, it was not overlooked by Mr. Bingley, who had gone quite suddenly pale.

When his dance with Jane Bennet ended, Bingley hastily rejoined his sister and friend, returning Jane to her young sisters Catherine and Lydia. "Come, Darcy," said he, "I must have you dance. I hate to see you standing about by yourself in this stupid manner." The words all but tumbled from him, so determined was he to remove his friend from Lady Caroline, and his hands flew about in an erratic fashion as he attempted to draw Mr. Darcy's attention toward Miss Elizabeth Bennet, who was seated nearby. Moments ago she had been engaged in conversation with her friend and neighbor Charlotte Lucas, but she was now quite alone.

"I certainly shall not," said Darcy. "You know how I detest it, unless I am particularly acquainted with my partner. There is not another woman in the room whom it would not be a punishment to me to stand up with." He looked toward Miss Bennet, who, owing to the scarcity of gentlemen, had been obliged to sit out each dance. However, no amount of extolling her virtues by Mr. Bingley could persuade him to take a turn with her. "She is tolerable, but not handsome enough to tempt *me*. I am in no humor at present to give consequence to young ladies who are slighted by other men," replied Darcy, whose insult did not go unheard by Elizabeth.

The ball proved most auspicious for the remaining Bennet sisters. Jane had been distinguished in the eyes of everyone by Mr. Bingley's attentions; Mary, despite her plainness, had been mentioned as the most accomplished girl in the neighborhood; and Kitty and Lydia had enjoyed no lull in dance partners. Were it not for the fact that Lydia was unable to abstain from pulling up her skirts and rubbing herself against every available object in the room as well as every gentleman who remained still long enough, Elizabeth and Mrs. Bennet would have considered the evening an absolute success. It had required them both to pry the youngest Bennet sister from the thigh of a handsome young officer, and not before she emitted a breathy cry of delight, grabbing hold of his backside with such force there came a corresponding cry from the recipient. The gentleman was left with a severely heightened countenance and a patch of damp on his breeches, the flap of which boasted a similar agitation as that which Mr. Darcy had suffered earlier, and he removed himself from the room shortly afterward with a plan to relieve himself with his hand the moment he found a quiet location in which to do so.

The officer would be spared the trouble, however, for within moments Lydia had followed him outside, whereupon she proceeded to complete the task for him, taking his manhood into her hand and massaging it with great enthusiasm. Her fingers moved along its length with an expertise that far surpassed his own, squeezing the exposed tip until he thought he would go mad from pleasure. The young redcoat closed his eyes and gave himself over to enjoyment, only just as quickly to reopen them when he felt Lydia placing herself once more on his thigh, resuming the earlier rubbing of her sex against it, her movements acting in accord with those of her hand. Her release was swift in arriving and she laughed loudly, shuddering against him. As the officer began to tremble with the beginnings of his own release, Lydia, to his astonishment, dropped to her knees to catch the rush of liquid in her mouth, her throat working noisily as she swallowed it. Indeed, he would have much of interest to report to his companions in the militia as regards the talents of Miss Lydia Bennet!

When the evening had concluded, the Bennet women returned home to Longbourn with exciting news for Mr. Bennet: Mr. Bingley had announced his intentions to give a ball at Netherfield. Mr. Bennet was made disconsolate by this information, as he continued to have misgivings about the perfect Mr. Bingley. Yet he became even more so aggrieved when he learned that his dear Lizzy had been slighted by none other than Bingley's close friend, Mr. Darcy.

Chapter Three

THAT NIGHT WHEN THE ELDER MISS BENNETS WERE ALONE, Jane expressed her admiration of Mr. Bingley to Elizabeth, extending this good opinion to his sisters Lady Caroline and Mrs. Hurst. Elizabeth, however, was skeptical. "You never see a fault in anybody. I never heard you speak ill of a human being in your life."

"I would not wish to be hasty in censuring anyone," countered Jane.

Elizabeth could not find censure with Mr. Bingley, but she remained unconvinced as regards his sisters. Although capable of good humor when they were pleased, their predisposition toward conceit and affectation made her little disposed to approve them. As for Bingley's friend Mr. Fitzwilliam Darcy, neither she nor Jane could fathom how two such extremes in temperament had established so close a bond. Whereas Bingley was sure of being liked wherever he appeared, Darcy was continually giving offense. It was a curious friendship indeed.

Their conversation was interrupted by the sound of

moans coming from Lydia's bedchamber. The sisters looked at each other and shook their heads. Despite Mr. Bennet's best efforts to remove most every item from her room, Lydia had undoubtedly found something of interest to rub against. Her breathy cries of "*oh! oh! oh!*" served to awaken both Kitty and Mary, and they shouted for Lydia to quiet down, which was followed by their mother's cry of "Oh, my nerves!" Shortly afterward, the elder Miss Bennets retired each to their beds. It had been an evening of much excitement, and fatigue had at last overcome them.

The ladies of Longbourn and Netherfield were soon reunited in a gathering that also included Charlotte Lucas and her father Sir William, Colonel and Mrs. Forster along with several young officers from the local regiment, and Mr. Darcy. Jane's pleasing manner began to win over both Miss Bingley and Mrs. Hurst, though Mrs. Bennet was deemed intolerable and the younger Bennet girls not even worthy of consideration. Lydia had found a small party of young officers to occupy herself with and had removed with them to a corner, where she proceeded to ride each of their thighs in turn, her moans of pleasure muted by the lively conversation taking place among the guests. That the officers did not remain unaffected by her activities was manifest, for their hands derived much merriment from her ample bosom, which swelled forth from the bodice of her gown, with the bolder gentlemen seeking to explore beneath her skirts. To Lydia's delight, a number of fingers had begun to make themselves familiar with the place of her womanhood and even the more illicit neighbor of her backside, and this served to greatly advance her bliss. She stood for some while between a pair of redcoats, allowing the fingers of one to explore her folds while those of his companion chose the less traditional route, applying so many that Lydia thought he had slipped his manhood inside her. Her pleasure was swift and strong as she bore down on their hands, her cry of such volume that several guests turned in their direction, their view of the proceedings blocked by a sea of redcoats. After a brief respite, she continued to seek out every available thigh, and by the close of the evening, the breeches of more than a few from Colonel Forster's regiment would be marked by Lydia's distinctive signature.

Though Elizabeth continued to maintain her earlier opinion of the Bingley sisters, she could not help but be pleased at the strength of feeling that appeared to be developing between Jane and Mr. Bingley. She mentioned this to her friend Charlotte, who held a rather different opinion of the matter. "There are very few of us who have heart enough to be really in love without encouragement," said Miss Lucas. "In nine cases out of ten a woman had better show *more* affection than she feels. Bingley likes your sister undoubtedly, but he may never do more than like her, if she does not help him on."

"But she does help him on, as much as her nature will allow," replied Elizabeth. "If I can perceive her regard for him, he must be a simpleton, indeed, not to discover it too."

Miss Lucas drew very close to her friend. "Remember, Eliza, that he does not know Jane's disposition as you do. Jane should therefore make the most of every half hour in which she can command his attention. When she is secure of him, there will be more leisure for falling in love."

"Your plan is a good one, where nothing is in question but the desire of being well married, and if I were determined to get a rich husband, or any husband, I daresay I should adopt it. But these are not Jane's feelings; she is not acting by design."

"Happiness in marriage is entirely a matter of chance," replied Miss Lucas. "If the dispositions of the parties are ever so well known to each other or ever so similar beforehand, it does not advance their felicity in the least. It is better to know as little as possible of the defects of the person with whom you are to pass your life."

Elizabeth decided it best not to argue with her friend, whom she thought rather curious in her views, which undoubtedly accounted for her lack of suitors. In all the time she had known Charlotte, she had yet to see her in the company of a gentleman other than her father, which, though unusual, was not entirely unexpected considering she was some years older than most young ladies in want of a husband. Elizabeth turned her attention instead to Miss Bingley, who was dressed in a fashion that left little to the imagination. The bodice of her gown was cut scandalously low, revealing nearly the entire expanse of her bosom, including the tips. Elizabeth wondered for whom this display was intended; Lady Caroline gave no indication of any interest in the young officers who, other than Mr. Darcy, made up the majority of unattached gentlemen present. She was occupying herself with a length of birch, which Elizabeth thought a most curious object to bring to a social gathering, her long fingers busily stroking the small branch, as if to buff smooth its surface. So busy was Elizabeth with her observations that she failed to notice that she herself was being observed.

Mr. Darcy had spent some while in his study of Miss Bennet, mortified to discover his original assessment of her much altered. What he formerly looked at only to criticize he now found possessed of great appeal. Her features, figure, and manners were most pleasing, her face rendered uncommonly intelligent by the beautiful expression of her dark eyes. There was a playfulness in her demeanor of which he very much wished to gain firsthand knowledge. His thoughts wandered toward an image of a smiling Miss Bennet lying unclothed beneath him save for a demure little bonnet on her head, her legs wrapped around his back as their loins joined, then unlocked, then rejoined, her fair bosom rising and falling like waves on a stormy sea until they had both achieved their joyous release. Darcy vowed to take her again and again, filling her and filling her until they were both too spent to walk. It was not often he entertained himself with such reflections, and he was forced to acknowledge that the recent overtures from Lady Caroline had been inspiring his thoughts toward those of a less wholesome nature. Though he continued to have no desire to experience her birch upon his backside, the thought of Miss Elizabeth Bennet applying it with somewhat more gentleness, and he to her, encouraged him to look more favorably on the matter.

Desiring to know more of Miss Bennet, Darcy moved toward where she was engaged in conversation with Sir William and Charlotte Lucas. Very few words beyond that of initial pleasantries were exchanged, however, for Elizabeth allowed herself to be persuaded by Miss Lucas to take a brief turn at the pianoforte and sing, after which she was eagerly succeeded by her sister Mary, who was always impatient to display. Her lukewarm performance and pedantic demeanor proved most tiresome to the guests, and her sonata was quickly interrupted by Kitty and Lydia, who insisted she perform something more suitable for the occasion.

A lively dance soon started up. "My dear Miss Eliza, why are you not dancing?" asked Sir William when she rejoined them. "Mr. Darcy, you must allow me to present this young lady to you as a very desirable partner. You cannot refuse to dance, I am sure, when so much beauty is before you."

Elizabeth drew back. "Indeed, sir, I have not the least intention of dancing. I entreat you not to suppose that I moved this way in order to beg for a partner." She had not forgotten the slight she had suffered from Darcy previously, and despite his now requesting to be allowed the honor of her hand, she would not be swayed. She turned away from the discussion, leaving Mr. Darcy to the determined approach of Miss Bingley.

"The insipidity, the nothingness, and yet the self-importance of all those people! What would I give to hear your strictures on them!" cried Miss Bingley, the length of birch in her hand twitching with the desire to mark the pristine flesh of Mr. Darcy's backside. It would make a pleasant change after the uninspiring version belonging to her brother-in-law Mr. Hurst, who appeared unable to get sufficient. She was growing quite weary of his plaintive pleas, to say nothing of his slavish lapping at her parts after she had drawn blood. When she finished a good birching it was usual for her to be ready for a gentleman's attentions, but on the last few occasions she had been forced to feign a few shudders if only to rid herself of the nuisance of an unskilled tongue when it was Darcy's she most desired. This, indeed, she could already feel working its way up and down her cleft, and she leaned in close, pressing her bosom against him. "Let us go outside, Mr. Darcy," said she. "I wish to see you with your breeches down and your backside raised high. You have kept me waiting long enough." Patience had never been Lady Caroline's strong suit. That Mr. Darcy was the only gentleman of her acquaintance who had not succumbed to her charms provoked her ire. He would be one conquest she vowed to take considerable delight from.

"Your conjecture is totally wrong, I assure you," replied Darcy. "My mind was more agreeably engaged. I have been meditating on the very great pleasure which a pair of fine eyes in the face of a pretty woman can bestow."

Encouraged that it was herself to whom he was referring, Miss Bingley let down her guard. "Pray, tell, Mr. Darcy, what lady has the credit of inspiring such reflections? Might this be the same lady who, if you go to your knees and beg, may be persuaded to strap a large wooden contraption to her loins and provide you with a good buggering?"

On hearing Darcy's reply, Lady Caroline went deathly pale.

"The lady is Miss Elizabeth Bennet."

Chapter Four

With Mr. Bingley installed at Netherfield and the arrival of Colonel Forster's regiment in Meryton, life for the ladies of the Bennet household became far livelier than usual. It was agreed that Jane was the object of Bingley's affections, and her mother considered it a matter of time before she saw her eldest daughter wed. The youngest Bennet sisters made frequent visits into Meryton, which was only a mile's walk, on the pretext of visiting their aunt, Mrs. Phillips, and Kitty and Lydia used these opportunities to gather intelligence about the officers. They could talk of nothing else; Mr. Bingley's large fortune, the mention of which gave animation to their mother, was worthless in their eyes when opposed to the regimentals of an ensign.

Unable to bear another morning filled with their ceaseless chatter, Mr. Bennet remarked, "You must be two of the silliest girls in the country. I have suspected it for some time, but I am now convinced."

His wife immediately came to their defense. "I remember the time when I liked a redcoat myself—and, indeed, so I do still at my heart. If a smart young colonel with five or six thousand a year should want one of my girls, I shall not say nay to him." Mrs. Bennet failed to report that she had been with child on wedding Mr. Bennet, having given her heart to a handsome young officer who was the image of Jane.

Marriage to Mr. Bennet had been a compromise of considerable proportions, and one from which Mrs. Bennet had never truly recovered. Though she had given her husband four daughters since, she could not recall a time when she had enjoyed performing her wifely duty. Mr. Bennet was a man with curious tastes, and it required much generosity of spirit to call him *handsome*. Whereas he was squat in figure and unremarkable of countenance, Mrs. Bennet's militiaman had been tall and well formed, a handsome golden Apollo perfect in every regard. His touches set fire to her flesh, stealing away all sense of propriety as she abandoned herself to his care, heedless to the repercussions. His manhood had risen out from beneath his belly with all the supremacy of a god's, and she had attended it in wonderment, even going so far as to place her mouth upon it. She believed at that moment they would be together forever; had she suspected otherwise, she might not have behaved with such boldness. He had moved inside her mouth with a frantic need, at first with great gentleness, then with an increasing disregard for decorum, urging his manhood further and further past her lips. She had felt it pulsing against her teeth and tongue, as if it possessed its own heartbeat, and she began to take control, holding the length of him steady with her hand so that she could move her head forward and back, her redcoat's sighs indicating that he considered her actions most pleasing. That they were likewise pleasing to herself was manifest, for she experienced a heartbeat of her own in the place of her womanhood, and as it gained in strength so too did the pulsing in her mouth, and within moments a hot liquid sprang forth from him. She drank all he had to give, his nectar of the gods leaving the taste of honey on her tongue.

When he had taken her for the first time, Mrs. Bennet felt as if a ray of sunlight were moving inside her. His kisses shimmered on her lips as she wrapped her legs around him, drawing him farther into her and giving herself over to his command. The source of the heartbeat hidden within the cleft of her womanhood was brought into exposure when he reached down and parted it, and she cried out with shock and delight as he placed his thumb against the fragment of flesh it found there and proceeded to move it about in a manner as pleasurable as it was vexing. It appeared to act as a sort of trigger, and she felt herself opening up to him and taking him deeper until at last he could go no farther. She knew instantly when he got her with child, for she had felt the sun exploding in her loins. The result was her beautiful Jane.

That all this recent excitement in the neighborhood proved very trying for Mrs. Bennet's already compromised nerves was but to be expected. Gypsies could be spied calling at the rear of the house with increasing frequency, bringing with them their mysterious potions and remedies. Mrs. Bennet's eyes took on a more unnatural gleam than typical, and her voice grew louder and more shrill, prompting Mr. Bennet to seek solace in his library. Another drawing had arrived by special post, and it surpassed in quality that of its predecessor. It depicted two charming young ladies on their knees positioned posterior to posterior. Some manner of contrivance had been fitted into their womanly openings, serving as a bridge to connect them together and, determining from the lewdness of their expressions, they appeared to find their predicament most pleasing. How Mr. Bennet wished to be the artist wielding the pen that had rendered such delights to paper! He had not even time to reach for his handkerchief before his pleasure burst forth, soiling his garments and leaving him in fear of Hill's knowing glance when laundering day next arrived. Though he looked forward with eagerness to the delivery of the next drawing, he wondered how long he could continue financing his habit. His source in London was increasing his fee to extortionate levels, and he might soon be forced to lessen the number of servants in the household if he hoped to pay it.

Later that morning a letter arrived for Jane. It was from Miss Bingley, and it contained an invitation to dine at Netherfield with her and Mrs. Hurst. When Jane asked if she could have the carriage, her mother replied, "No, my dear, you had better go on horseback, because it seems likely to rain, and then you must stay all night." She then solicited acknowledgment from Mr. Bennet that the horses were, indeed, needed in the farm, at which point she attended Jane to the door with many cheerful prognostics of a bad day.

The elder Miss Bennet had not been gone long before it rained hard, and it continued for the whole of the evening. "This was a lucky idea of mine indeed!" said Mrs. Bennet more than once, as if the credit of making it rain were her own. Her scheme had worked: Jane would be forced to stay the night.

The next morning a servant arrived from Netherfield with a note for Elizabeth. Jane was most unwell, and the apothecary had been summoned. "Well, my dear," said Mr. Bennet to his wife after Elizabeth had read the note aloud, "if your daughter should have a dangerous fit of illness—if she should die, it would be a comfort to know that it was all in pursuit of Mr. Bingley, and under your orders."

"Oh, I am not afraid of her dying! People do not die of little trifling colds. She will be taken good care of," replied Mrs. Bennet.

Elizabeth, feeling quite anxious, was determined to go to Jane, though the carriage was not to be had. As she was no horsewoman, walking was her only alternative, despite Mrs. Bennet's protests that it would be unseemly for her to do so.

Kitty and Lydia accompanied their sister as far as Meryton, where they set off in eager pursuit of officers. Elizabeth continued on to Netherfield, arriving muddied and unkempt, her face glowing from the exercise. She was shown into the breakfast parlor, where all but Jane were assembled. That she should have walked three miles so early in the day, in such dirty weather, and by herself, was almost incredible to Mrs. Hurst and Miss Bingley, whose expressions indicated their contempt for her appearance. Mr. Bingley was more gracious, though Mr. Hurst and Mr. Darcy said little.

From her brief meeting with Jane in her sickroom, then with the others at breakfast, it became clear to Elizabeth that the Bingley sisters held genuine warmth for Jane, and she softened her opinion of them. However, her concern was not alleviated from having seen her sister. Jane was loath to let her leave, and an invitation was extended for Elizabeth to remain at Netherfield until her sister had recovered.

That evening at dinner, still more solicitude was made of Jane's condition by Miss Bingley and Mrs. Hurst, though Elizabeth noted an indifference in their demeanor that restored her former opinion of the women. The only genuine concern for Jane's well-being came from Mr. Bingley, though this too began to wane as Lady Caroline's attentions became focused increasingly on Mr. Darcy, near whom she had positioned herself, giving him the full effect of her bosom and her wit. That she had chosen again so inappropriate a gown to wear in mixed company was a source of amazement to Elizabeth, who considered it most impolitic for a lady to place on display the areolae. Unless she was very much mistaken, Miss Bingley appeared to have applied some form of rouge to them, drawing yet further attention to those places that modesty dictated should be seen only by a husband. Darcy's heightened countenance and agitation of manner appeared to indicate that he, too, found such displays inappropriate, as did the increasingly anxious bearing exhibited by Bingley.

After dinner, Elizabeth left the room to check on her sister, and the conversation immediately turned to a condemnation of the now-absent Miss Bennet, which was begun by Miss Bingley.

"I shall never forget her appearance this morning. She really looked almost wild."

"I hope you saw her petticoat, six inches deep in mud, I am absolutely certain," offered Mrs. Hurst.

"*You* observed it, Mr. Darcy, I am sure," said Miss Bingley; "and I am inclined to think that you would not wish to see *your* sister make such an exhibition." She urged her bosom toward him, lowering her voice to a whisper. "I should more wish to make an exhibition of your fine backside, sir." Her hand slipped beneath the table to seek out Darcy's lap, where she was pleased to discover the flap of his breeches in a state of disturbance. She skillfully unbuttoned it and grasped hold of his burgeoning manhood. "How I shall make you suffer for your pleasure!" she whispered, pinching the tip and receiving for her troubles a stream of moisture on her fingertips. She brought them up to her mouth and proceeded to lick them with all the languor of a cat, then returned her hand back to Darcy's manhood, which had by this time begun to throb.

"It shows an affection for her sister that is very pleasing," said Bingley, whose generally cheerful countenance began to change as he closely monitored his sister and Darcy. Although he was not ignorant of Lady Caroline's intrigues, he remained for the most part unaffected by them. Seeing her in such close proximity to his friend, however, he experienced a turmoil of emotions that, had he not known better, could only have been described as jealousy. He noted the way in which Darcy's dark hair curled against the nape of his neck and wondered how it might be to twine his fingers in it. Indeed, the thought caused him to feel quite faint, and a disturbance made itself known inside his own breeches for which he could not account.

Miss Bingley had still more to say on the rich subject of Miss Bennet, and as she continued to find fault with all manner of Elizabeth's appearance and deportment, she squeezed Darcy's manhood in her hand, concentrating her effects at the crown. He was very near to achieving release, and she vowed to take him just to the brink, at which time she would stop, knowing that this was the ultimate of torments. She knew from experience that he would then be unable to resist submitting to her, and no manner of activity, regardless of how base, would be beneath his regard. "I am afraid, Mr. Darcy, that this adventure has rather affected your admiration of her fine eyes," she said, her tone teasing.

"Not at all," replied he. "They were brightened by the exercise."

Lady Caroline reclaimed her hand from Darcy's lap, her irritation manifest as she wiped her fingers on the hem of her petticoat. Indeed, she would spare him nothing; the birch would be the least of his problems when she finished with him!

The conversation moved on to the unsuitability of the Bennet sisters' relations, which included an uncle in Cheapside—an area of London they considered well beneath them. Miss Bingley, Mrs. Hurst, and Mr. Darcy all concurred that such low connections would very much materially lessen the sisters' chances of marrying men of any consideration in society. To all this Bingley remained silent, though whether from his earlier reverie or from the opinions being expressed was uncertain.

Elizabeth returned downstairs quite late, having stayed with Jane until she was given the comfort of seeing her sleep. A game of loo was already underway in the drawing room, but Elizabeth, suspecting them to be playing high, declined to join their table, expressing instead a preference to read a book—a pursuit whose singularity did not go unremarked upon by both Mrs. Hurst and Miss Bingley. The discussion moved from the enjoyment of books to the library at Mr. Darcy's estate Pemberley, whereupon Miss Bingley inquired of his young sister, Georgiana. "How I long to see her again!" she cried. "I never met with anybody who delighted me so much. Such a countenance, such manners! And so extremely accomplished for her age! Her performance on the pianoforte is exquisite."

At this, Mr. Bingley joined in the conversation. "It is amazing to me how young ladies can have patience to be so very accomplished as they all are. They paint tables, cover screens, and net purses. I scarcely know anyone who cannot do all this, and I am sure I never heard a young lady spoken of for the first time, without being informed that she was very accomplished."

A lively debate ensued, with Mr. Darcy dismissing his friend's definition of "accomplished," which he believed was applied to *any* woman who could net a purse or cover a screen. "I cannot boast of knowing more than half a dozen, in the whole range of my acquaintance, that are really accomplished," said he.

"Nor I," offered Miss Bingley, seizing the opportunity to return herself to Darcy's attentions. Lowering her voice so that only he could hear, she added, "I am sure there are very few young ladies so accomplished with the birch as I, nor indeed, whose womanly parts taste so sweet." She glanced down at his lap, noting that her words had achieved the desired result. The breeches of her brother's friend boasted a most impressive specimen—in fact, one of the finest she had ever encountered, and she very much wished to avail herself of it in a variety of ways. Perhaps after she had finished disciplining his backside, she might be persuaded to offer indulgences of a more tender sort, providing there was any vigor remaining in him. The gentlemen of Lady Caroline's acquaintance rarely lasted beyond a good thrashing.

That Miss Bingley had orchestrated it so that she could

be seated beside him at loo Darcy had no doubt, and he shifted uneasily in his chair, struggling to keep his thoughts on what Bingley was saying. It never ceased to astonish him how a brother and sister could be so very unalike, and not for the first time did he wonder if their mother had strayed from the marital bed.

"A woman must have a thorough knowledge of music, singing, drawing, dancing, and the modern languages, to deserve the word," offered Bingley; "and besides all this, she must possess a certain something in her air and manner of walking, the tone of her voice . . ." He trailed off, noting that his sister had once more set her sights on his friend, whose heightened countenance indicated that he was not entirely unaffected. Bingley experienced a dark rage at Darcy's reaction. To his knowledge, the two had never engaged in activities beyond those of polite society, which offered him some consolation. On observing, however, that it was now Miss Bennet who appeared to have become the object of Darcy's attention, his concerns were renewed in abundance.

"All this she must possess," concurred Darcy, directing his words pointedly toward Miss Bennet, "and to all this she must yet add something more substantial, in the improvement of her mind by extensive reading."

Elizabeth set down her book. "I am no longer surprised at your knowing only six accomplished women, Mr. Darcy. I rather wonder now at your knowing *any*."

The Bingley sisters cried out against the injustice of her implied doubt, and were both protesting that they knew many women who answered this description, when Mr. Hurst called them back to the game. Shortly afterward, Miss Bennet quit the room.

"Elizabeth Bennet," said Miss Bingley when the door had closed, "is one of those young ladies who seek to recommend themselves to the other sex by undervaluing their own, and with many men, I daresay, it succeeds. But, in my opinion, it is a paltry device, a very mean art."

"Undoubtedly," replied Darcy, to whom this remark was chiefly addressed, "there is a meanness in *all* the arts that ladies sometimes condescend to employ for captivation."

That he intended this as a rebuke was not lost on Lady Caroline. Never had she encountered so difficult a challenge as Mr. Darcy, and the recent addition of Miss Bennet to their society vexed her no end. If she was to succeed, she would need to alter her tactics, or perhaps take them to a more advanced level.

Later that night while Darcy slept, a figure stole into his room. He did not so much as stir, having enjoyed a fine meal and, owing to his friend Charles Bingley, a good many libations to follow it with. He had also enjoyed a most stimulating discourse, much of which he credited to Miss Elizabeth Bennet, whose conversation and deportment proved most refreshingly improved from those whom he typically met in society. He breathed evenly and with contentment, unaware that anyone had joined him. Were he to open his eyes, he would have seen no one, for by then his visitor was settled beneath the bedcovers in well-situated proximity to his loins.

Darcy had been in a state of provocation for most of the evening—a situation brought on by the wickedness of Bingley's sister, who was likewise quite skilled in her repartee, though in an altogether different manner from that of Miss Bennet. He had considered taking matters into his own hands on retiring, then decided better of it. The seeking of self-relief did not seem at all proper when a guest in another's home; therefore he had gone to sleep in the same condition in which he had spent his time awake. It would not last for long, however. In the deep haze of sleep, Darcy dreamed that his manhood was entering something warm and wet and, indeed, most pleasing, and it involved yet another guest at Netherfield. He sighed heavily and allowed himself to be led into this delightful bliss by Miss Bennet, whose mouth moved with great eagerness on his manly flesh. For it to be her lips and tongue that performed the task rather than those of Miss Bingley was no surprise; Elizabeth had occupied his thoughts from the moment of her arrival that morning. Darcy imagined her fine eyes looking up at him from her place at his loins, as if seeking his approval, which he would most wholeheartedly give as she licked his length with extravagant swipes of her tongue, seeming to wish to taunt him before taking the entirety of him into her throat, leaving not so much as a trace of flesh remaining in view, only to repeat the process all over again till he feared he would go mad from the agonies of pleasure. Her tongue would even lave the pouch below, drawing it into her mouth before returning her attention to his manhood. That Miss Bennet's keen mind should also possess such an abundance of licentiousness was a prize Darcy dared not have hoped to win. His release would not be long in arriving, and when it did, it went on for some while and seemed to come from the very core of him, though perhaps it only felt so from the depths of his slumber. He emitted a satisfied cry and fell into an even deeper sleep than before, whereupon the figure beneath the bedcovers finally emerged.

With a pounding heart, Mr. Bingley wiped his lips on the cuff of his nightshirt, quitting the room with haste.

Chapter Five

THE FOLLOWING MORNING MR. DARCY AWAKENED RESTED and refreshed, the fragments of an agreeable dream teasing his mind. Though he recalled that the subject was one Miss Elizabeth Bennet, further details eluded him. It had, however, left him feeling that he very much desired to return to that place again.

Elizabeth had remained with her sister till she slept, then returned to her room, where exhaustion led her to fall quickly asleep. As for Jane, she had spent a most fitful night, and the next day complained to Elizabeth of hearing curious noises, like that of something being struck again and again, followed by a considerable amount of moaning, as if someone suffered grievously. So concerned was the elder Miss Bennet that she had roused herself from her sickbed and moved to the window, which looked down into the garden. The moon was out in full, illuminating two figures whom she eventually recognized as Miss Bingley and her brother-in-law Mr. Hurst. Lady Caroline wore only her short stays from which the entirety of her bosom spilled out, and slippers. She was standing over Mr. Hurst, who lay facedown on the grass. He was dressed in a nightshirt, the hem of which had been raised to his waist, bringing into full exposure his backside, which reminded Jane of an overstuffed game pie that had not been given sufficient time to bake.

Miss Bingley held a rod fashioned from a length of wood, and she brought it down repeatedly against Mr. Hurst's bare backside, which lifted itself up from the surrounding grass as if to welcome the blows. This went on for some while until Lady Caroline appeared to grow rather bored with the endeavor. Turning so that her back was now to Jane, she stretched her arms high above her head and sighed. When she brought them back down again, her hands alighted on the meeting place of her thighs, and proceeded to busy themselves with all manner of complex movements. It was difficult for Jane to determine precisely what Miss Bingley was so industriously engaged with, though a series of moans soon began to issue from her throat. Her head lolled about on her neck as if it had suddenly come loose, her hands a blur as they moved with such swiftness that she gave out a sharp cry, appearing on the verge of collapse.

Having apparently completed this occupation, Miss Bingley made some manner of adjustments to herself, then mounted Mr. Hurst as one might a horse, whereupon she began to propel her loins at him in a most curious fashion. He appeared to suffer a great deal as she did so, though surprisingly he made no move to escape. Instead he thrashed about beneath her, his fingers tearing at the grass, his cries becoming ever more anguished as Lady Caroline's movements increased in their rigor until at last he grew still. As she rose up from his whimpering figure, Jane noted that some form of object had been fixed below her waist with a strap. It was cylindrical in shape, and quite long and thick. It did not take long for her to realize that Miss Bingley had been attending the opening of Mr. Hurst's backside with it, which undoubtedly accounted for the anguish of his cries.

Jane, her face coloring with embarrassment, confessed all this to Elizabeth, who dismissed the story as the result of fever and thought it wise to send for their mother to offer her own assessment of the situation. A note to Longbourn was immediately dispatched, and its contents as quickly complied with; Mrs. Bennet, accompanied by her two youngest girls, reached Netherfield soon after breakfast.

Their arrival did little to elevate the Bingley sisters' low opinion of the family. Only Mr. Bingley behaved with grace and civility, insisting that Jane remain for as long as necessary, to which they coldly concurred. Mrs. Bennet had no wish for her daughter's speedy recovery, however, or her removal from Netherfield. "If it was not for such good friends I do not know what would become of her, for she is very ill indeed, and suffers a vast deal, though with the greatest patience in the world," she proclaimed. "Such is always the way with her, for she has, without exception, the sweetest temper I have ever met with!" Mrs. Bennet then proceeded to question Mr. Bingley about his plans to remain in the neighborhood. Her voice had taken on a shriller note of hysteria than usual, and Bingley, visibly alarmed, swiftly assured her of his intentions to stay.

Mrs. Bennet next managed to enter into an argument with Mr. Darcy over the merits of country life and society, which he considered confined and unvarying. Their exchange resulted in much rolling of the eyes by Miss Bingley and a mortified intervention on the part of Elizabeth, who assured her mother that she had misunderstood Mr. Darcy. To divert the conversation, she inquired as to whether her friend Miss Lucas had called, which provided inspiration for Mrs. Bennet to offer a discourse on the family.

"What an agreeable man Sir William is," she declared. "So much the man of fashion! So genteel and easy! *That* is my idea of good breeding, and those persons who fancy

themselves very important and never open their mouths"—
she looked pointedly at Mr. Darcy—"quite mistake the matter." Mrs. Bennet moved on to a discussion of the Lucas
girls, directing her comments toward Mr. Bingley. "It is a
pity they are not handsome! Not that I think Charlotte so
very plain, but Lady Lucas herself has often said how she
envied me Jane's beauty. I do not like to boast of my own
child, but to be sure, one does not often see anybody better
looking. It is what everybody says!"

Satisfied that all was well with Jane, Mrs. Bennet ordered
her carriage. The younger Miss Bennets had been whispering to each other during the whole of the visit as to which of
them should remind Mr. Bingley of his promise to give a ball
at Netherfield. It was Lydia who finally spoke out, her voice
breathless and excited at the prospect of so many handsome
young officers assembled in one place. Perhaps she might
manage to surpass her own record as to how many men she
could take into her mouth on the same occasion.

"I am perfectly ready to keep my engagement," replied
Mr. Bingley, all amiability. "And when your sister is recovered, you shall, if you please, name the very day of the
ball."

Lydia, squealing with delight, raised up her skirts and
launched herself at a marble statue, rubbing against it in
earnest and encircling it with her arms. Were it not for the
fact that she was facing away from the guests, everyone in
the room would have been made privy to the specific nature
of her activities. Mrs. Bennet and Kitty managed to collect
Lydia before she had created a disturbance. With repeated
thanks to the Bingleys from the mother, the three departed
with haste to their waiting carriage, Lydia in markedly ill
temper from having been thwarted from her pleasure.

Mortified beyond all imaginings, Elizabeth hurried upstairs
to Jane, leaving her relations' behavior to the tongues of Lady
Caroline and Mrs. Hurst, both of whom had much to offer

on the subject. Despite Miss Bingley's repeated witticisms to Mr. Darcy that "fine eyes could never compare to a good thrashing," he could not be prevailed on to join in.

That evening Elizabeth joined the party in the drawing room, where Mr. Bingley and Mr. Hurst were engaged in a game of piquet, which Mrs. Hurst was closely observing. Mr. Hurst kept shifting about in his chair as if it pained him greatly to sit, his actions drawing the displeasure of his wife, who admonished him that if he wished to be the victor, he had best cease with his fidgeting and concentrate on the game. Mr. Darcy was occupied in the writing of a letter to his sister, Georgiana. Miss Bingley sat close by, watching his progress and continually requiring that messages be inserted to Miss Darcy on her behalf. Elizabeth took up some needlework, quietly amusing herself with the exchanges between Lady Caroline and Mr. Darcy, whose bearing indicated his displeasure. She did not, however, notice the teasing caresses of that lady's hand in his lap, for their backs were turned to her.

"I beg you, madam, to be so kind as to allow me to finish this letter," said Darcy so that only Miss Bingley could hear.

"Sir, at last I have heard you beg!" she whispered, pressing the bare expanse of her bosom against his arm. "What a delight it shall be to witness you on your knees, presenting your pristine backside to my birch. Then you shall *truly* beg," said she, "beg me not to stop! My womanhood is weeping with desire at the image. Do you not desire to taste it?" Lady Caroline grabbed hold of Darcy's hand and placed it high up beneath her skirts, urging his fingers into her wet folds, very nearly succeeding in directing one inside herself. Had he not just as swiftly reclaimed them, she might have reached rapture.

"You are most persistent, Miss Bingley."

"Indeed, I am so, Mr. Darcy."

"One can only wonder why, when you appear to have

the patronage of so many gentlemen at your disposal." At that moment Mr. Hurst chose to let out an anguished groan, shifting yet again in his chair and receiving a further scolding from his wife.

Darcy folded his letter and set it aside. "Ladies, may we prevail upon you to indulge us with some music?"

Irritated at having been so summarily dismissed, Miss Bingley got up and moved directly to the pianoforte, where she was joined by Mrs. Hurst. The pair began by singing some Italian melodies, then launched into a lively Scottish tune, which was followed by a spirited solo by Miss Bingley that contained some rather curious mentions of birches and backsides that no one could recall being present in the original lyric. During the performance, Elizabeth could not help but notice how frequently Mr. Darcy's eyes were fixed on her. Certain that she was not an object of admiration, she concluded that she had drawn his attention because there was something reprehensible about her in accordance to his standard. The supposition did not pain her. She liked him too little to care for his approbation.

Darcy chose this moment to draw near. "Do you not feel a great inclination, Miss Bennet, to seize such an opportunity of dancing a reel?" When Elizabeth did not speak, he repeated himself.

"Oh!" said she, "I heard you before, but I could not determine what to reply. You wanted me, I know, to say 'Yes,' that you might have the pleasure of despising my taste. I always delight in overthrowing such schemes and cheating a person of their premeditated contempt. I have, therefore, made up my mind to tell you that I do not want to dance a reel at all. Now despise me if you dare."

Darcy began to recollect the details of his dream from the night before, and he stood there in silence, captivated by the loveliness of Miss Bennet's mouth, the lips of which reminded him of a spring rosebud just coming into bloom.

He cursed the turmoil taking place in his breeches as he envisioned his manhood slipping past her lips, its length resting most agreeably on the soft bed of her tongue. He recalled the delightful sensation of it licking him from tip to pedestal until, at last overcome with pleasure, he had released himself into her mouth. Though it had been but a dream, it felt so real. Never had Darcy been so bewitched by any woman as he was by Miss Bennet. Were it not for the inferiority of her connections, he believed he should be in some danger.

Their exchange did not go unobserved by Miss Bingley, who prayed for her friend Jane's speedy recovery and subsequent departure from Netherfield, along with that of Miss Elizabeth Bennet.

That evening after dinner, Jane was well enough to join everyone in the drawing room. Pleasantries were put forth by all as to her recovery, after which Miss Bingley's attentions were drawn to Mr. Darcy, whose were, in turn, drawn toward Elizabeth. Much fuss would be made of building up the fire, lest Jane suffer a chill, and Mr. Bingley attended to her for most of the evening, feeling both guilty about his actions of the night before and relieved by his friend's indifference to his sister, though he experienced some uncertainty as to that gentleman's interest in Miss Bennet. He had acted with foolishness when he had stolen into Darcy's room; he had committed an unspeakable act that would have very likely resulted in his being ostracized from society, save for that of the basest sort. Yet Bingley could neither forget the taste of him nor the hot rush of liquid that had flooded his mouth, and he wondered how something of such depravity could feel so wonderful and true. As he looked at Darcy's handsome figure, he felt overwhelmed by emotion and even experienced the sting of tears in his eyes. If he might be strong enough to resist temptation were it to present itself again he did not know. Indeed, he feared greatly for the direction of his thoughts, for he had begun to desire far more from his friend than a taste of his manhood.

When tea was over, Mr. Hurst reminded those gathered of the card table, but in vain. It appeared that no one wished to play; therefore he stretched out on the sofa, endeavoring to make himself as comfortable as possible under the circumstances. His backside pained him greatly and was likely to for several days, though he had been assured of his reward by his sister-in-law, who promised to seat herself on his face after everyone had retired for the night, remaining until he had taken his fill. With thoughts of being suffocated by Lady Caroline's moist sex, Mr. Hurst sighed with contentment and promptly fell asleep.

Darcy took up a book, as did Miss Bingley and Elizabeth, leaving Mrs. Hurst to join in her brother's conversation with Jane. Rather than reading her own book, Lady Caroline observed Mr. Darcy's progress through his, repeatedly trying to engage him in conversation. He mostly chose to ignore her, and she eventually abandoned her attempts and employed another tactic. She rose from her chair to walk about the room, hoping that this might attract his notice and move matters in the direction she most desired. Although she had entered into an engagement with Mr. Hurst for later, she suspected that it would be over with quite quickly, and she would afterward require further manner of amusement. Perhaps Mr. Hurst's face would not be the only one she sat on this evening!

Miss Bingley's figure was elegant, and she used it to her advantage, exaggerating the sway of her backside each time she passed Darcy's chair. This evening she had forgone wearing a chemise and petticoat, and the shapely halves of her backside along with the triangle of dark at the fore were visible through the thin fabric of her gown, which had been her intention. Mr. Darcy, at whom all this was aimed, was still inflexibly studious and remained absorbed in his book.

In the desperation of her feelings, she resolved on one effort more. "Miss Eliza Bennet, let me persuade you to follow my example and take a turn about the room. I assure you it is very refreshing after sitting so long," she invited, certain the contrast between them would convince Darcy that *she* was the superior of the two women. Whereas Miss Bennet was dressed in a simple gown cut with a modest décolletage, the full of Miss Bingley's bosom was on display, projecting proudly out from the bodice of her garment. For the occasion she had applied extra rouge to her tips—a slight artifice that had heretofore proved successful in attracting a gentleman's eye. Though many of her acquaintance wished to suckle there, Lady Caroline was most particular as to whom she invited to do so. She was not one to enjoy the uncouth slavering of overstimulated men.

Mr. Darcy was directly invited to join the ladies in their promenade, but declined, observing that he could imagine but two motives for their choosing to walk up and down the room together, both of which his joining them would interfere with. When asked by Miss Bingley to explain his meaning, he replied, "You either choose this method of passing the evening because you are in each other's confidence and have secret affairs to discuss, or because you are conscious that your figures appear to the greatest advantage in walking. If the first, I would be completely in your way, and if the second, I can admire you much better as I sit by the fire."

"Oh, shocking!" cried Miss Bingley, pleased by what she perceived to be a personal victory. She could already hear the sweet sound of her birch striking Darcy's backside, and was convinced that his gaze was fixed on the place of her womanhood. Had the room been empty but for them, she would have raised up her skirt and displayed it to him. "I never heard anything so abominable," she added. "How shall we punish him for such a speech?"

"Nothing so easy," replied Elizabeth. "We can plague

and punish him. Tease him—laugh at him. Intimate as you are, you must know how it is to be done."

"Indeed, I do!" Miss Bingley's countenance was bright with excitement, and she felt her womanhood growing quite moist. "Mr. Darcy is above diversion and merriment, but I shall break him down. He will humble himself before me and beg for my punishment, which I shall offer in abundance. I will break him of his pride and conceit. When I am finished, he will be mine to do with as I choose, my own private plaything."

All eyes were suddenly trained on Miss Bingley, who realized that her impatience to seduce Darcy before matters with Miss Bennet escalated any further had loosened her tongue far more than was prudent; therefore she endeavored to curtail her commentary before her motives became more widely known. "Do let us have a little music," said she. "Louisa, you will not mind my waking Mr. Hurst?" Receiving no objection from her sister, Miss Bingley moved to the sofa on which her brother-in-law slept and shook him awake.

"Is it time for my reward?" cried Mr. Hurst, who had been sleeping so soundly that for a moment he knew not where he was. "Shall I ready myself to worship at your altar? My dear Lady Caroline, my manhood is near to bursting with delight at the thought of my tongue in your sweet folds!"

No one spoke. The pianoforte was hastily opened, and the party experienced great relief when the music commenced.

Despite her annoyance with Mr. Hurst's rather impolitic outburst, Miss Bingley afterward made good on her promise and passed the remaining hours of darkness seated on her brother-in-law's face. Though he was delighted beyond all description, he believed that she did so far longer than he required, and he frequently found himself gasping for air and envisioning his own demise as Lady Caroline bore down against his mouth and nose, as if seeking to punish him for some wrongdoing. Mr. Hurst licked at her parts as if his life depended on it, as perhaps it did, hoping he might inspire some result that would oblige her to remove her sodden folds from his face and allow him to breathe, yet nothing he did seemed to give her the release she sought. He even endeavored to apply his tongue to her backside, which, rather than accelerate the process, inspired his sister-in-law to urge herself against him with greater fury until he thought his heart would burst. The contact of his tongue with this illicit opening, combined with a lack of air, brought about a release that shot forth from his manhood with a force that caused Mr. Hurst to momentarily lose consciousness. He was quickly roused by an insistent pressure against his face, and resumed where he had left off.

It would not be until the light of morning when Lady Caroline at last rose up from her brother-in-law's face, only to discover that he had fallen asleep beneath her, the rattling of his snores against her folds apparently having been successful in bringing forth a finale, though her countenance indicated little in the way of satisfaction.

The departure of Jane and Elizabeth from Netherfield provided Darcy and Bingley with much to reflect on. Miss Elizabeth Bennet attracted the former a good deal more than he liked, resulting in an increase of Lady Caroline's unsolicited and increasingly imprudent attentions toward him. Darcy wisely resolved to be particularly careful that no sign of admiration should now escape him, nothing that could encourage Miss Bennet with the hope of influencing his felicity. As for Bingley, he very much enjoyed the society of Miss Jane Bennet, but was confused as to both his emotions and his intentions regarding her. Though he knew what he felt for his friend was most impolitic for a gentleman of his standing, he could no longer deny its existence. Therefore he decided to follow a more sensible course and engage in the appearance of courtship with Jane. Perhaps, in time, matters might right themselves.

Chapter Six

ONE MORNING MR. BENNET ANNOUNCED TO HIS FAMILY that a guest would be arriving at Longbourn. "I have received a letter from my cousin, William Collins, who, when I am dead, may turn you all out of this house as soon as he pleases," said he.

"Pray, do not talk of that odious man," cried his wife. "I do think it is the hardest thing in the world that your estate should be entailed away from your own children. If I had been you, I should have tried long ago to do something about it!" Mrs. Bennet spent several moments railing against the injustices being perpetrated on her girls, her demeanor alarming both her husband and their daughters. The gypsies had been calling at Longbourn with increasing frequency, and she had begun to take a most foul-smelling herb in her tea, which had caused her eyes to grow so large they appeared ready to leave their sockets. The family could scarcely bear to look at her.

Hoping to stave off further hysteria, Mr. Bennet read aloud his cousin's letter, which explained the gentleman's wish to make amends. In addition to recently being ordained in the clergy, Mr. Collins was so fortunate as to be distinguished by the patronage of the Right Honorable Lady Catherine de Bourgh, to whom he owed thanks for having been made rectory of Hunsford parish. *I cannot be otherwise than concerned at being the means of injuring your amiable daughters, and beg leave to apologize for it, as well as to assure you of my readiness to make them every possible amends*, wrote Mr. Collins, his words inspiring great speculation as to their meaning. He would be arriving that day for dinner, and planned to stay a week. Although it was agreed that his desire to extend an olive branch was creditable, as was his value as an acquaintance, some question remained as to how he planned to make the atonement to which he referred.

Mr. Collins arrived punctually. A plain-featured young man of stoutish build, he possessed a grave and stately manner and a tendency toward obsequiousness that did much to try the patience of those with whom he engaged. He had not been long seated at the dinner table before he complimented Mrs. Bennet on having such fine daughters, adding that he did not doubt her seeing them all in due time disposed of in marriage. Though she accepted his words with pleasure, Mrs. Bennet was quite frank in her expression of concern for their imminent destitution should this situation not transpire. Her hand hovered over the carving knife, giving everyone cause for alarm, particularly Mr. Collins, who added, "I am very sensible, madam, of the hardship to my fair cousins and could say much on the subject, but that I am cautious of appearing forward and precipitate. I can assure the young ladies that I come prepared to admire them. At present I will not say more."

The remainder of Mr. Collins's conversation was occupied with the subject of Lady Catherine de Bourgh, of whom he was highly eloquent in his praise. He described in detail her fine residence Rosings Park, where he had the good fortune to both be invited to dine and make up her pool of quadrille in the evening, for he lived very close by, his humble parsonage separated from Rosings only by a small lane. Lady Catherine had even condescended to advise him to marry as soon as he could, provided he chose with discretion.

On hearing this, Mary, who had offered very little to the conversation, straightened in her chair, thrusting her flat chest forward and fixing Mr. Collins with a keen gaze. A bookish and pedantic young woman with little in the way of prospects, she found Mr. Collins an object of considerable interest. She knew her plainness in appearance and character was unlikely to attract the likes of a Charles Bingley. With a simple and more modest gentleman such as Mr. Collins, she might have a chance. Throwing back her shoulders, she attempted to exaggerate her bosom, staring resentfully at her four sisters, all of whom had been abundantly blessed in this region. Her efforts to engage Mr. Collins's attention with her lack of attributes nevertheless failed, for he was still discoursing on his favorite subject: Lady Catherine de Bourgh.

"I think you said she was a widow, sir? Has she any family?" asked Mrs. Bennet.

"She has only one daughter, the heiress of Rosings. Miss de Bourgh is far superior to the handsomest of her sex, because there is that in her features that marks the young lady of distinguished birth. She is unfortunately of a sickly constitution."

"Has she been presented? I do not remember her name among the ladies at court."

"Her indifferent state of health unhappily prevents her being in town," replied Mr. Collins. "And by that means, as I told Lady Catherine one day, has deprived the British court of its brightest ornament. Her ladyship seemed pleased with the idea. I am happy on every occasion to offer those little delicate compliments that are always acceptable to ladies."

"You judge very properly. It is happy for you that you possess the talent of flattering with delicacy," said Mr. Bennet. Indeed, his cousin was as absurd as he had hoped, and he listened to him with the keenest enjoyment, as did Elizabeth, who shared in the assessment. Mr. Collins passed the remainder of the day complimenting the meal, the furnishings in the household, and anything else he could find to praise.

By the end of teatime the dose had been enough, and Mr. Bennet invited his cousin to read aloud to the ladies in the drawing room. A selection of books had been hastily procured from the library by Mr. Bennet, who did not wish for Mr. Collins, or anyone else, to enter his private sanctum. With much portentousness, his cousin began reading from the book nearest to hand, which bore the rather curious title *A Strumpet's Pleasure.*

> *"The rain pounded hard against the stable roof as Angus, the stableman, thrust his throbbing member deep into Annabel's sopping chasm, eliciting from her an anguished shriek. There was nothing he enjoyed more than taking a young woman's maidenhood, especially when she was the daughter of his employer Lord Tingeford, and the tightness of her sheath further inflamed his passions, inspiring him to do his worst. 'Beg for your reward, strumpet!' growled Angus, tearing the bonnet from Annabel's head. The ivory pillows on her chest bounced wildly as he repeatedly plunged his great member inside her, displaying no mercy. 'Oh, oh, oh!' cried Annabel, clawing at his back and drawing blood. 'I shall surely die of pleasure!' The horses in the stable whinnied and neighed in unison with Angus and Annabel's howls until the final ecstasy arrived and, with one*

final howl, they fell away from each other, lying
spent in the hay, Angus's spunk trickling down
the insides of Annabel's thighs."

Mr. Collins paled as sharp intakes of breath were heard all around the room. Mary herself seemed particularly moved; her complexion glowed, as did her eyes, which never left Mr. Collins, who had been so engrossed in his performance that he had failed to take note of the words he recited. Mr. Bennet made haste to intervene before the fact that such salacious reading material occupied his library could be remarked upon. "Cousin, perhaps you might wish to select a passage from a different book?"

Rather than entertaining the ladies with another novel, Mr. Collins chose a book of sermons. He had not even managed three pages before Lydia interrupted with news about Colonel Forster's regiment and, in particular, a Mr. Denny, for whom she displayed a keen interest. Indeed, it was his "spunk" from which she most took inspiration, and she wished only for the evening to be over with and for the next day to begin so that she might go out in search of it. She had been in a heightened state of excitement ever since the militia had first come to Meryton, and with the arrival of still more redcoats, Lydia could scarcely sit still.

Never in her life had she seen so many handsome young men! She had already enjoyed several agreeable engagements with members of the regiment in a hired room at the town's tavern, where Lydia entertained any number of officers who sought out her society. A lively and sociable young woman, she had no trouble in keeping them all amused, often taking them three at a time, since she saw no point in possessing three openings if they could not all be applied to at once. Wearing only her short stays, she took to the bed with a trio of gentlemen, one lying beneath her, another on top, and still another positioned at her face, their eager members conveniently located within their opening of choice.

With officers filling her womanhood, backside, and mouth, Lydia was happier than she had ever been, and her moans of ecstasy would have deafened the ears of those gathered in the room had her mouth not been so busily engaged. As her lips drew upon the length of flesh being offered to her, that belonging to the others pushed deeper and deeper into her front and hind passages till they could go no farther. Lydia found the orchestration most pleasing, particularly when the officers worked in harmony, driving themselves in and out of her respective openings and forcing from her release after release—until they too experienced their own, discharging their pleasure inside her to the merriment of the other officers who stood impatiently by, awaiting their turn. It was a rare occasion when a gentleman was not given an opportunity to avail himself of all the openings on offer. By the time everyone had finished, Lydia would be near to fainting, and as she rolled off the redcoat lying beneath her, his manhood exited her backside with a most unceremonious noise, prompting from her a lusty bout of laughter that could be heard all the way to the tavern's front door.

Mr. Collins was clearly affronted by Lydia's lack of interest in his selection of reading matter, and made it known. "I have often observed how little most young ladies are interested by books of a serious stamp, though written solely for their benefit. It amazes me, for certainly there can be nothing so advantageous to them as instruction. But I will no longer importune my young cousin."

When Lydia replied that his earlier selection of reading matter had been far more instructional, her elder sisters admonished her. A game of backgammon was then suggested between Mr. Collins and Mr. Bennet, leaving the ladies free to their own pursuits. Mrs. Bennet removed herself to a shadowy corner with a cup of her foul-smelling tea, her eyes growing wider and brighter with each sip. Elizabeth and Jane occupied themselves in quiet conversation while Lydia entertained herself by rubbing against the back of a chair. Kitty took up a piece of needlework, leaving Mary to gaze with hopeless ardor at Mr. Collins.

The remainder of the evening passed without further drama.

Chapter Seven

BEING IN POSSESSION OF A GOOD HOUSE AND A SUFFICIENT income from the living of Hunsford, Mr. Collins intended to marry, and in seeking a reconciliation with the Longbourn family he had a wife in view, as he meant to choose one of the daughters, if he found them as handsome and amiable as they were represented by common report. This was his plan of atonement for inheriting their father's estate, and he thought it excessively generous and disinterested on his own part. He settled on the eldest, Jane, whom he felt certain would meet the approval of Lady Catherine de Bourgh. He only hoped her presence would be adequate to distract him from pursuits of a rather less wholesome nature, of which his patroness had recently been made aware.

Hunsford was a small parish, and scandal was something it could ill afford. An unmarried clergyman did not inspire confidence, particularly when he had a tendency toward inappropriate engagements with certain members of the parish. In an attempt to ingratiate themselves with Lady Catherine, a number of individuals had come forth with intelligence of Mr. Collins having been seen emerging from the shrubbery with young men, all of whom were in various stages of undress and appeared to be walking with difficulty, as if they had been sitting on hot coals. Several members from the choir were also sighted, some bent forward on their knees with their breeches at their ankles and their exposed backsides raised high as a figure resembling that of Mr. Collins passed from one to another, his disjointed movements eliciting much in the way of groans and lamentations from the choristers. When the same reports began to involve the stables at Rosings, Lady Catherine felt it incumbent on her to intervene. Thus it was decided: Mr. Collins would be married as quickly as possible.

The morning after his arrival at Longbourn, Mr. Collins made his intention known to Mrs. Bennet, and it was greeted with much joy, though he received a caution as regards Jane, who she hinted was likely to be very soon engaged. Undaunted, Mr. Collins decided instead upon Elizabeth. With the prospect of having two daughters married, the gentleman whose name Mrs. Bennet could not bear to pronounce only the day before was now high in her good graces. This went no way toward calming her nerves, however, and she was forced to obtain still more remedies from the gypsies, financing her treatment by instructing Cook to use cheaper cuts of meat, and in so doing returning to her the sum that remained.

After breakfast, Lydia announced that she desired to walk to Meryton. Every sister except Mary agreed to go with her. Mr. Collins was to attend them, at the request of Mr. Bennet, who was anxious to be rid of him, for yet another drawing had arrived, and he was most keen to examine it. He was not, however, keen to examine the household accounts, which had been dwindling considerably in recent weeks—a state of affairs for which he blamed himself.

Although Mary might have seized this opportunity to

be with Mr. Collins, his inattention to her the previous day had proved dispiriting. If she hoped to attract his notice, she would need to make herself more prepossessing. Her face, she realized, could not be much improved on, but her figure was another matter. Mary was not indisposed to some degree of feminine deception, providing it put her on equal footing with her sisters; therefore she visited the kitchen and, while Cook's back was turned, helped herself to two apples. As she did so, her attention was caught by an odd sort of wooden contrivance. It looked to be something one might employ for crushing or grinding. That Mary could make more interesting use of it she had no doubt. Removing its wooden cylinder, she hastened with the three items to her room and would not be seen again till dinnertime.

Mr. Collins's reading of the evening before had put some curious ideas into Mary's head, and she felt obliged to follow where they led. What she proposed to do astonished even herself, but she was determined to provide satisfaction to the need that had been growing inside her ever since she heard Mr. Collins speak with such rawness of language as he had done in the drawing room. The fact that they were not his own words mattered not a jot. Settling herself on her bed, Mary raised up her skirts and parted her thighs, offering up her maidenhead to Mr. Collins, whom she imagined there in the room with her. Perhaps he was not so handsome a figure as Angus the stableman, but in her eyes he was completely without fault. She placed the wooden object at the entrance to her womanhood and began to urge it inside, the sound of Mr. Collins's voice as he narrated Angus and Annabel's passion still in her ears.

That Mary had not given proper consideration to the matter swiftly became manifest, and she was required to content herself with only a partial consummation of her ardor for Mr. Collins. Her participation in the more studious pursuits of life had ill prepared her for what she now proposed to do, and the object's progress was halted by the refusal of her body to accept it fully. Rather than abandoning her plan altogether, she directed the object as she imagined Mr. Collins might do, were it the length of his manhood rather than a shaft of wood endeavoring to penetrate her. After a time matters became more agreeable, and she began to experience a pulsing within the folds of her womanhood that compelled her to place her hand there, her finger alighting on a highly sensitive ridge of flesh. This she paid much heed to, moving it about every which way until she found a method that pleased her.

As Mary found herself being overcome by an increasing sense of urgency for which she could not account, she increased the speed of her finger, along with the object located part of the way inside her. It now moved with greater ease, though she could not as yet accommodate the entirety of it. As her hands continued to occupy themselves, her breath suddenly caught in her throat as she experienced a sensation like that of a match being struck. Mary cried out with the wonder of it, soon afterward falling into repose. She felt no regret in not having dispensed with her maidenhood and was now more than ever determined to award it to Mr. Collins at the first opportunity, hoping he would dispense with it in the same brutish manner as Angus had done with Annabel.

Owing to Mr. Collins's unceasing conversation and pompous nothings, the remaining Bennet sisters found themselves much vexed on their walk to Meryton. When the party at last reached town, Kitty's and Lydia's eyes were immediately wandering up the street in quest of officers, with the latter seeming especially affected. Lydia's breaths became increasingly labored, as if she had been running, her bosom rising and falling with great agitation. The attention of every lady was soon caught by a young man whom they had never seen before, walking with the very Mr. Denny Lydia wished to inquire after. All were struck with the stranger's air and fine countenance and wondered who he could be. Kitty and Lydia, determined to find out, crossed the road on the pretense of investigating bonnets in a shop window. The ruse was successful; the officers were shortly upon them, and Mr. Denny introduced his friend, Mr. Wickham, who had accepted a commission in their corps and would be staying on in Meryton. The remainder of the party joined the quartet, and a happy conversation ensued. Mr. Wickham, in particular, showed himself to be most charming, and Elizabeth, of all her sisters, was quite taken with him.

The sound of horses soon drew their notice. Mr. Bingley and Mr. Darcy, on distinguishing the ladies of the party, rode toward them, where Bingley took the lead in the usual civilities, directing most of them to Jane. Darcy bowed, determining not to fix his eyes on Elizabeth, when they were suddenly arrested by the sight of Mr. Wickham. Elizabeth, happening to see the countenance of both as they looked at each other, was all astonishment at the effect of the meeting. Both men changed color, and Mr. Wickham, after a few moments, touched his hat in salutation, which Mr. Darcy just deigned to return. The exchange went unnoticed by Mr. Bingley, who took leave and rode on with his friend. Indeed, Elizabeth knew not what to make of it.

The Bennet sisters decided to call on their uncle and aunt, Mr. and Mrs. Phillips, and Mr. Denny and Mr. Wickham continued on their way, despite invitations to join them. Mrs. Phillips was pleased to see her nieces, particularly Jane and Elizabeth, and they chatted amiably as Kitty and Lydia secured a place at the window, watching in the event the officers might reappear. Mr. Collins was received by the Phillipses with the very best politeness, though his habit of admiring the furnishings was not agreeably looked upon, his manner more that of a lowly country trader assessing their value than a respected member of the clergy. His continual apologies to Mrs. Phillips for intruding without any previous acquaintance were eventually ignored when the conversation turned to the latest arrival to Meryton, whereupon it was agreed that the next day the Bennets were to join the Phillipses in an evening of cards and supper, and Mr. Phillips would call on Mr. Wickham with an invitation to join them.

With so much lively discussion over the prospect of the planned gathering, no one observed when Mr. Collins had removed himself from the vicinity. He had earlier spied the figure of a young man, the son of one of the maids, carrying a stack of linen up the stairs. He had the face of a cherub, and it was framed by golden curls. His eyes, which were the blue of a summer sky, reminded Mr. Collins of an angel's. The boy cast a glance over his shoulder, indicating that Mr. Collins should follow him upstairs, where they quickly availed themselves of a storage cupboard. The linens were dropped, without ceremony, to the floor, and much clumsy fondling ensued within the cramped space, most of it engaged in by Mr. Collins, who found the boy's manhood to be of pleasing stature. That it also possessed great appeal he could not deny, and, feeling quite suddenly impetuous, he fell to his knees and took it into his mouth, not entirely certain what to expect. His encounters had always involved the application of his manhood to the hind openings of young men rather than the more insalubrious activities he was now about to embark on. Indeed, Mr. Collins was most particular in his habits and considered such practices far beneath a gentleman of his standing. As he felt the boy's flesh begin to twitch against his tongue, he drew hard upon it, his lips eliciting from it the first release, which arrived swiftly, as is the custom of the very young, and it prompted much coughing and sputtering from the recipient, who did not find the resulting rush of liquid into his mouth at all disagreeable.

Mr. Collins turned the housemaid's son around to face

the wall, his heart beating with ferocity when he feared that his overtures might be met with resistance. But the boy seemed not unaccustomed to such appointments, and he lowered his breeches and bent forward quite readily, his hands reaching back to part the cleft of his backside. Until now, Mr. Collins had been forced to refrain from pursuing his curious desires, the eyes of his patroness Lady Catherine having grown more vigilant since the matter with the choristers from his parish in Kent. However, the excitement of being presented with what had for too long been denied him proved overwhelming and, rather than savoring the moment, he entered the boy with one great thrust, eliciting not the slightest complaint. On the contrary, his companion afforded him a most friendly reception, and Mr. Collins indulged himself for as long as he deemed prudent, certain his absence would be noticed and that someone would soon be dispatched to locate him, perhaps one of his charming cousins. The thought of being found by either Miss Jane or Miss Elizabeth added much to his pleasure and he hastened his movements, driving his manhood into the opening before him with as much force as he could muster, energized by the low groans of the housemaid's son, who appeared to be enjoying himself considerably, if the renewed length of his manhood was to be believed. Mr. Collins, who was not indisposed to such manner of engagements in public places or, indeed, the thrill of possible discovery, often took his companions into the shrubbery adjacent to the vicarage, the thorns on the branches adding an ecclesiastical element to the experience that proved highly inspirational.

Mr. Collins reached around to grasp hold of the boy's manhood and began to work it with rapid up-and-down motions, feeling himself on the brink of release. He sallied forth with one final thrust, his portly form shuddering as his fluids were depleted from him, at which point his recently gained acquaintance reached his own conclusion, depositing his contribution onto the clean stack of linen, where it would remain until dry, only later to make up the bedding of Mr. and Mrs. Phillips. Mr. Collins withdrew from the source of his pleasure and, after attending to his garments, quit the cupboard and returned downstairs in time for the Longbourn party's departure. To his disappointment, no one had noticed him gone, though his heightened countenance elicited more than one curious glance in his direction.

The following evening the coach conveyed Mr. Collins and his five cousins to the Phillipses. No sooner were they in the door than the girls had the pleasure of hearing that Mr. Wickham had accepted their uncle's invitation and was already present. Such news was of little consequence to Mary, who planned to spend the evening in pursuit of Mr. Collins, from whom she was never very far. On this occasion, her plain figure appeared remarkably altered. Her bosom projected out at a precarious angle, the two apples she had removed from the kitchen now secreted into her corset and affording her a contour that she believed was more womanly. The ruse might well have been a success had she not looked near to toppling over.

Mr. Collins, unmoved by Mary's attempts to engage his attention, cast his eyes about in hopes of seeing his young friend from the cupboard, whose muscular backside having provided much in the way of heavenly delights that he very much wished to sample again. This evening, however, the boy was nowhere to be seen; therefore Mr. Collins instead attached himself to Mrs. Phillips and her nieces. He resumed his discourse from the day before, describing the grandeur of Lady Catherine and her mansion and the cost of various furnishings, with occasional digressions in praise of his own humble abode and the improvements it was receiving, thanks to her ladyship's generous patronage. To the girls, who could not bear to listen to their cousin, the interval felt very long until the gentlemen appeared.

It was over at last when the officers entered the room with Mr. Phillips, leaving Mr. Collins to sink into insignificance. Mr. Wickham was the happy man toward whom almost every female eye was turned, and Elizabeth the happy woman by whom he finally seated himself. After supper, a game of whist was proposed by Mrs. Phillips, to which Mr. Collins eagerly assented, and card tables were set up all around. Elizabeth and Mr. Wickham were joined at another table by Lydia, who was as fond of placing bets as she was of riding a young officer's thigh; therefore the danger of her monopolizing their conversation was short-lived.

Since Mr. Wickham did not play, he was at leisure to talk to Elizabeth, who was most curious to learn of his acquaintance with Mr. Darcy, though she dared not mention the gentleman. Her curiosity, however, was unexpectedly relieved when Mr. Wickham introduced the subject by inquiring how long Darcy had been staying at Netherfield. The discussion then progressed to his estate in Derbyshire, where, to Elizabeth's astonishment, Wickham had spent his youth. "I have been connected with his family in a particular manner from my infancy," said Mr. Wickham. "You may well be surprised, Miss Bennet, at such an assertion, after seeing, as you probably might, the very cold manner of our meeting yesterday. Are you much acquainted with Mr. Darcy?"

"As much as I ever wish to be," replied she. "I have spent four days in the same house with him, and I think him very disagreeable. He is not at all liked in Hertfordshire. Everyone is disgusted by his pride."

"The world is blinded by his fortune and consequence, or frightened by his high and imposing manners, and sees him only as he chooses to be seen," added Mr. Wickham, displaying a keen inclination to speak further on the subject. "The late Mr. Darcy bequeathed me the best living. He was my godfather and excessively attached to me. He meant to provide for me amply, and thought he had done it, but it was removed elsewhere exactly as I was of an age to hold it."

"Good heavens! Surely you do not mean it fell to Mr. Darcy?"

"Indeed, you have not heard the worst, Miss Bennet. Though I fear you may be too delicate for such confidences."

"Pray, Mr. Wickham, I very much wish to know the full extent of Mr. Darcy's wickedness."

"I fear it is quite abominable. Mr. Darcy took a goodly portion of the income which I was bequeathed and used it to open a bawdy house in London. Miss Bennet, I am a man of the world, and realize such modes of commerce exist; however, I have heard that activities of a particularly unwholesome nature take place at this establishment, some of which involve farm animals."

"Say it isn't so!" cried Elizabeth, thinking with fondness of the sheep that grazed in the surrounding countryside. Mr. Wickham's revelation prompted a suffusion of color to spread over her features and she cast her eyes downward, at which point she noted a movement in Mr. Wickham's breeches, as if something contained therein were endeavoring to escape. She could not account for it, though she found herself becoming very much affected as she experienced a curious sensation like that of a heartbeat in the place of her womanhood.

"I fear it is, Miss Bennet. Although he is a gentleman of considerable wealth from his family's estate, Mr. Darcy's fortune has increased significantly since entering into . . ."— he struggled to finish the sentence—"*trade*."

Elizabeth's attention was momentarily caught by Lydia, whose excitement at the card table had prompted her to raise up her skirts and wriggle about in her chair, which she straddled in a rather unladylike manner, laughing and talking loudly. So distressed was Elizabeth by Wickham's report that she had not the strength to admonish her sister.

"But you have not heard the worst. Are you acquainted with Mr. Darcy's sister, Georgiana?"

"I regret not, though I have it on good authority that she is a very fine young lady," replied Elizabeth.

Wickham nodded gravely. "She was most assuredly, Miss Bennet, until her brother dispatched her to work in this very same bawdy house to which I referred earlier."

While Wickham had been speaking, the flap of his breeches had begun to expand outward, prompting a dampening to take place on the seat cushion beneath Elizabeth. She shifted position to remove herself from it, her color heightening still further as she felt his eyes on her. "These are villainous crimes indeed!" she cried. "Mr. Darcy deserves to be publicly disgraced!"

"Some time or other he will be, but it shall not be by *me*. Till I can forget the father, I can never defy or expose the son."

Elizabeth honored him for such feelings and considered him handsomer than ever as he expressed them. "I had not thought Mr. Darcy so bad as this, though I have never liked him. I am astonished at Mr. Bingley's intimacy with him! How can he be in friendship with such a man? He cannot know what Mr. Darcy is."

"Probably not, but Mr. Darcy can be pleasing to whom he chooses. Among those who are his equals in consequence, he is a very different man from what he is to the less prosperous."

The whist party soon broke up, and Mr. Collins resumed his monologue on Lady Catherine and Rosings Park, at which point Mr. Wickham imparted to Elizabeth an amusing piece of intelligence. "You know of course that Lady Catherine is aunt to the present Mr. Darcy. Her daughter, Miss de Bourgh, will have a very large fortune, and it is believed she and her cousin will unite the two estates through marriage."

Elizabeth thought of Miss Bingley and smiled. In vain

were all her attentions to that quarter, if Darcy was already destined for another. The news left her feeling quite satisfied as she recalled the rouged tips of Lady Caroline's bosom, which, no matter how beguiling their shade of red, could never compete with the likes of such a fortune.

That night Elizabeth took to her bed, her head full of Mr. Wickham. He had impressed her greatly with his frankness and ease of manner—so much so that she could scarcely wait to see him again. She had likewise been quite taken with the activity within his breeches, of which she was curious to learn more. The thought of what was contained there caused her to cry out with what sounded like pain as she recalled the rather unsavory nature of their discussion and how it had seemed to affect them both. The tips of Elizabeth's bosom pressed against the thin fabric of her sleeping garment and she placed her hands there, then allowed them to travel down her body, her flesh dimpling from her touch. She could still hear the fine timbre of Wickham's voice in her ear, and for a moment she believed him to be with her—indeed, very much wished it so, despite the impropriety of her desires. The pulsing she had experienced earlier had returned, and as it gained in strength she felt her thighs parting and raised up her hem, her fingers discovering a silken wetness. That Wickham had inspired it she had no doubt, for it was the same as that which had transpired earlier while in conversation with him.

Elizabeth felt quite wicked as, with one hand, she unlocked the cleft of her womanhood, a finger from the other alighting on the secret flesh that had been brought into exposure. As she began to stroke it, she felt it growing beneath the pad of her finger in a manner most extraordinary, and she increased the tempo till she could scarcely draw a breath. Suddenly she experienced a sensation of flying, then just as suddenly of being dropped. It was unlike anything she had ever known, and she was so overwhelmed that she fell very quickly asleep, dreaming of Mr. Wickham's handsome figure and pleasing manner.

When Elizabeth related to Jane the next day her conversation with Wickham, her sister listened with astonishment and concern; she knew not how to believe that Mr. Darcy could be so unworthy of Mr. Bingley's regard, yet it was not in her nature to question the veracity of a young man of such amiable appearance as Mr. Wickham. Therefore nothing remained for her but to think well of them both and throw into the account the possibility of accident or mistake for what could not be otherwise explained. Elizabeth, however, remained unconvinced, and her partiality toward Mr. Wickham was evident as she spoke. "I can much more easily believe Mr. Bingley's being imposed on, than that Mr. Wickham should invent such a history of himself as he gave me last night. If it be not so, let Mr. Darcy contradict it."

Although hesitant to accept the veracity of Mr. Wickham's story, Jane held one certainty—if Mr. Bingley *had* been imposed on, he would have much to suffer when the affair became public.

The two young ladies were summoned by the arrival of the very person of whom they had been speaking. Mr. Bingley was accompanied by his two sisters, who had come to give their personal invitation to the ball at Netherfield. Delight was expressed in abundance by Miss Bingley and Mrs. Hurst at seeing their dear friend Jane again; to the rest of the family they paid little attention. They were soon gone, rising from their seats with an action that took their brother by surprise, and hurrying off as if eager to escape from Mrs. Bennet's civilities.

The prospect of the ball caused much excitement at Longbourn House. Mrs. Bennet considered it a compliment to herself that her eldest had been invited personally. Jane anticipated a pleasant evening enjoying the company of her two friends and the attentions of their brother, while Kitty and Lydia entertained thoughts of dancing with any number of handsome young officers, the latter talking incessantly of Mr. Denny, who had become her personal favorite. Even Mary indicated that she had no disinclination for the event, particularly with the added presence of Mr. Collins in the party. Elizabeth thought with pleasure of dancing most of the evening with Mr. Wickham and of seeing a confirmation of all she had been told in Mr. Darcy's look and behavior. It appeared that the entire household looked forward with great eagerness to the evening, but for Mr. Bennet.

The subject of so much endless discussion of balls and officers had driven him to increase his hours of solace in the library, where he continued to occupy himself quite happily with his drawings, reemerging only to take meals and occasionally wash. Mr. Bennet had been so fortunate as to locate a very fine butternut squash, which he had hollowed out with a knife while still leaving the skin and much of the pulpy interior intact. This he used in place of his hand, and as he stood before his escritoire, on which he had placed a drawing, his manhood engaged itself most agreeably with the interior of the fruit, imagining it to be the interior of the young lady on whose pleasing form he gazed. Within moments the squash had heated sufficiently to render the illusion complete, and Mr. Bennet found that it felt quite authentic, if one did not mind encountering the occasional seed along the way. Only a short series of thrusts would be required before his pleasure emerged from him with a force he had never imagined possible. Indeed, he much preferred the squash to Mrs. Bennet, who had never once accepted him into the marital bed without some manner of complaint.

When Elizabeth asked Mr. Collins whether he intended to accept Mr. Bingley's invitation, and if he did, whether he would think it proper to join in the evening's amusement, she was eagerly assured by him of his opinion that a ball of this kind, given by a young man of character, could not have any evil tendency. "I am so far from objecting to dancing myself," he added, "that I shall hope to be honored with the hands of all my fair cousins in the course of the evening; and I take this opportunity of soliciting yours, Miss Elizabeth, for the two first dances especially."

Only at this moment did Elizabeth realize that it was *she* who had been singled out from among her sisters to be the future mistress of Hunsford parsonage, the idea soon reaching to conviction as she noted Mr. Collins's increasing civilities toward herself and heard his frequent attempt at a compliment. It was not long before her mother gave her to understand that the probability of their marriage was extremely agreeable. Elizabeth, however, chose not to take the hint and instead ignored the situation. Perhaps Mr. Collins might never make the offer.

Chapter Eight

THE LONGBOURN PARTY ARRIVED AT NETHERFIELD IN animated spirits. Kitty and Lydia immediately set upon a cluster of redcoats, one of whom was Mr. Denny. Mary endeavored to attach herself to Mr. Collins, hoping that the circumstances of a ball might allow them the opportunity for more intimate acquaintance. She had chosen a gown most suited to the occasion and one that she thought would emphasize her figure. Instead it brought to light the apples she had placed in her corset, which were of varying size, giving her bosom a curiously misshapen appearance. Her wiles were lost on Mr. Collins, however, for this evening he had eyes only for Elizabeth, who he felt assured would make a suitable wife and meet the approval of his discerning patroness, Lady Catherine.

Elizabeth had dressed with particular care, and she looked about in vain for Mr. Wickham, her excited anticipation changing to disappointment when she realized he was not present. She suspected that Mr. Bingley had omitted his invitation out of deference to his friend Darcy. The fact of his absence was later pronounced by Denny, who told them that Wickham had been obliged to go into town. "I do not imagine his business would have called him away just now," he added, "if he had not wanted to avoid a certain gentleman here."

Such intelligence confirmed what Elizabeth already suspected—that Mr. Darcy was in great part to blame for Wickham's absence, and she could hardly reply with tolerable civility to the polite inquiries that he afterward approached to make, instead turning away, resolved against any sort of conversation. When she looked at Darcy, she saw only the fallen of her sex who were forced to sell their bodies to any man with enough coins in his pockets to pay for them. To imagine that he should have engaged his own sister into such iniquity was more than she could bear, and she gazed with a fond heart at her own dear sisters Kitty and Lydia, rejoicing in their blissful innocence as they conversed happily with several young officers. Elizabeth's vantage point did not allow her to see the latter's hand inside the breeches of the officer nearest her, where it was busily working the length of his manhood.

Noting the presence of her friend Miss Lucas, Elizabeth moved to join her and informed her of her griefs, much of which concerned the absent Mr. Wickham. As if her mood was not already disposed toward displeasure, Mr. Collins chose that moment to appear before her with the request that she make good on her promise of honoring him with the first two dances, both of which gave Elizabeth all the shame and misery a disagreeable dance partner can give.

Till now Mary had been standing with Mr. Collins, and his abrupt removal from her side provoked nothing less than rage toward Elizabeth and dismay at her own physical shortcomings; she could not compete for Mr. Collins's attention when she had sisters so much more prepossessing in face and figure than herself. He was due to depart Longbourn in a matter of days, which left her very little time to secure his affection. Mary decided that she had no recourse but to apply to the gypsies for a beauty potion. She was weary of always being the plain Bennet sister; it was time to do something about it.

While Elizabeth was being tormented on the dance floor by Mr. Collins, Lydia stepped out into the gardens with Mr. Denny. It was a fine evening lit by a full moon, and they strolled along a pathway, moving farther away from the house. They soon arrived at a small clearing, whereupon Lydia, lifting up her skirts, flung herself against her companion's thigh and proceeded to rub vigorously against it. Denny's mouth came down over hers, the movements of his tongue highly agreeable, its tip fluttering against her own as if to offer provocation. Lydia, being Lydia, however, required no provocation. She unbuttoned his breeches and reached inside, taking his manhood into her hand, laughing happily when she discovered what she held. That Denny was much more generously proportioned than the other gentlemen with whom she had engaged in this manner was a source of much delight, and as she measured his girth with the circumference of her fingers, found herself eager to empty from it his pleasure. The skillfulness of Lydia's hand had often been remarked upon, and she very much wished to make her talents known to the handsome Mr. Denny.

Denny, however, had desires of an altogether different nature, for he had heard a good deal more about Lydia's accomplishments than those which she now proceeded to demonstrate to him. He pushed her backward onto the grass, where she lay sprawled in some disarray, the hems of her skirts nearly to her waist. Grasping hold of her thighs, he parted them wide, bringing the full of her womanhood into view. Lydia cast her eyes up at him, her tongue licking with deliberateness over her lips. To Denny's astonishment, she reached down with her fingers to pull open the cleft of her sex with a lasciviousness the likes of which even a gentle-man of his experience had never encountered, not even in a bawdy house. She proceeded to manipulate herself without so much as a blush of shame heightening her cheeks, her fingers flying about in her folds and occasionally vanishing inside her. Within moments Lydia was propelling her loins upward, crying out and laughing at the same time, until at last her hands grew still, only to resume their activities with even greater zeal.

Unable to endure this lewd performance any longer, Denny dropped to his knees and, in one quick movement, instilled the full length of himself inside her, not in the least surprised by how accommodating she was. A number of his fellow redcoats from other regiments that had passed through Meryton had spoken quite frankly of Miss Lydia Bennet's eagerness for the fleshly pursuits, and he did not find himself disappointed. Lydia wriggled about beneath him, meeting his thrusts with those of her own, some of which were so full of vigor that they nearly sent him fly-ing backward. He was finally forced to grab hold of her backside in order to prevent his manhood from becoming dislodged.

The sound of footfalls alerted Denny that someone was fast approaching. As he tried to quiet Lydia's loud giggles with his mouth, he put forth one final thrust that prompted her to scream with delight against his lips, releasing into her the full consignment of his fluids. He removed himself from Lydia with scarcely enough time remaining for her to tidy her skirts before they were joined by a third party. As Denny struggled without success to return his waning manhood to his breeches, the sound of a familiar voice reached his ears. "I daresay, you two appear to be most agreeably engaged," greeted Captain Carter with a smile. "Miss Bennet, might your generosity of spirit be likewise extended to myself?"

Lydia raised her skirts high in reply, exposing herself to Captain Carter. Her thighs continued to lie open, and the light from the moon left him with little need to tax his imagination. Not the sort of gentleman to refuse a lady's invitation, Captain Carter undid the buttons on his breeches and fell upon Lydia, sliding into her with ease and resuming where Denny had left off until there was a sufficient renewal of interest indicated from that quarter. Decorum had not yet been returned to Denny; his manhood continued to remain in full view of all, having returned to its previous state from his observations of Captain Carter applying himself to Miss Bennet.

Although superior in rank, Captain Carter was not quite so superior in stature; however, Lydia appeared not to mind in the least, and she met his thrusts with the same lustiness she had shown to those of Mr. Denny. Noting that gentleman's forlorn expression, she beckoned him to join her on the grass, where she turned her face toward him, her open mouth indicating that she required something to be placed inside it. Denny instantly comprehended her meaning, and within moments his manhood was being agreeably entertained. He was pleased to discover that the high praise for Miss Bennet's abilities in this area had also not been exaggerated. Captain Carter released his pleasure inside her a short while later, and she soon followed, her cry of rapture stifled by the flood of liquid on her tongue as Denny experienced his own. The two officers spent the next hour enjoying her in turns, after which they all returned to the house in time for more dancing.

Elizabeth experienced her own form of release when her obligation to Mr. Collins was at last concluded. She returned to Miss Lucas when the music was stopped momentarily and was in conversation with her when she found herself suddenly addressed by Mr. Darcy, who took her so much by surprise in his application for her hand that, without knowing what she did, she accepted. Her regret was immediate, and she made her feelings known with some force to Miss Lucas. When the dancing recommenced and Darcy made his approach, Charlotte touched Elizabeth's arm, cautioning her in a whisper not to allow her fancy for Wickham to make her appear unpleasant in the eyes of a man ten times his consequence. Elizabeth said nothing in reply, though she was rather puzzled by the curious manner in which her friend's fingers lingered on her flesh.

As Elizabeth took her place in the set, she was amazed at the dignity to which she was received in being allowed to stand opposite to Mr. Darcy. They began their dance in silence, which she imagined might last for the entirety of the two dances, and she resolved not to break it until she decided that obliging Darcy to engage in conversation might prove a greater punishment to him. She therefore put forth a series of light remarks, which were met, followed by more silence. Addressing Darcy again, Elizabeth assured him that they could now remain silent, to which he replied, "Do you talk by rule, then, while you are dancing?"

"One must speak a little. It would look odd to be entirely silent; and yet for *some*, conversation ought to be so arranged that they may have the trouble of saying as little as possible."

"Are you consulting your own feelings, or do you imagine that you are gratifying mine?"

"Both," answered Elizabeth. "I have always seen a great similarity in the turn of our minds. We are each of an unsocial, taciturn disposition, unwilling to speak unless we expect to say something that will amaze the whole room."

After another exchange, followed by more silence, Darcy inquired if Elizabeth and her sisters very often walked to Meryton. This she affirmed, unable to resist adding, "When you met us there the other day, we had just been forming a new acquaintance."

Mr. Darcy's features became overspread with color, and

it took some time before he spoke. "Mr. Wickham is blessed with such happy manners as may ensure his making friends. Whether he may be equally capable of retaining them, is less certain."

"He has been so unlucky as to lose *your* friendship," replied Elizabeth, "and in a manner that he is likely to suffer from all his life." Although she very much wished to say more—to denounce Darcy for his theft of Wickham's living and for his iniquitous application of it, she found that she could not go on.

As they moved through the dance, Sir William appeared close to them, offering Darcy a bow of deferential courtesy. "Such very superior dancing is not often seen," he praised. "Allow me to say, however, that your fair partner does not disgrace you, and that I must hope to have this pleasure often repeated, especially when a certain desirable event," he paused, glancing at Jane and Mr. Bingley, "takes place."

Darcy, his expression grave, directed his eyes toward his friend and Jane, who were dancing together. Recovering himself, he turned back to Elizabeth. "Sir William's interruption has made me forget what we were talking of."

"I do not think we were speaking at all. Sir William could not have interrupted two people in the room who had less to say for themselves. We have tried two or three subjects already without success, and what we are to talk of next I cannot imagine."

Smiling, Mr. Darcy asked her opinion of books, occupying a few more moments of conversation, most of which involved Elizabeth's discourse on the delights of her father's library. A blush marked her features as she recalled the novel that had been given a brief recitation by Mr. Collins, though he no doubt lived such a sheltered existence that he understood very little of what he read. As Elizabeth thought of Angus and Annabel's encounter in the stable, the disturbed flap of Mr. Wickham's breeches entered her mind, prompting the heat from her face to travel to her loins, and she very nearly cried out with the need to reach down and touch herself through the fabric of her gown. On noticing her dance partner looking at her with some curiosity, Elizabeth, wisely deciding to change the subject, turned the discussion to matters of more consequence. "I hear such different accounts of you as puzzle me exceedingly, Mr. Darcy."

"I can readily believe that reports may vary greatly with respect to me," he replied. "I could wish, Miss Bennet, that you were not to sketch my character at the present moment."

They moved down the line of dancers and parted in silence, on each side dissatisfied—Elizabeth, for not having forced Darcy into a confirmation or denial of Wickham's story, and Darcy, who had been left with a powerful feeling toward Miss Bennet.

They had not long separated when Miss Bingley moved toward Elizabeth with an expression of civil disdain. The low décolletage of her elegant gown revealed the full expanse of her bosom, the tips of which, rather than being tinted with rouge, had now been encrusted with brightly colored beads. Not for the first time did Elizabeth wonder why no one had seen fit to check her on the continued inappropriateness of her apparel. "Miss Eliza, I hear you are quite delighted with George Wickham!" cried Lady Caroline. "Your sister has been talking to me about him and asking me a thousand questions. Let me recommend you, however, as a friend, not to give implicit confidence to all his assertions. As to Mr. Darcy's using him ill, it is perfectly false. I pity you, Miss Eliza, for this discovery of your favorite's guilt."

"And pray, what is it he should be guilty of?" asked Elizabeth angrily. "That he is a gentleman of honor?—that he possesses an absence of deceit? Are these suddenly crimes in our society?"

"I beg your pardon," replied Miss Bingley with a sneer.

She thrust her chest outward, the sudden movement dislodging several of the beads, one of which flew into Elizabeth's more modest décolletage, where it remained for the rest of the evening. "Excuse my interference—it was kindly meant."

Elizabeth went to seek out Jane, who had undertaken to make inquiries on the same subject of Mr. Bingley. He remained ignorant, however, as to the history of Wickham and the circumstances that had caused such a powerful rift in his relationship with Darcy. Jane was quite clear in her report that Bingley vouched for the good conduct, probity, and honor of his friend, but Wickham was another matter. "I am sorry to say by his account as well as his sister's, Mr. Wickham is by no means a respectable young man. I am afraid he has been very imprudent and has deserved to lose Mr. Darcy's regard."

When Elizabeth asked if Mr. Bingley was himself acquainted with Wickham, she was told that Bingley had never seen him till the other morning at Meryton. Elizabeth smiled indulgently at Jane. "I have no doubt as to Mr. Bingley's sincerity," said she, "but you must excuse my not being convinced by assurances only. Mr. Bingley's defense of his friend was a very able one, but since he is unacquainted with several parts of the story, and has learned the rest from that friend himself, I shall venture to think of both gentlemen as I did before."

Elizabeth, finding herself rather annoyed at her sister, rejoined her friend Miss Lucas, more certain than ever that this condemnation of Wickham was a ruse put forth by Darcy to deflect guilt from himself. Charlotte's fingers once more sought out Elizabeth's arm, stroking the exposed flesh above her glove in a manner that was not at all displeasing, particularly when they quite by accident brushed against her bosom, seeming to remain in that vicinity far longer than was prudent. Elizabeth felt the tips stiffening and had the most curious image of her friend's lips upon them. Her night of self-pleasuring enjoyed in the privacy of her bed returned to her, and she felt her body tingling with the remembered sensations. These were further encouraged by Charlotte's touch as it grew bolder, her fingertips employing feathery motions on her flesh that brought forth the same manner of wetness from Elizabeth's womanhood as had been inspired by Mr. Wickham. That she should, at this moment, experience so impolitic a desire as to reach beneath her skirts and touch herself was a revelation, and she felt a powerful clutching in her loins, nearly crying out as she grabbed on to Charlotte's arm for support. How she wished for Mr. Wickham to appear! Elizabeth shut her eyes, willing it to be so. When she reopened them, rather than that gentleman's tall handsome figure, she was instead confronted by Mr. Collins's short, portly form.

"I have found out," said he with great excitement, "that there is now in the room a near relation of my patroness. Who would have thought of my meeting with a nephew of Lady Catherine de Bourgh in this assembly! I am most thankful that the discovery is made in time for me to pay my respects to him."

Horrified, Elizabeth tried to dissuade her cousin from such a scheme, assuring him that Mr. Darcy would consider Mr. Collins addressing the nephew without introduction as an impertinent freedom rather than a compliment to his aunt; should there be any notice, it must belong to Mr. Darcy, the superior in consequence, to begin the acquaintance. Her efforts were ineffective, however; Mr. Collins remained convinced of his right, for he considered his rank in the clergy equal with that of the highest rank in the kingdom, and he set off with determination to where Mr. Darcy was seated. Elizabeth observed with astonishment as he offered Darcy a solemn bow, the words "Hunsford parish" and "Lady Catherine de Bourgh" carrying to her across the room. Darcy eyed him with unrestrained wonder, which turned to contempt, whereupon he rose from his chair and moved off in another direction, leaving Mr. Collins in conversation with himself. Despite Elizabeth's strong dislike of Darcy, it gave her pain that she should be known by him to be linked to such a foolish gentleman as Mr. Collins.

When everyone sat down to supper, Elizabeth's mood improved at seeing how well suited her sister and Mr. Bingley were, and she felt nothing but the utmost joy for Jane and her future happiness in that quarter. Mrs. Bennet appeared to share the sentiment and had begun to speak very freely and loudly of her expectation that her eldest daughter would soon be married to Mr. Bingley. She went on to enumerate the many advantages of the match, adding that he was charming, rich, and well connected in society, which should also bode well for her other daughters. Mrs. Bennet's eyes gleamed with an unnatural brightness and were so wide that it was quite by chance they did not escape from her head. The excitement of the ball had been more than her nerves could endure, and she had been required in the days leading up to the event to summon the gypsies to Longbourn.

In vain did Elizabeth endeavor to temper the volume of her mother's enthusiasm, for Mr. Darcy was seated directly across from her and had overheard the entire exchange, but her mother would have none of it. "What is Mr. Darcy to me, pray, that I should be afraid of him?" cried Mrs. Bennet even more vociferously. "I am sure we owe him no such particular civility as to be obliged to say nothing *he* may not like to hear."

Loud laughter erupted from the opposite end of the table. The youngest Miss Bennet lolled about in her chair, her features heightened in color, her gown in some disarray. Earlier, while she had been dancing, Elizabeth had noted a large patch of damp on the back of her sister's gown. Lydia looked as if she had been rolling about in the grass; there were even smudges of what appeared to be mud on the hem of her petticoat, which had been immaculate on leaving the house. Mr. Denny presented a similar exterior, with occasional spots of dirt darkening his garments, his friend Captain Carter equally untidy, both men's complexions as red as their coats.

Lydia was seated between Denny and another officer, her hands beyond the view of the others at the table, for she had one each inside the breeches of her two dinner companions, where she was busily working the lengths of their manhood between bites of food, her ample bosom bobbing up and down from her efforts. The officers' faces had taken on a faraway expression as Lydia's fingers squeezed and pulled at their flesh, tormenting them still further by rolling the pad of her thumb in the moisture at the crown, which she then brought up to her lips, putting forth an extravagant display of licking it with her tongue. Each time she did so, the gentlemen emitted a plaintive groan, their upstanding members twitching wildly in their laps and threatening to erupt with their fluids, which would have ended up in their plates of food had matters not taken a different turn. More than once could Lydia be seen making a great fuss of dropping her serviette to the floor, at which point she bent sidewise to collect it, taking first one officer into her mouth, then the other, drawing upon their flesh most cheerfully until a servant was finally summoned by Mrs. Bennet to provide her daughter with a clean serviette. It would afterward be used to collect the pleasure of the two officers, who put forth their release just in time for dessert.

At the conclusion of supper, singing was talked of, and without waiting for an entreaty, Mary hastened to the pianoforte. The two apples protruding from the décolletage of her gown were of much curiosity to the guests, Miss Bingley and Mrs. Hurst finding them of particular amusement, and they spent some while in whispering to each other and laughing. During her song, Mary kept her eyes fixed on Mr. Collins. His were, in turn, fixed on Elizabeth, who could not help but glance at Mr. Darcy, whose contempt for her relations was manifest in his countenance. Despite the agonies suffered by those being treated to her performance, Mary began another melody, until Mr. Bennet at last intervened. "You have delighted us long enough," said he. "Let the other young ladies have time to exhibit."

Mr. Collins chose that moment to move toward the instrument. "If I were so fortunate as to be able to sing, I should have great pleasure, I am sure, in obliging the company with an air," he began, "for I consider music as a very innocent diversion, and perfectly compatible with the profession of a clergyman." Thereupon he launched into a ponderous speech on the duties of life in the clergy. Many stared, and still more smiled, but no one looked more amused than Mr. Bennet himself, while his wife, with rather more enthusiasm than was required, commended Mr. Collins for having spoken so sensibly.

Had Elizabeth's family made an agreement to expose themselves as much as they could during the evening, it would have been impossible for them to play their parts with more spirit or finer success. Elizabeth wished for nothing more than to be away from Netherfield, but Mr. Collins continued to recommend himself to her for the remainder of the evening, and she owed her greatest relief to Miss Lucas, who joined them and good-naturedly engaged Mr. Collins's conversation to herself. The caresses of Miss Lucas's fingers at Elizabeth's arm were not resumed.

Owing to a maneuver on the part of Mrs. Bennet, the family was the last to depart, and it was to the delight of everyone when their carriage arrived to transport them home to Longbourn.

Chapter Nine

THE NEXT DAY BROUGHT WITH IT ANOTHER MANNER OF grief for Elizabeth when Mr. Collins finally gave voice to his proposal. Observing proprieties, he first addressed Mrs. Bennet in requesting a private audience with her daughter, to which she offered her immediate affirmation. To all this Mary would not be privy; she had gone into Meryton in search of the gypsies, determined to seek a cure for her plainness.

On hearing of Mr. Collins's intent, Elizabeth, blushing with surprise, beseeched her mother to remain, adding that Mr. Collins could have nothing to say to her that anybody need not hear. Mrs. Bennet, however, would not be swayed, and her tone verged on hysteria as she insisted her daughter remain to hear him out.

Elizabeth sat down, sensible that it was wisest to get it over with as soon as possible. She wished to return to her room and resume her nocturnal activities, her increasing regard for Wickham now transferring them to the daytime. The shame brought on by the Netherfield ball had tarnished her pleasure the night before, and no amount of clever manipulations from her fingers inspired a result. They employed every rhythm and orchestration, but not the slightest hint of delight could be coaxed from her folds. She had even engaged a small candle, sliding it inside the opening of her womanhood and imagining it to be Wickham, whose breeches had indicated great promise. This, too, failed to bring relief, and Elizabeth at last abandoned her attempts. A good night's sleep and the start of a new day had refreshed her considerably, however, and she looked forward with eagerness to an afternoon spent in happy stimulation of her parts. Perhaps she might prevail upon two candles, since it seemed improvident to make use of only one aperture when she had another located in convenient proximity!

Such a pleasing appointment was not to be, for no sooner had Mr. Collins begun his speech than all thoughts of desire left her. "Almost as soon as I entered the house, I singled you out as the companion of my future life," he avowed. "But before I am run away with by my feelings on this subject, perhaps it would be advisable for me to state my reasons for marrying." Mr. Collins then proceeded to list the advantages to himself for securing a wife, the most pertinent of which related to his patroness, Lady Catherine de Bourgh. "Twice has she condescended to give me her opinion on this subject. 'Choose properly, choose a gentlewoman for *my* sake; and for your *own*, let her be an active, useful sort of person, not brought up high, but able to make a small income go a good way. Find such a woman as soon as you can,' were her precise words on the subject." He paused momentarily, as if allowing Elizabeth to comprehend the full honor of having been singled out by him as being worthy to gain the approval of such a noble personage as her ladyship.

Mr. Collins next began to outline the merits of enjoying such an alliance with Lady Catherine, his effusive praise inspiring in Elizabeth an intense dislike of a woman whom she had not even met. He then explained his other motive, that being his generosity to select a wife from Longbourn to mitigate the loss when he inherited the estate on the death of Mr. Bennet. "And now nothing remains but for me to assure you in the most animated language of the violence of my affection. To fortune I am perfectly indifferent, and shall make no demand of that nature on your father, since I am well aware that it could not be complied with."

Elizabeth could bear no more. "You are too hasty, sir!" cried she. "You forget that I have made no answer. Accept my thanks for the compliment you are paying me. I am very sensible of the honor of your proposals, but it is impossible for me to do otherwise than to decline them."

Mr. Collins was unperturbed by the rejection; he had heard that young ladies were disposed to rejecting the initial addresses of a gentleman they secretly planned to accept, and he continued undaunted, prompting Elizabeth to temper her words with rather less diplomacy. Yet despite the frankness with which she spoke, Mr. Collins remained convinced hers was a feminine ruse designed to encourage him and raise her in his esteem, and he continued with his argument until Elizabeth, perceiving the hopelessness of the situation, quit the room.

A number of days would pass before she felt able to indulge herself in private pleasure, and when she did, it was not of the quality she desired. Rather than envisioning the handsome Mr. Wickham, it was Mr. Collins whom Elizabeth kept seeing in her mind's eye. No matter how industriously her fingers labored or how many candles she applied, she could not inspire that wondrous sensation of flight she had enjoyed previously. Indeed, she had all but exhausted the household's supply of candles in her quest to seek fulfillment, later taking a mirror to herself to ascertain whether all was as it should be, relieved to find that the flesh within her cleft appeared intact, though it still stubbornly refused to respond. She found this latest turn of events most worrisome and hoped for another meeting with Mr. Wickham to take place without delay, before any further harm was done.

Mrs. Bennet did not take well to the news of Elizabeth's refusal, which she received firsthand from Mr. Collins, who had begun to express some misgivings as regards Miss Bennet's suitability as a wife. Assuring him that her daughter would be brought to reason, she took it upon herself to call uninvited on her husband in his library. "Mr. Bennet, you are wanted immediately! We are all in an uproar!"

Mr. Bennet was seated at his writing desk, studying some manner of drawing, his hands happily pumping away in his lap when his wife interrupted. "Mr. Bennet, whatever are you doing there?" cried she, her voice unnaturally shrill. Ever since she had begun increasing the dosage of her special medicine, the volume of her conversation had become greatly amplified.

"Of what are you talking, Mrs. Bennet?" replied Mr. Bennet, secreting the drawing into a drawer with the others. His astonishment at the intrusion quickly turned to annoyance, some of it directed toward himself for neglecting to lock the door. He had been enjoying a particularly pleasurable interlude with the latest addition to his collection, this one depicting a young lady passing a few moments with two African fellows, both of whom were servicing her at the same time. Till now, Mr. Bennet had been unaware that such a manner of activity was even possible, though the drawing was scrupulous in every detail as it displayed the subject lying on her back atop one man, her feet held high in the air by the other, who knelt between her thighs. The fellow beneath her had fitted the entirety of his manhood into her backside, while his companion was in the process of introducing himself into the opening of her womanhood, which had been rendered so succulent a shade of pink that

Mr. Bennet desired from it a taste. The expression on the young lady's face was nothing less than pure lust, and Mr. Bennet, wishing that he could gain the society of such a lady, had benefited from four spells of pleasure in rapid succession courtesy of his hand, having been forced to dispense with his specially prepared squash owing to its falling apart, before his solitude was interrupted by his wife. His contact in London had outdone himself on this occasion, despite the increased fee he had been made to pay. Mr. Bennet only hoped that his family had not noticed the recent absence of Bessie, Kitty's favorite horse, which he had sold to the knackerman so that he had enough for payment.

"Oh, Mr. Bennet!" cried Mrs. Bennet. "Lizzy declares she will not have Mr. Collins, and Mr. Collins begins to say that he will not have Lizzy! Tell her that you insist upon her marrying him."

Mr. Bennet, momentarily forgetting himself, rose from his chair, exposing the full extent of his manhood to Mrs. Bennet, who had not encountered these parts for many years, nor wished to. "Oh, my nerves!" she screamed, running from the room, her flight leaving Mr. Bennet to reflect on what was a very simple solution to his privacy concerns. Were it not for the presence of his five daughters, he might well have considered forgoing the wearing of breeches altogether.

To Elizabeth's good fortune, her father sided fully with her in her refusal of his cousin's offer, though Mrs. Bennet continued to plague her daughter on the matter at every available opportunity. Mr. Collins, despite the wounding to his pride, thought too well of himself to suffer the rejection. His regard for Elizabeth was quite imaginary, just as it had been for Jane. Were it not for the insistence of his patroness Lady Catherine, he would have been quite satisfied to pass his days as a bachelor, happily serving the people of his parish, particularly those young men who most required his guidance.

Charlotte Lucas chose that day to call with an invitation to Lucas Lodge, and had barely entered the vestibule before receiving the news from Lydia and Kitty that their sister had rejected a proposal of marriage from Mr. Collins. She was then met by Mrs. Bennet, who reiterated the same sad tale, which was made all the more sorrowful by the delicate state of her nerves. Before Charlotte could speak, Jane and Elizabeth appeared. "Aye, there she is," said Mrs. Bennet. "Miss Lizzy, if you take it into your head to go on refusing every offer of marriage, you will never get a husband at all, and I am sure I do not know who is to maintain you when your father is dead." The room next admitted Mr. Collins, who, when Mrs. Bennet drew him aside, made it clear that his offer of marriage to Elizabeth had been fully rescinded.

Mary, who had been made ecstatic by the news of her sister's refusal, joined her family downstairs in anticipation that her new appearance might persuade Mr. Collins to transfer his proposal to herself. The two apples had once more been placed inside her corset, and the bodice of her gown stuck out like a shelf, minus a vase of flowers. That her features were markedly improved she had no doubt. Her search that morning for the gypsies had proved successful. She had been walking through the town when she saw them being removed from the tavern by its proprietor, who shouted words of the sort Mary had never heard in her life. For a moment she thought she heard familiar laughter coming from an upstairs window, but quickly dismissed it as she got on with the business at hand. She had brought with her what few coins she had managed to pilfer from the pockets of her father's coat, along with a necklace, all of which she used in exchange for a foul-smelling potion she had been assured would work immediately on its consumption. She drank it then and there, her throat burning as if she had swallowed fire, hastening home before her absence was noticed.

The moment Mary entered the room, all eyes were drawn

toward her, and she thrust out her bosom with pride, certain that the looks she received were those of admiration and, in the case of her sisters, *envy*. She moved directly toward Mr. Collins, who had begun to back away. Mary offered him a reassuring smile, believing that he was so overcome by her newfound beauty that he could no longer trust himself to remain a gentleman in her presence. As she envisioned him tearing off her gown and ravishing her on the floor in full view of everyone, she experienced a powerful ache in the place of her womanhood, and it was all she could do not to reach for the nearest and most suitably shaped object to relieve it. "Angus!" she whispered, drawing closer to Mr. Collins, her only thought that of her nails dragging down his back as he roughly dispensed with her maidenhood.

Mr. Collins's reaction was most curious and, to Mary, quite unexpected, for he gave the appearance of a man stricken with terror, casting his eyes about as if seeking escape. As she drew determinedly nearer to the object of her affection, she caught sight of a figure in the mirror hanging on the wall behind him. Though she recognized the gown, there was little else familiar about the image. It took several moments for her to realize that it was herself. The smile on Mary's face suddenly reversed course, and she screamed so loudly on seeing the black mustache situated at her upper lip that the glass of the mirror shattered.

The following day produced no abatement of Mrs. Bennet's ill health or ill humor. Mr. Collins continued to remain in the same state of injured pride, avoiding any manner of engagement with Elizabeth, who had expected his resentment of her to necessitate his early departure to Kent. He was determined, however, to fulfill the full obligation of his visit; therefore she had no recourse but to abandon any plans toward a resumption of pleasurable self-indulgences. His presence in the house was sufficient to quell any hope of reinvigorating her desire.

After breakfast, the Bennet sisters walked to Meryton to inquire if Mr. Wickham had returned. The party was minus Mary, who had locked herself in her room, where her screams continued to be heard. To everyone's delight, Mr. Wickham joined up with the girls as they entered the town, and he attended them to their aunt's, where everyone lamented his absence at the Netherfield ball. His appearance caused a suffusion of color to erupt on Elizabeth's face and chest, and she was most flattered when he elected specifically to sit with her, his nearness prompting a tingle to manifest itself in the cleft of her womanhood. Overcome by the need to attend to it and equally relieved by its reappearance, she pressed her thighs tightly together, endeavoring to focus her attention on their conversation.

Wickham acknowledged to Elizabeth that his absence from the ball had been self-imposed and, as she suspected, owing to Mr. Darcy, whose presence in the same room for so many hours he felt was more than he could bear. His willingness to spare others any unpleasantness only increased her high opinion and admiration, and she was pleased when he appeared eager to resume their previous discussion. "Miss Bennet, are you aware that Miss Darcy is now returned to the guardianship of her brother?" When Elizabeth replied that she was not, he continued. "Indeed, it is of a highly confidential nature, but the truth is, Miss Georgiana is now addicted to opium."

Elizabeth gasped, whereupon Wickham shifted his chair nearer so that they would not be overheard. As he did so, she noted the same manner of movement in his breeches as that which she had observed on their last meeting, and she felt a clutching in her loins as she experienced a most impolitic desire to place her hand on the cause of it. As Wickham continued to chronicle the tragic plight of Darcy's sister, a shape began to appear beneath the fabric, growing larger and larger until the threads securing the buttons at the flap threatened to break. "Alas, it is a similar situation with many of the young ladies who are forced to work in such unsavory establishments. Miss Darcy, being perhaps of a more tender age than most, was ill prepared to engage with the nature of her . . ."—Wickham paused, swallowing hard—"*duties*. It is not uncommon for those of her ilk to turn to opium for comfort."

"Oh, the horror of it all!" cried Elizabeth. "How can such things be allowed to go on? Those poor, poor girls!" She was near to tears as she imagined her younger sisters being taken into such insalubrious establishments, only to have their innocence stolen by men who perhaps had daughters their age. The thought of Lydia, especially, tore at her heart, and it took several moments before she could regain her composure.

Wickham shook his head sadly, his breathing increasingly labored. "You may well ask, Miss Bennet, but I fear we live in cruel times, and there are some of my sex who will use a young woman without regard to her sensibilities, or those of her family. And for these men there are men like Mr. Darcy, who are more than happy to provide young women to these wicked devils."

"Is there nothing that can be done?"

"Not as long as there are men willing to pay for these wretched creatures. Many die of the pox, though death, perhaps, is a blessing. The others, such as Miss Darcy, become too deranged to be of service and are either cast out into the streets or returned to their families, many of whom sold them into service in the first place. Indeed, Miss Darcy might be considered one of the more fortunate souls."

Elizabeth found her gaze being repeatedly drawn toward the turmoil transpiring in Wickham's breeches. She was able to establish still more of the shape therein, particularly that of a bulb-like protuberance that seemed to throb quite violently whenever she looked upon it. Suddenly she experienced the most unprecedented urge to seat herself in his lap and press her parts against it, though she knew to do so would be most unseemly. Wickham's face had grown quite flushed, and a sheen of moisture appeared on his brow as he continued to avail himself of her confidence. "I have it on good authority that Miss Darcy was being engaged in a manner of a particularly unnatural nature to which no lady should be made privy."

"I do not understand to what you refer," replied Elizabeth in genuine confusion.

"Miss Darcy . . ." Wickham's voice broke. He reached into his pocket for a handkerchief, which he employed to mop his brow. That he was highly distressed by what he was about to relate to Miss Bennet was conspicuous by his lapse of composure, and he struggled to continue. "The men who called on Miss Darcy did so for one specific purpose, that being to—"

"Yes?" encouraged Elizabeth.

"—to take their pleasure in her hind entry!" A low moan escaped from Wickham's lips as a dark circle began to form on the flap of his breeches. Elizabeth observed with a keen interest as it spread increasingly outward, Wickham's eyes rolling upward until all that could be seen were their whites. He looked very much in danger of toppling over backward in his chair. At that moment a loud bout of laughter erupted from another part of the room. It came from Lydia, who was occupied in conversation with her aunt and Jane, the disruption seeming to cause Wickham to remember himself, at which point he made some subtle adjustments to his garments.

Elizabeth could not speak; nor did she know what to say. Though it was admittedly a most reprehensible crime, she could not help giving it some careful reflection. Perhaps in the correct circumstances, such an activity need not be so very odious, particularly when she imagined being engaged in similar circumstances with Mr. Wickham. The thought would afterward go some way toward inspiring many nights of pleasure in the privacy of her room.

It had come time to quit her aunt's, and Elizabeth regretfully took her leave of Wickham, whose breeches were still in a rather dubious state. He put forth his farewell to the ladies with an extraordinarily low bow, from which he appeared unwilling to recover.

The party returned to Longbourn, where a letter awaited the eldest Miss Bennet. The envelope contained a sheet of elegant paper covered with a lady's fine flowing hand, and Elizabeth saw her sister's cheerful countenance change as she read it. "It is from Caroline Bingley, with news that the whole party has left Netherfield for London—and without any intention of coming back." As Jane related the contents, Elizabeth listened with distrust, particularly to Miss Bingley's declaration as to the pain of her separation from her dear friend, knowing that the only pain to be suffered would be borne by Jane for the loss of Mr. Bingley. Lady Caroline went on to write that her brother's business in town could not be concluded with swiftness, and it was certain that, once there, he would not be inclined to leave.

Jane turned to her sister. "It is evident that Mr. Bingley has no intention to return this winter."

"It is only evident that Miss Bingley intends it to be so."

"But Lizzy, you have not heard the worst of it! She goes on to say that everyone is most eager to meet Miss Darcy again. Here, let me read: *My brother admires her greatly, and her relations all wish the connection as much as his own. With all these circumstances to favor an attachment, and nothing to prevent it, am I wrong, my dearest Jane, in indulging the hope of an event that will secure the happiness of so many?*"

Elizabeth was all astonishment. A match between Miss Darcy and Mr. Bingley! It sounded most improbable, particularly with the intelligence she had gained from Mr. Wickham, to whom she had pledged her silence on the matter. Had Bingley's trust for his friend Darcy made him so blind as to be unaware of the sordid details of Miss Darcy's recent past? As regards Jane, Elizabeth very much doubted that Bingley's affections could be so easily swayed; therefore she offered another explanation. "Miss Bingley sees that her brother is in love with you, and wants him to marry Miss Darcy. She follows him to town in hope of keeping him there, and tries to persuade you that he does not care about you. She is anxious to get Miss Darcy for her brother on the notion that, when there has been *one* intermarriage, she may have less trouble in achieving a second. I daresay it would succeed, if Miss de Bourgh were out of the way."

Jane, in her willingness to think only good of everyone, refused to believe her friend Miss Bingley capable of a moment's duplicity, and it required much effort from Elizabeth to cheer her from what she perceived to be a hopeless situation. It was decided that news of the party's departure from Netherfield would be relayed to the family, but not the particulars. Jane and Elizabeth knew too well the delicacy of Mrs. Bennet's nerves, and thought it wise to spare her from further distress.

Chapter Ten

ON THE EVENING IN WHICH THE BENNETS DINED WITH THE Lucases, Miss Lucas displayed the utmost agreeableness in her attentions toward Mr. Collins, for which Elizabeth expressed her gratitude. Charlotte's kindness extended further than Elizabeth had any conception of, however, its object being to engage Mr. Collins's addresses toward herself. Her scheme proved so successful that it led that gentleman to hasten to Lucas Lodge the next morning to throw himself at her feet.

Matters were swiftly settled, and the couple received the joyful consent of Sir William and Lady Lucas. Mr. Collins's present circumstances made it a most eligible match for their daughter, to whom they could give little fortune, and his future inheritance of the Longbourn estate and his association with Lady Catherine added further to their felicity. Charlotte herself was tolerably composed. Mr. Collins, to be sure, was neither sensible nor agreeable; his society was irksome, and his attachment to her imaginary. Without thinking highly either of men or of matrimony, she had nevertheless made marriage her object. It was the only provision for well-educated young women of small fortune. Concerned for her friend Elizabeth, she exacted a promise from her betrothed to keep the affair secret until she herself could inform the Bennets of their impending nuptials.

Mr. Collins's relief at having finally secured the hand of a suitable young woman—one who would most assuredly meet the approval of her ladyship—inspired in him a desire for celebration. He had earlier spied one of the grooms from Lucas Lodge, a handsome boy with flashing dark eyes and the wild hair of a gypsy. A meaningful look had passed between them as he had walked by, and rather than return directly to Longbourn House, Mr. Collins sought out the stables, his heart pounding with a furiousness he assured himself was the result of his recent success with Miss Lucas.

The stableman loitered outside, lounging against a bale of hay. At Mr. Collins's approach, he stood up to display the full of his height, offering a smile that indicated much languorousness of spirit. Neither party spoke as the young man unbuttoned his grass-stained breeches and pushed them down, allowing his manhood to spring free. Mr. Collins fell to his knees in praise, certain that on this fine day every last one of his prayers had been answered. He reached out with trembling fingers to stroke the gift that had been presented to him, its beauty surpassing all his expectations. The groom's manhood was of significant length and thickness, its surface smooth and without flaw, and Mr. Collins pressed his face into the black curls from which it sprung, smelling leather and hay. He had barely time to open his mouth before the groom hoisted himself inside it, all but cutting off his breaths.

Mr. Collins accepted the stableman's flesh without complaint, taking great joy from the sensation of it slipping along his tongue. He reached around to grasp hold of the young man's muscular backside, his fingers acting on instinct as they sought out the cleft, which seemed to part most willingly, particularly when he endeavored to insinuate a finger inside the opening he found there. The stableman reacted with the wildness of an animal, driving his manhood into Mr. Collins's mouth with little regard for his anguished gasps and severely reddened countenance. As a respected member of the clergy under the patronage of Lady Catherine de Bourgh, Mr. Collins was unaccustomed to such an absence of refinement and for a moment knew not what to do. That he found such behavior most exhilarating, however, was manifest from the response in his breeches, and he allowed the groom to do as he wished, knowing that he was on the verge of soiling his garments.

Charlotte chose that moment to look out from the upstairs window of her room, which boasted a pleasing vista of the stables and the fields beyond. As she did so, she recognized the handsome figure of one of the stable hands—a gypsy boy whose family often traveled through Hertfordshire, plying their various wares and potions. Something of a rather curious nature appeared to be transpiring as she noted the figure of a second man, who was positioned on his knees before the stableman. The bobbing motions of his head reminded her of a marionette, and she squinted to better see what manner of activity could be occasioning these movements. The groom's manhood projected out from his loins, and he forced it repeatedly into the other man's mouth. Indeed, his actions appeared quite brutal, though the kneeling figure made no move to escape. Charlotte thought there was a familiarity to his coat and hat, but it would require several more moments of rigorous observation before she realized that the man taking the gypsy boy into his mouth was none other than her betrothed, Mr. Collins.

Charlotte was astonished, yet she did not experience any manner of distress from what she witnessed. Her match with Mr. Collins was not, at least on her side, born of the heart, but rather of practicality, and she now had affirmation that it was similarly on his side as well. Perhaps it had been wiser to accept his proposal than she had first believed. If the eagerness with which Mr. Collins applied himself to the groom's manhood was any indication, it was most unlikely that he would impose too stringently upon her the performance of her matrimonial duty. To Charlotte, who preferred to partake of fleshly pleasures with those of her own sex, this knowledge provided great relief, and she smiled with contentment, observing the gypsy's final shudders as he deposited his pleasure into her future husband's mouth.

Mr. Collins departed from Longbourn the next morning, giving numerous hints of being obliged very soon to revisit Hertfordshire, and leaving the Bennets to meditate the reasons why he should desire a return after having a proposal of marriage spurned. Mrs. Bennet wished to understand by it that he thought of paying his addresses to one of her younger girls, and Mary, in particular, was eagerly disposed to accept him, despite his recent reaction to her appearance. His quitting Longbourn had at last brought her forth from her room, where she had remained until now, refusing to speak to anyone or even take meals. The beauty potion obtained from the gypsies had failed. It had encouraged hair to sprout forth on her face and chest, rendering her ugly instead of merely plain. That morning while everyone was gathered at breakfast, Mary had availed herself of her father's razor, taking it to her upper lip, her inexperienced hand inspiring a considerable amount of bloodletting to take place. She eventually succeeded in doing away with the unsightly growth, and arrived downstairs in time to bid Mr. Collins farewell. The depilation would, however, be only temporary, for rather than eliminating this scourge to Mary's face, it only served to stimulate it.

The following morning every hope that Mr. Collins intended to return to Longbourn to choose another wife was done away with. Miss Lucas called soon after breakfast, and in a private conference with Elizabeth, related the event of the day before. Her fingers once more sought out Elizabeth's arm as if to give emphasis to her words, brushing repeatedly against Elizabeth's bosom. Her friend was so surprised by the news that she scarcely noticed, though this surprise was more at Charlotte's acceptance of the proposal than at Mr. Collins having offered it. "My dear Eliza, I am not romantic," said Charlotte. "I ask only a comfortable home, and considering Mr. Collins's character, connection, and situation in life, I am convinced that my chance of happiness with him is as fair as most people can boast on entering the marriage state."

It was a long time before Elizabeth became reconciled to the idea of so unsuitable a match. The strangeness of Mr. Collins's making two offers of marriage within three days was nothing in comparison to his being now accepted. Charlotte as the wife of Mr. Collins was a most humiliating picture. Perhaps Elizabeth understood less of her friend than she imagined.

Uncertain whether she was authorized to mention the matter to her family, Elizabeth chose to say nothing. However, Sir William arrived a short time later to announce the engagement, meeting with protestations that he must be entirely mistaken. Mrs. Bennet, in particular, was highly vexed by the news and, after Sir William's departure, insisted that Mr. Collins had been the victim of duplicity. "I never trusted that girl. There is something of an unwholesome nature in her eye," said Mrs. Bennet, her own exhibiting a manic gleam. Mary took the announcement of Mr. Collins's engagement to Miss Lucas stoically and made no further attempt to alter her appearance. The apples were returned to the kitchen.

Mrs. Bennet became convinced that her family was cursed, and this was further corroborated by one of the gypsies to whom she had turned for counsel. Not only were the Bennets eventually to be turned out of their own home by Charlotte Lucas, but Mr. Bingley had gone away to London, bringing into question the future happiness of her dear Jane. Her nerves suffered most grievously when, for nearly a fortnight, the Longbourn estate was littered with the corpses of small animals, for which no one could offer explanation. When Mary eventually came to be observed at Lucas Lodge marking the front door with fresh animal blood, Mr. Bennet felt it his duty to intervene, and he locked his daughter in a cupboard until the occasion arose to warrant her release.

Nothing more was heard of Mr. Bingley's return. Jane had written to his sister, and was counting the days till she might reasonably hope to hear again, the lack of reply indicating, at least to Elizabeth, a most calculated rudeness. Mr. Bennet received the promised letter from Mr. Collins, who wrote that he planned to return shortly to Longbourn; Lady Catherine so heartily approved his marriage that she wished it to take place as soon as possible. The news of a guest, particularly as it was to be Mr. Collins, did not bode well with Mrs. Bennet, and she was forced to enter into further bargains to locate the funds with which to pay for the increased dosage of her nerve medicine. She instructed Cook to reduce the portions of food served to her family, and to refuse Mr. Collins should he request additional meals during his stay.

Mr. Collins's reception at Longbourn was not quite so gracious as it had been on his first introduction. He was too happy, however, to require much attention. The chief of every day was spent by him at Lucas Lodge, and he often returned only in time to make an apology for his absence before the family retired for the night. Though the distance between the two properties was not great, Mr. Collins did not pass directly from the door of Lucas Lodge to the door of Longbourn House. Rather he called in at the stables first, where the gypsy stableman would be waiting. As before, he granted Mr. Collins the privilege of serving him on his knees, a position for which he was most cheerfully inclined. After a few minor preliminaries that consisted of Mr. Collins placing kisses along the length of the other's manhood until he reached the pouch below, the entirety of which he endeavored to draw into his mouth until his cheeks bulged outward like those of a squirrel storing food, the dose of worship had been enough. The groom returned his member to Mr. Collins's lips, which parted without delay, whereupon he proceeded to put forth a series of punishing thrusts until he released himself into Mr. Collins's mouth. Despite the latter's highly stimulated state, the gypsy indicated that he was neither to touch himself nor bring his manhood into exposure; therefore Mr. Collins was forced to endure the indignity of discharging his pleasure into his breeches, which he considered an appropriate penance for the manner of worship in which he engaged. There was no shame too great for him to endure, and he desired but to experience still more of it. Were it not for the condescension of his patroness and his situation at Hunsford parish, he would have been tempted to remain forever in Hertfordshire, for life at Lucas Lodge was proving most agreeable indeed.

The gloom that had fallen over the Bennet household increased with the long-awaited arrival of a letter for Jane from Miss Bingley, announcing that the party was happily settled in London for the winter. Miss Darcy's praise occupied the chief of it, as Lady Caroline boasted joyfully of their increasing intimacy, venturing to predict the accomplishment of the wishes that had been unfolded in her former letter as regards Mr. Darcy's sister and her brother, who was now Mr. Darcy's guest. Elizabeth, to whom Jane communicated the letter's contents, heard all in silent indignation. To Caroline's assertion of her brother's being partial to Miss Darcy she paid no credit. Unlike Jane, Elizabeth knew the truth about Miss Darcy. As much as it pained her not to be able to relay the information to her sister, she had given Mr. Wickham her word that it would go no farther, and her feelings for him were such that she dared not lose his good favor. Instead she attempted once more to persuade Jane toward her belief that Bingley's sisters, in conjunction with Darcy, were influencing his feelings away from her and toward another whom they held in greater regard. Jane nevertheless refused to accept that those she esteemed could be capable of such deceitful behavior and continued to place the blame on herself for not having been successful in securing Bingley's affections. Elizabeth dropped the matter, and from this time Mr. Bingley's name was scarcely ever mentioned between them.

The mood at Longbourn House was momentarily lightened in an unexpected manner by Mr. Collins, who had been calling in at the stables with increasing urgency. Until recently, he had always adopted a more dominant stance in his dealings with certain young males who had caught his eye. The gypsy stableman, however, displayed an assertiveness of demeanor he found most inspirational; therefore, rather than bestow the bounties of his manhood onto another, Mr. Collins was happy to receive them, and he did so in abundance, his generosity of spirit leading him to offer his mouth to the groom as often as circumstance permitted. The time of his visit to Hertfordshire was drawing to a close, and he wished to take full advantage of the treasure he had discovered before returning to his parish in Kent. He feared that his days of indulging in such pleasing diversions were nearing an end, particularly with his approaching marriage and the watchful eye of Lady Catherine upon him.

On what would be their final moments together, Mr. Collins brought forth from the stableman no fewer than three liquid bestowals of pleasure, the last of which required a most rigorous effort from both parties. The groom attacked his mouth with increasing fervor, as desperate to reach fulfillment as Mr. Collins was to provide it, the groom's movements of such force that Mr. Collins's hat was knocked to the ground. The parson held on mightily to the gypsy's hind cheeks so that he could accept the full length of his manhood into his throat, experiencing no fewer than three releases of his own inside his breeches. Mr. Collins became so occupied with the business of bringing matters to an agreeable conclusion that, when it finally arrived, he failed to notice the loss of a front tooth, which would be brought to his attention the following morning by Lydia when the family gathered at breakfast. She made much merriment of it, causing considerable embarrassment to Mr. Collins, who, for the first time, suffered from an absence of words. Both Mr. Bennet and Elizabeth found their cousin's new appearance as ridiculous as the man himself, and even Jane was unable to resist a smile. From that point forward, Mr. Collins paid no more visits to the stables at Lucas Lodge.

For the future Mrs. Collins to partake similarly of her own impending farewells with the object of her desire would have astonished not only Mr. Collins but the whole of Meryton and, in particular, her friend Elizabeth. While Mr. Collins had been busily engaging in activities that resulted in the loss of a tooth, Miss Lucas was involved in activities of more genteel nature with the daughter of the local costermonger, whose delicate female folds she had been availing herself of in their place of rendezvous—a small woodland conveniently situated between Lucas Lodge and the town. Charlotte took particular delight in attiring herself in the garb of a gentleman and stealing up on the young woman, accosting her, and pulling her into a dense undergrowth, where her tongue became one with the softness it located between the girl's thighs. It fluttered most agreeably within the moist cleft, paying extra heed to its fleshy center, until the young woman was near to fainting. It was a game they both very much enjoyed playing. For Charlotte, she could for a short time become the master of her own destiny rather than being restricted to a life that was always in the control of a father, brother, or husband. For the costermonger's daughter, Miss Lucas's costume eliminated any sense of wrongdoing for partaking in pursuits of the flesh with a member of her own sex.

That Mr. Collins's betrothed was highly accomplished was manifest as her companion underwent a succession of releases, benefiting from many years of practice by Miss Lucas, whose fingers preferred the delights of the female form to that of the pianoforte. In keeping with the masculine guise she had adopted, she applied a clustering of fingers to the opening of the girl's womanhood, moving them about in a tolerable imitation of a gentleman's member. Her fingers' employment, though at first slow, gained in speed until the recipient was eagerly returning their thrusts, the guttural groans issuing from the girl's throat growing in volume till she suddenly went limp, trapping Charlotte's fingers inside her.

Charlotte, having situated her other hand within her breeches, had been all the while steadily manipulating herself until she was trembling with her own ecstasy. At the moment of its arrival, she drove her fingers inside herself, feeling the pulsations of her pleasure as well as those of her companion. It was not without regret that Charlotte would shortly be required to leave Hertfordshire, and she could but hope that Mr. Collins's predilections bode favorably on the resumption of her own in Kent.

With the absence of the Netherfield party, Mr. Wickham's society was of material service in dispelling some of the gloom that continued to hang over Longbourn House. The family saw him often, and to his other recommendations was added that of general unreserve, for he now spoke quite freely of his dealings with the Darcy family. Indeed, much of what Elizabeth had heard of his assertion both to Mr.

Darcy's cheating him of the fortune bequeathed to him and to that gentleman's trade in the bodies of young women was now openly acknowledged and publicly canvassed, barring only the revelation of Miss Darcy's downfall. To all except Jane, who urged the possibility of error, Mr. Darcy was condemned as the worst of men. Elizabeth continued to hold her tongue concerning his sister, her regard for Wickham by this time so great that there was little she would have refused him, had he asked.

Chapter Eleven

MR. COLLINS TOOK LEAVE OF HIS RELATIONS IN Hertfordshire, declaring a speedy return, at which time he hoped the day would be fixed for his marriage to Miss Lucas. Despite the felicity of his upcoming nuptials, he wore a grave countenance owing partly to the absence of a front tooth, though more so that his delightful indiscretions with the stableman at Lucas Lodge were unlikely to recur.

For the family, the pleasure of the departure of Mr. Collins was shortly replaced by the pleasure of the arrival of Mrs. Bennet's brother and his wife, who had come to spend Christmas at Longbourn. A well-bred and agreeable couple, Mr. and Mrs. Gardiner were held in high regard by the Bennets, and Mrs. Bennet, in particular, had been looking forward to the visit. She had many grievances to relate and much to complain of, most of which was bound for her sister-in-law's ear.

Mrs. Gardiner listened with sympathy, the news being relayed by Mrs. Bennet already having been provided by both Jane's and Elizabeth's correspondence. Though the future happiness of the two eldest Bennet girls was of concern to her, even more so was the appearance of her husband's sister, whose nervous temperament had become much amplified since the last time they had met, as had the volume of her conversation, and Mrs. Gardiner was repeatedly forced to clap her hands over her ears to shield them lest her hearing be damaged. Yet it was Mrs. Bennet's eyes that caused the most unease, for they possessed a most unnatural glow and bulged outward, as if seeking to escape from her head. Mrs. Gardiner later employed her husband to speak in confidence about his sister to Mr. Bennet, who, after hearing him out, locked himself inside his library and was not seen again until supper.

The conversations between Elizabeth and her aunt focused mostly on Jane, whose increasing wretchedness could not be ignored. "It seems likely to have been a desirable match," said Mrs. Gardiner. "But these things happen so often! A young man, such as you describe Mr. Bingley, so easily falls in love with a pretty girl for a few weeks, and when accident separates them, so easily forgets her."

"And it does not often happen that the interference of friends will persuade a young man of independent fortune to think no more of a girl whom he was violently in love with only a few days before," countered Elizabeth, who continued to maintain that Mr. Bingley had been genuine in his feelings toward her sister and was as much a victim as Jane.

After further discussion, Mrs. Gardiner suggested that Jane return with them to London for a change of scene and, though she did not mention this, a relief from home, for a young woman suffering from a broken heart would not be much improved in the company of Mrs. Bennet. She added that she hoped Jane's decision would not be influenced by the possibility of a chance encounter with Mr. Bingley, to which Elizabeth replied as to the unlikeliness of this event. "Mr. Darcy may perhaps have *heard* of such a place as

Gracechurch Street, but he would hardly think a month's ablution enough to cleanse him from its impurities, were he to enter it," replied she, "and depend upon it, Mr. Bingley never stirs without him."

Jane accepted her aunt's invitation with pleasure. She hoped, by Lady Caroline's not living in the same house with her brother, she might occasionally spend a morning with her without any danger of seeing him. Indeed, she fully expected Miss Bingley to welcome her society and looked forward to seeing her dear friend again.

The Gardiners stayed a week at Longbourn, and with the Phillipses, the Lucases, and the officers, of whom Mr. Wickham was sure to be one, not a day went by without some form of engagement. Elizabeth was delighted to have the advantage of Wickham's company, and they resumed their previous discussion, to which she supplied the recent intelligence of the Netherfield party's departure for London. When she put forth her observations as regards her sister and Mr. Bingley, Wickham did not appear at all surprised, adding his own opinion on the subject. "Such an alliance, although unpleasant, makes perfect sense. Should Miss Darcy wed a gentleman of Bingley's stature, it will remove from her the taint of the bawdy house. So, too, will it do for her brother. For indeed, who would believe that the wife of Charles Bingley should have been previously engaged in the trade of her own body—*and* at the behest of her brother, the esteemed Mr. Fitzwilliam Darcy?"

Elizabeth saw the logic in the argument, but she found fault with a portion of it. "But what of her condition? To be sure, Mr. Bingley would not take for a bride a young woman who has been so well used in this manner." That Elizabeth felt she could speak so plainly about such matters with Wickham only attested to his amiability and character, and her heart warmed still further toward him, though she felt a flush manifest itself on her face and neck as she thought of the unwholesome means in which Miss Darcy had been employed. That Wickham's color also appeared heightened indicated to her that perhaps they were joined in thought on the subject, and she wondered if he imagined himself applying his manhood to her in the same manner as that which so many men had to Miss Darcy.

"Darcy will have persuaded him," said Wickham matter-of-factly. This Elizabeth could well believe, knowing the influence he had over his friend. "And unless Bingley is of a nature to, shall we say, *use* a female in a particular fashion—and by that I refer to the unnatural deed to which Miss Darcy was most applied, it is quite unlikely he will ever become aware of the situation."

To Elizabeth, Wickham's reply had been sufficient confirmation of his thoughts, and she found herself becoming curiously excited at the prospect of him introducing his manhood to her in this most "unnatural" fashion. As she envisioned him raising up her skirts and bending her forward so that he could insert himself into the opening at her backside, her attention was caught by a familiar presence making itself known inside his breeches, and for several moments she was unable to speak. The restless stirrings behind the flap provoked a corresponding restlessness in the place of her womanhood, and she pressed her thighs together, her face growing quite hot as the urge to apply a hand to herself took hold of her.

Wickham, appearing to accept her reticence as an indication of shock, quickly apologized for his frankness of speech. When Elizabeth offered her assurances that she much preferred forthrightness to subterfuge, the mass in his breeches grew larger, the bulb-like shape at the end twitching beneath the fabric, at which point he eagerly resumed his conversation, his tone by now quite animated. "Miss Darcy hails from a long line of sodomites, including her brother and his father before him. It is not a fact widely known or, indeed, spoken of, but I came to witness a good deal while at Pemberley, which is where Miss Darcy's tutelage in these aberrant arts began." In reply to Elizabeth's sharp intake of breath, Wickham added, "Miss Bennet, I can see that I have trespassed on your delicate sensibilities far more than I have any right to. I shall say no more on the subject."

"Indeed, sir, I am shocked, but I insist on knowing the entire sordid history, so that I might become more convinced of my aversion to Mr. Darcy. I beg that you do not spare me the details!"

Before he could elaborate further, they were interrupted by Lydia. "Lizzy, you have kept Mr. Wickham to yourself long enough. It is time for your sisters to enjoy his society as well!" She pulled him from his chair and whisked him off to dance, leaving Elizabeth to ponder the nature of Miss Darcy's conscription into a life of baseness, the details of which she found oddly thrilling. As her mind conjured up engagements with any number of ruffians with an inclination toward the more unnatural pursuits of the flesh, she shifted in her chair, arranging her positioning so that she could employ the cleft of her womanhood against it without being observed to do so. Though not as direct a method as that which she employed in private, it provided sufficient stimulus for the occasion, and she augmented this by placing her hand on the cushion of the chair recently vacated by Wickham, the heat he had deposited there warming her palm. Elizabeth reflected again on the havoc she had observed in his breeches. As she envisioned him fitting their contents into her backside, she moved about in her seat, urging her folds against the cushion. She had found of considerable interest the series of twitches put forth by the topmost portion of Wickham's manhood, and as she wondered how it might be to feel that same twitching deep inside the place she now imagined him occupying, Elizabeth was overwhelmed by the same sensation of soaring she experienced in private, obliging her to press her hand to her mouth to quiet her moan lest someone take notice.

Laughter rang out loudly in the room, startling her from the aftermath of her furtively gained pleasure. She immediately recognized it as belonging to Lydia, whom she now observed rubbing against Wickham's thigh, which she held trapped between her own. The bulge in his breeches was still evident and, unless Elizabeth was very much mistaken, had grown larger still. Were it not for the innocence of her youngest sister, she might have resented her. She soon lost sight of the dancing couple and, before she could set off to locate them, was joined by her aunt, who took Wickham's chair.

Mrs. Gardiner, rendered curious by Elizabeth's warm commendation of Mr. Wickham, had been narrowly observing them both before he had been removed by Lydia. Their preference for each other was plain enough to make her a little uneasy, and she resolved to represent to Elizabeth the imprudence of such an attachment. Before her marriage, she had spent a considerable time in that very part of Derbyshire to which Wickham belonged. She had seen Pemberley and known the late Mr. Darcy by character perfectly well; Wickham's claim to such connections was not in question. Nevertheless, Mrs. Gardiner advised her niece to be on her guard. "He is a most interesting young man, and if he had the fortune he ought to have, I should think you could not do better. But you must not let your fancy run away with you."

Elizabeth did not take offense, knowing the warning was kindly meant. "At present I am not in love with Mr. Wickham," replied she. "But he is, beyond all comparison, the most agreeable man I ever saw. Though I recognize the imprudence of it, since we see every day that where there is affection, young people are seldom withheld by immediate want of fortune from entering into engagements with each other, how can I promise to be wiser than so many of my fellow creatures if I am tempted? All that I can promise, therefore, is not to be in a hurry."

They parted amiably, and Elizabeth went in search of Wickham, whom she had not seen since his dance with Lydia. Believing he had grown tired of her sister's silly chatter and had joined with the other officers, she moved in their direction, observing Kitty among the party. But there was no sign of either Lydia or Mr. Wickham, and no one could offer any account of their whereabouts. Mr. Denny seemed unusually cheerful and proceeded to engage Elizabeth in conversation until they were at last joined by Wickham, whose features were suffused with color. A smile of acknowledgment passed between the two men, after which Lydia arrived, all out of breath, her hair and gown disheveled. The occasion, at least for now, had passed for Elizabeth to learn the full history of Miss Darcy's descent into disgrace.

Mr. Collins returned to Hertfordshire soon after it had been quit by the Gardiners and Jane, this time taking up his abode at Lucas Lodge, as his marriage was fast approaching. He refused to go anywhere near the stables, making certain always to be accompanied by Miss Lucas while on the property. That this went some way toward thwarting Charlotte's woodland trysts was a cause of much displeasure to her, and she used every opportunity to encourage her future husband to take his walks in solitude, where he might be allowed to engage in quiet reflection. Mr. Collins, however, would have none of it. Therefore Charlotte began to slip from the house in the dead of night after everyone was asleep, her tongue pining for a taste of the costermonger's daughter. Though she felt no fear in the dark, her friend was quite alarmed and took to bringing along a pretty female companion. Both would be shared equally by Miss Lucas, whose fingers and tongue labored with much industriousness beneath their skirts, bringing forth a number of satisfied cries that caused her to question the wisdom of her forthcoming marriage.

In the darkness there was no need for donning the costume of a man, and Charlotte, feeling emboldened beneath the moon, removed the entirety of her garments. She stood proudly before the two women as they kissed and stroked her, their hands alighting repeatedly on her bare bosom as if never before having witnessed such splendor, teasing the tips with their fingers until Charlotte felt as if her womanhood had begun to melt. They sought out the source of this moisture with their fingers; then, as they became bolder, their tongues took turns in their explorations, enthusiasm overcoming inexperience as they endeavored to coax the rapture from Charlotte's folds until she could scarcely stand upright. Her companions seemed incapable of fatigue as they continued to taste the delights of their mentor, dipping their tongues into the opening of her womanhood and stealing away the sweetness they discovered there, laughing happily when they were greeted with the arrival of still more.

Sensing an opportunity, Charlotte offered instruction to her two apprentices until there was every manner of activity taking place. They were all on the ground, the fingers and tongue of one entertaining the womanhood of the second, while she, in turn, engaged similarly with the third, the three linked together in a single chain of pleasure that neither of them desired to break. Charlotte felt a sense of pride that she could impart her skills to those who were decidedly beneath her in society, and their appreciation was manifest as they rewarded her with release after release. She believed she might not live to see daybreak, her ecstasy was so great. In this manner all three were most agreeably occupied until the sun began to appear, at which point each was obliged to go her own way.

The wedding between Miss Lucas and Mr. Collins took place, and the bride and bridegroom set off for Kent from the church door, their departure witnessed with equal measures of sadness by the gypsy stableman and the costermonger's daughter, watching from a safe distance, wearing matching expressions of gloom. Elizabeth soon afterward received a letter from Mrs. Collins. Charlotte wrote cheerfully of her new life and there was nothing beyond her praise; the house, furniture, neighborhood, and roads were all to her taste, and Lady Catherine's behavior was most friendly and obliging. Elizabeth perceived that she must wait for the time of her own visit to discover the rest.

Jane wrote often from Gracechurch Street, expressing that she had been a week in town and had neither seen nor heard from Lady Caroline. Presuming her earlier letter had been lost, she took the opportunity to call in Grosvenor Street to see her friend, whom she reported was very glad to see her, and who had reproached Jane for not giving notice of her coming to London. *I was right, therefore, that my last letter had never reached her,* wrote Jane. *I inquired after her brother, of course. He was well, but so much engaged with Mr. Darcy and his sister that they scarcely ever saw him.* To this Elizabeth experienced no surprise, though she did wonder at the appearance of Miss Darcy, who, to be sure, bore the marks of her disrepute.

Jane's correspondence continued to indicate that she had seen nothing of Mr. Bingley or his sister until, after she had waited at home every morning for a fortnight, her friend at last appeared, but the shortness of her stay and the alteration of her manner gave Jane to deceive herself no longer. *Caroline did not return my visit till yesterday; and not a note, not a line, did I receive in the meantime. When she did come, it was very evident that she had no pleasure in it. Mr. Bingley knows of my being in town, I am certain, and yet it would seem, by her manner of talking, as if she wanted to persuade herself that he is partial to Miss Darcy. If I were not afraid of judging harshly, I should be almost tempted to say that there is a strong appearance of duplicity in all this.*

The letter gave Elizabeth some pain, though her spirits

returned as she considered that Jane would no longer be duped, at least not by Miss Bingley. All expectation from Mr. Bingley was now at an end, and as a punishment for him, Elizabeth hoped he might really marry Darcy's sister. Indeed, she found the prospect of the fickle Mr. Bingley's marriage to an opium-eating creature from a bawdy house very pleasing. As for the fickleness of her own admirer, she had recently observed Mr. Wickham's attentions toward another, the sudden acquisition of ten thousand pounds adding much to the charm of one Miss King, the young lady to whom he was now rendering himself agreeable. Although her heart had been bruised, Elizabeth was satisfied with believing that *she* would have been his only choice, had fortune permitted it. The appearance of Miss King, however, did much to thwart her nocturnal self-pleasuring and this, more than anything, put Elizabeth in a state of ill humor. Therefore when Charlotte's invitations to visit Hunsford became more insistent, she finally consented. She was to accompany Sir William and his second daughter, Maria, the entire party to spend a night in Gracechurch Street before continuing on to Kent. She looked forward with eagerness to seeing Jane and hoped to find her sister with her spirits much improved.

Chapter Twelve

THE FAREWELL BETWEEN ELIZABETH AND MR. WICKHAM
was perfectly amiable, on his side even more, and he wished
her every enjoyment for her journey, expressing in a heartfelt tone that he would greatly miss the pleasure of their
conversations. Elizabeth, recalling the nature of these conversations, noted only a modicum of activity in his breeches,
though she did not take it too much to heart. In the course
of their meeting, Lydia appeared. She chastised her sister for
abandoning Longbourn, then, laughing breathlessly, dragged
Wickham away by the arm. He glanced back at Elizabeth
with an expression of helpless amusement, to which she
smiled, pleased that, despite recent events with Miss King,
he still had time for her family.

Wickham's sorrow at the departure of his friend Miss
Bennet would be much improved when he accompanied
Lydia to the undergrowth, where she proceeded to apply
her hand to his manhood. She grasped hold of it with an
assuredness that could only have come from years of practice, employing it in swift up-and-down motions, which were

interspersed with visits to her mouth, her tongue repeatedly teasing the tiny opening at the tip until he was very close to achieving release, whereupon she raised up her skirts and bent over, her head nearly touching the ground. That Lydia felt not the slightest shame in exposing herself in this manner was evident as she reached back to part her hind cheeks, displaying to him both her openings, as if offering a choice. Wickham, finding the selections most tempting, paused to consider which he preferred on this occasion. Having only recently partaken of the backside belonging to Miss King, he opted for the more traditional thoroughfare, and he hoisted himself inside the opening of Lydia's womanhood, not at all surprised to find by his ease of passage that she had recently been enjoyed by another. He had earlier spied her walking with Captain Carter, with neither party reappearing for the best part of an hour. The knowledge that his superior had entertained himself in advance of his arrival gave Wickham an illicit thrill, and he held tightly to Lydia's waist, launching into her his full length with little thought toward courteous or gentlemanly behavior. He cast upon her every manner of foul name, which, rather than necessitating a slap to his face, caused Lydia to act with even greater abandonment as she began to manipulate those parts of her that were not already engaged.

The volume of Lydia's enjoyment prompted Wickham to make haste before they were discovered, for he did not relish the prospect of a duel with Mr. Bennet, though he had no doubt as to which of them would be the victor. With one final movement, he lodged himself inside her as deeply as he could go, condemning her with an epithet of such coarseness that she cried out with delight. Wickham's pleasure erupted from him, and it was joined in equal measure by Lydia, who squealed so loudly that a flock of birds in a nearby tree took flight. He had barely time to disengage himself from her before he recognized Denny coming up the pathway toward them. They touched their hats in greeting, at which point Wickham left Lydia to the company of his friend, returning to the house in time for tea.

Elizabeth and her party set off early the next morning, arriving at Gracechurch Street by noon. She was overjoyed to be reunited with her sister, whom she found looking as healthful and lovely as ever, though there were periods of dejection, for which Elizabeth held responsible Mr. Bingley. She provided Jane with all the particulars of Wickham's desertion, hoping her own misfortune in love might distract her sister from hers. On hearing that her niece had been so swiftly replaced, Mrs. Gardiner went so far as to suggest that Wickham was mercenary in his affairs. "He paid Miss King not the smallest attention till her grandfather's death made her mistress of this fortune," said she. "There seems an indelicacy in directing his attentions toward her so soon after this event."

"A man in distressed circumstances has not time for all those elegant decorums that other people may observe. If *she* does not object to it, why should *we*?" replied Elizabeth in his defense. She knew that had it not been for her own lack of fortune, matters between herself and Mr. Wickham would have turned out very differently indeed.

The subject was swiftly changed to more agreeable topics, including an invitation to Elizabeth to join the Gardiners in the summer on a tour to the Lakes. She readily accepted, grateful for any opportunity to remove herself from both the dramas at Longbourn and the disappointments brought on by young gentlemen.

Elizabeth's party arrived the next day at Hunsford parish, where Mrs. Collins greeted her friend with the liveliest pleasure, her fingertips once again managing to alight upon Elizabeth's bosom and remain in the vicinity for as long as practicable. With ostentatious formality, Mr. Collins welcomed his guests to his humble abode, offering them the full glory of his gap-toothed smile, though he seemed to be distracted by his right ear, which he kept prodding with a fingertip. Refreshments were brought out, after which he proceeded to give his guests a very thorough tour of the rooms, continually making reference to Rosings Park and the generous patronage of Lady Catherine, who had done much to see to his comfort at Hunsford House. Elizabeth could not help thinking that by displaying the assets of the house, Mr. Collins addressed himself particularly to her, as if wishing to make her feel what she had lost in refusing him. The house, though small, was well built and convenient, and everything was arranged with a neatness and consistency for which she gave Charlotte all the credit.

Mr. Collins next invited them to take a stroll in the garden, where he could smoke from his pipe, for his wife did not approve the pastime indoors. As everyone arose from their chairs, the slamming of a door was heard, and Elizabeth observed through the parlor window three young men running from the house. One was attired only in a long shirt, though his two companions were lacking in any garments at all, save for their boots. Their figures were handsomely formed, and the sight of their merrily bouncing members provided Elizabeth with much in the way of amusement, as did the pleasing shape of their backsides, which came into view as they turned toward the direction of the park. One of the party in particular possessed the most impressive of manly attributes, and she was momentarily reminded of Mr. Wickham and the intimacy of their conversations, which she ascribed to agitating him in this very same region. The memory would encourage her to embark on a renewal of her nocturnal self-pleasuring when she retired to bed that night.

All eyes looked toward Mr. Collins for an explanation, and he forced another gap-toothed smile, his features suffusing with color as he replied that members of the choir often practiced at Hunsford House, as they found the setting most inspirational. Charlotte remained silent all throughout, though Elizabeth could discern a blush that equaled her husband's.

The garden was one of Mr. Collins's most respectable pleasures, and he worked in it as often as his duties allowed. Charlotte spoke happily of the healthfulness of the exercise, and owned that she encouraged it in her husband as much as possible. Of such encouragement Elizabeth had no doubt, though she could not help wondering if a *lack* of encouragement as regards certain other matters was creating a situation that might cause them both considerable embarrassment. She thought it best to say nothing, however, for her friend seemed content with life at Hunsford, and it was not Elizabeth's place to discuss the intimate engagements that took place between a husband and wife.

Mr. Collins led the way through every walk in the garden, scarcely allowing his guests an interval to utter the praises he solicited. He could number the fields in every direction and account for how many trees there were. But of all the views of which his garden or any in the kingdom could boast, none were comparable to the prospect of Rosings as it came into view through an opening in the trees bordering the park opposite his house. Elizabeth had already learned that she would, according to Mr. Collins, have the honor of seeing its owner on the ensuing Sunday at church. "I need not say you will be delighted with her ladyship," said he. "She is all affability and condescension." Elizabeth decided to reserve forming an opinion until the time of their meeting.

That night she took to her bed, replacing in her mind Mr. Wickham with the abundantly endowed chorister she had seen running from the house that day. His image had inspired her to return to the parlor after everyone had retired, where she decided to avail herself of the pipe Mr. Collins had deposited there earlier. The fire in the hearth had died out, but enough heat still remained for Elizabeth to dispense with the bedcovers, and she pulled up her nightdress and parted her thighs, exposing herself to the air. The sense of freedom it brought was most refreshing, the cool air licking over her uncovered parts like a phantom tongue. She imagined that the tongue of the handsome chorister had taken to them, finding the scenario highly pleasing and allowing her finger to explore her folds as the tip of his tongue might do, teasing the wetness from her opening until she was nearly mad with the need to have something filling it.

It had been some while since Elizabeth had engaged in such manner of activities, particularly with any level of success, and it required several attempts before her fingers located an appropriate rhythm within the cleft of her womanhood. She then took the pipe in her unoccupied hand and guided it inside herself until nothing remained but the bowl, which she kept hold of with her fingers. She began to employ the stem using gentle motions, pushing forward, then drawing back, at first slowly, then with increasing speed, her other hand matching the pace as it manipulated the flesh it was attending to. Elizabeth found the combination a most agreeable enterprise, and she closed her eyes, envisioning the pipe to be the rather more substantial version she had spied projecting out from beneath the chorister's belly. As she did so, a very pleasing tension began to make itself known in her loins, and it grew and grew until at last she cried out, the sensation of soaring into the heavens returning to her once more. Elizabeth fell quickly asleep, awakening in time to return the pipe to the parlor before the others appeared.

Later that day a commotion from below seemed to place the whole house in confusion. Elizabeth was in her room getting ready for a walk and, believing it to be the choristers she had seen the previous afternoon, she hastened to the window, hoping to be granted another glimpse of the one whose finely proportioned manhood had occupied her fantasies for most of the night. Instead she observed two ladies stopping in a phaeton at the garden gate. She then heard somebody running upstairs in a violent hurry. It was Maria who, breathless with agitation, called out, "My dear Eliza! There is such a sight to be seen! Make haste, and come with me this very moment."

Elizabeth concluded by the level of commotion that the callers were none other than Lady Catherine de Bourgh and her daughter, only to be informed by Maria that the woman accompanying Miss de Bourgh was not her ladyship, but a Mrs. Jenkinson, who lived with them. Mr. Collins and Charlotte were standing at the gate in conversation with the ladies, leaving Sir William stationed in the doorway in earnest contemplation of the greatness before him, constantly bowing whenever Miss de Bourgh looked in his direction. "She is abominably rude to keep Charlotte out of doors in all this wind," Elizabeth replied to Maria. "Why does she not come in?"

"Oh, Charlotte says she hardly ever does. It is the greatest of favors when Miss de Bourgh comes in."

"I like her appearance," said Elizabeth, mostly to herself. "She looks sickly and cross. Yes, she will do for Mr. Darcy very well. She will make him a very proper wife."

The phaeton rode off, and Mr. Collins hastened back to the house to offer both Elizabeth and Maria his congratulations. It appeared that the whole party was invited to dine at Rosings the next day.

Chapter Thirteen

MR. COLLINS'S TRIUMPH COULD NOT HAVE BEEN MORE complete. The power of displaying the grandeur of his patroness to his visitors, and of letting them see her civility toward himself and his wife, was exactly what he had wished for. That an opportunity of doing it should be given so soon was such an instance of Lady Catherine's condescension, and Mr. Collins carefully instructed his guests in what they were to expect in order that such splendor might not wholly overpower them. He experienced great relief in having occasion to draw away attention from the rather awkward departure of the parish choristers the previous afternoon, and was similarly vexed that he had not been given time to fully indulge himself with them before the arrival of his guests. Indeed, they had interrupted a particularly enjoyable union between his mouth and the manhood of the chorister who had caught Elizabeth's eye. Mr. Collins had already drained the pleasure from his companions, having moved from one to the next, taking them in turns till his knees threatened to give way beneath him before placing himself at the upstanding member of his favorite. By now the muscles of his jaw ached most grievously, yet still he succeeded in swallowing the entire length of the delightful object being presented to him, working it in and out of his mouth as eagerly as if being granted his first taste. The sound of the coach caused him to turn his face abruptly away, whereupon the chorister deposited his pleasure into Mr. Collins's right ear. He still could not hear properly with it.

"My dear cousin, do not make yourself uneasy about your apparel," said he to Elizabeth. "Lady Catherine is far from requiring that elegance of dress in us which becomes herself and her daughter. She will not think the worse of you for being simply dressed."

Elizabeth held her tongue, though she vowed to make more frequent use of Mr. Collins's pipe, perhaps even applying it to those parts for which her conversations with Wickham had given her much cause for contemplation.

On the day of their engagement with her ladyship, the party enjoyed a pleasant walk across the park to Rosings. Mr. Collins called their attention to every detail of the vista along the way, which continued long after they had crossed the threshold as, with a rapturous air, he pointed out the fine proportion of the structure and the superior quality of the ornaments and furnishings, enumerating on their cost. During their tour of the house, Elizabeth thought she heard what sounded like human screams, though everyone excepting herself seemed too mesmerized by their stately surroundings to notice.

They followed the servants to the room where Lady Catherine, her daughter, and Mrs. Jenkinson awaited them. Her ladyship had only recently arrived and could be seen fanning herself from some form of exertion known only to herself. Sir William was so completely awed by the magnificence surrounding him that he had just courage enough to make a very low bow and take his seat. Maria, frightened almost out of her senses, sat on the edge of her chair, not knowing which way to look. Elizabeth found herself quite equal to the scene, and observed the three ladies with composure. Lady Catherine was a tall woman with strongly marked features that might once have been handsome, and neither her air nor her manner was such as to make her visitors forget their inferior rank. Elizabeth, detecting some of Mr. Darcy in her appearance, turned her attention to his future bride, Miss de Bourgh, who was pale and sickly, her features insignificant. She spoke very little, except in a low voice, to Mrs. Jenkinson, who spent her time fussing and fretting over her charge's well-being.

The dinner was exceedingly excellent, and there were all the servants and articles of plate that Mr. Collins had promised. He took his seat at the bottom of the table, by her ladyship's desire, and looked as if life could furnish nothing greater. There was little conversation to be enjoyed, and what existed of it was mostly borne by Lady Catherine, save for a few humble words of praise contributed by Mr. Collins. After dinner the party returned to the drawing room, where there was nothing to be done but to hear Lady Catherine talk, which she did without intermission, delivering her opinion on every subject, including the domestic affairs at Hunsford House, for which she provided Mrs. Collins copious advice. Elizabeth found that nothing was beneath this great lady's attention, particularly if it furnished her with an occasion to dictate to others.

Lady Catherine addressed a variety of questions to her guests, though most specifically to Elizabeth, who, despite their impertinence, endeavored to answer composedly. From her replies, however, it was evident that her ladyship regarded the Bennets as little more than savages. "Five daughters brought up at home without a governess! I never heard of such a thing!" cried she, her noble countenance distorted from the horror of such a prospect. After a lengthy discourse on the benefits of being educated by a governess, she inquired if any of Elizabeth's younger sisters were out, expressing great shock at learning that they all were. "How very odd! And the younger ones out before the elder ones are married!"

"I think it would be very hard upon younger sisters that they should not have their share of society because the elder may not have the means or inclination to marry early. The last born has as good a right to the pleasures of youth as the first," replied Elizabeth.

"Upon my word," said her ladyship, "you give your opinion very decidedly for so young a person. Pray, what is your age?"

"With three younger sisters grown up," said Elizabeth, smiling, "your ladyship can hardly expect me to own it."

Lady Catherine seemed quite astonished at not receiving a direct answer. Elizabeth suspected she was the first creature who had ever dared to trifle with so much dignified impertinence, and she found herself the recipient of a number of irritated glances from her ladyship throughout the evening.

The remainder of the visit was spent at cards, after which the party gathered by the fire to hear Lady Catherine determine what weather they were to have on the morrow. They were then summoned by the arrival of the coach, and with many speeches of thankfulness on Mr. Collins's side and as many bows on Sir William's, they took their leave.

That night Elizabeth followed through with her plan to employ Mr. Collins's pipe in a rather unwholesome manner, taking much delight not only from imagining it to be the chorister but from knowing that her cousin would, on the following day, be smoking from it. Until Mr. Wickham had confided in her the details relating to Miss Darcy's life of ill repute, she had never considered the matter, and she could not help wondering whether, had circumstances been more favorable as regards a match between them, she might be similarly occupied with Wickham's manhood. The possibility that he might at this moment be engaged with the backside of Miss King did not fail to inspire regret in her heart, and she tormented herself briefly with an image of the young woman bending forward with her skirts upraised while Wickham repeatedly inserted his manhood into her rear opening, his face glowing with delight.

Elizabeth found the pipe a most agreeable visitor to her hind portions, particularly when combined with the manipulations of her fingers on her more womanly parts, the moisture from which trickled down to the opening that now concerned her, aiding in the pipe's facilitation. She took to applying the object with greater haste, urging it as far as it would go and wishing for something larger, feeling quite wicked when she was forced to acknowledge that what she desired most was the length of a gentleman's member filling her rather than the fantasy of one. The movements of her fingers at her folds grew increasingly desperate as she felt herself being lifted higher and higher till she knew not whether she desired Wickham or the chorister—if not, perhaps *both*. The possibility of entertaining them in turns so excited Elizabeth that she nearly lost consciousness from the force of her pleasure, and it would be some while before she had regained sufficient strength to return Mr. Collins's pipe to the parlor.

Very few days passed in which Mr. Collins did not walk to Rosings, and his household was now and then honored with a call from her ladyship, from whose observation nothing escaped. She criticized their every manner of activity, found fault with the arrangement of the furniture, detected the housemaid in negligence and, if she accepted any refreshment, did so only for the sake of pointing out that Mrs. Collins's joints of meat were too large for her family. It soon became clear to Elizabeth that, though this great lady was not in commission of the peace of the county, she was a most active magistrate in her own parish. Whenever any of the villagers were disposed to be quarrelsome or discontented, she sallied forth to settle their differences, silence their complaints, and scold them into harmony. Though Elizabeth refused to be intimidated by Lady Catherine, she was little inclined for her society.

The entertainment of dining at Rosings was repeated about twice a week and was always prefaced with the same manner of screams that had welcomed the party initially. Elizabeth spent the remainder of her time in Kent in pleasant conversation with Charlotte and taking enjoyment out of doors. Her favorite walk was along a grove edging one side of the park, where there was a nice sheltered path. Despite its proximity to Rosings, here she felt beyond the reach of Lady Catherine's curiosity and sharp tongue.

One afternoon while Elizabeth was taking just such refreshment, she heard again those screams that had so much become part of the fabric of Rosings, and to which no one dared draw attention. They seemed to be coming from very close by, and as she moved in their direction, she caught herself stepping lightly so as not to be heard, the screams becoming more tortured with her every footfall. She now stood opposite the grand structure of the house, facing the rear gardens, in which several posts constructed from timber had been secured into the ground. Elizabeth, unable to recall having noticed them during any of her previous visits, might have expected to see roses climbing up them were it not for the unclothed figures of three men and one woman bound to them. A black hood covered each of their heads, and openings had been cut for the eyes, nose, and mouth.

An imposing figure concealed from head to toe in black and wielding a horsewhip was moving from one figure to the next, bringing the whip down sharply against their exposed hindquarters. Each lash brought about a scream of the most grievous nature, and Elizabeth winced in pain as if she herself had been struck. She was certain she recognized the voice of the man screaming the loudest as the villager Lady Catherine had accused of overcharging her for feed. Elizabeth had been in the village that morning with Charlotte and witnessed with heightened amusement the entire exchange. She recalled Miss de Bourgh cowering behind her mother and looking more unwell than usual, and she bit back a recommendation that her ladyship's daughter might perhaps find her health greatly improved were she to eat the feed herself.

Elizabeth turned her attention to the others in the party. The next man was quite squat in stature, reminding her of dough that had been left for too long to rise. As she continued with her inspection, she was moved to press her hand to her mouth to quell her laughter, lest she be heard, for his manhood—or rather what she could discern of it—resembled a garden snail barely emerged from its shell. She pitied his wife, should he, for that matter, even be in possession of one. The third man, by contrast, had much to recommend him. Elizabeth, realizing that this was not the first time she had seen him, experienced a renewal of the sensations she had enjoyed the night before. She was unlikely to forget the handsome specimen of the chorister's manhood as he had gone running from the parsonage, and she admired it once again as it rose upward from his loins with a superiority that belied the humiliation of his punishment, its topmost portion like that of a fist raised in protest. To him were directed the majority of the lashes, and with each that marked his flesh, his manhood grew more prideful than ever, as if seeking to spite his tormenter, until at last it brought forth its finale, some of which splashed onto his portly neighbor, whose decidedly less worthy specimen gave forth its own paltry offering.

The horsewhip was next turned on the woman, at which point Elizabeth at last ascertained its owner's identity. That stateliness of carriage could belong to no one but the owner of Rosings Park herself, and she cursed her folly at not having realized it at once. Elizabeth was astonished that her ladyship should deign to involve herself in matters pertaining to the discipline of those in the parish, though she would be even more so astonished on perceiving the identity of the figure to which Lady Catherine had now taken her horsewhip, for it was someone with whom she had been acquainted her entire life.

Elizabeth observed the pleasing curve of Charlotte's backside as the lashes from Lady Catherine's whip marked it. Her friend's softly pleading voice could be heard beneath each sharp crack of the leather as she tried to escape her punishment, her bosom swaying in a most engaging manner as she struggled against her bonds. Elizabeth found her shapely form most agreeable to the eye, and as she studied the dark triangle of her sex through which the daintiest hint of pink like that of a rose could be seen, she felt great pity that it should be given in intimacy to Mr. Collins by order of a marriage decree. She began to wonder about all those occasions of Charlotte's fingers on her arm and how they always seemed to travel toward her bosom, where they lingered for some while. Whatever could be the meaning of it?

Charlotte appeared to be straining toward the dough-like man beside her, as if she wished to seek his protection, though he looked barely capable of providing defense even for himself. On those few occasions when he endeavored to put forth a feebly uttered protest, Lady Catherine's whip came down with more force than ever, eliciting a grimace of teeth beneath his hood, the solid white line of which was suddenly interrupted by black, indicating that one was missing.

Elizabeth chose to say nothing to Charlotte of the puzzling events she had witnessed, considering it best to keep matters between them light and pleasant. Sir William returned home to Lucas Lodge, satisfied that all was well with his daughter and her new husband. However, the household had barely time to draw a breath before news of another arrival was forthcoming. Mr. Darcy was shortly expected at Rosings, and Lady Catherine, who talked of his coming with the greatest satisfaction, seemed almost angry to find that he had already been frequently seen by Mrs. Collins and Miss Bennet in Hertfordshire. Though Elizabeth wished she could confide in her friend as to the intelligence gained from Mr. Wickham, she continued to honor her promise of silence. Despite his defection to Miss King, Elizabeth considered Wickham in every way a gentleman, and she had no reason to call him anything other than her friend.

Mr. Darcy's arrival was soon known at the parsonage; Mr. Collins was walking the whole morning within view of the lane in order to have the earliest assurance of it, and the following morning he hastened to Rosings to pay his respects. Mr. Darcy had brought with him a Colonel Fitzwilliam, the younger son of his uncle, and to the great surprise of all, when Mr. Collins returned, both gentlemen accompanied him. To Elizabeth Charlotte said, "I may thank you, Eliza, for this piece of civility. Mr. Darcy would never have come so soon to wait upon *me*."

Elizabeth had scarcely time to disclaim all right to the compliment before the gentlemen entered the house. Colonel Fitzwilliam, though not as handsome as his cousin, was pleasant in countenance and, in person and address, most truly the gentleman. Elizabeth was momentarily reminded of Mr. Wickham, which immediately placed him in good stead. Mr. Darcy paid his compliments, with his usual reserve, to Mrs. Collins, and met Elizabeth with every appearance of composure. She curtseyed to him without saying a word, resisting the urge to announce to the entire room the whole of his crimes. After some conversation, most of which had been entered into by Colonel Fitzwilliam, Darcy inquired after the health of Elizabeth's family, to which she replied, "My eldest sister has been in town these three months. Have you never happened to see her?"

She was perfectly sensible that he never had, but she wished to see whether he would betray any consciousness of what had passed between the Bingleys and Jane, and she thought he looked a little confused when he answered that he had not been so fortunate as to meet Miss Bennet in London. The subject was pursued no further, and Darcy spent the remainder of the visit staring intently at her. Had her disdain for him not been so strong and, she believed, his for her, Elizabeth might have believed him to be in admiration of her. As regards Colonel Fitzwilliam, of his interest she had no doubt. It was evident in his breeches each time he spoke with her, much as it had been with Wickham, and she looked forward to a further acquaintance with it.

Chapter Fourteen

WITH THE ARRIVAL OF LADY CATHERINE'S NEPHEWS, SEVERAL days would pass before another invitation to Rosings was extended. The honor finally came as they were leaving church, where they were merely asked to join Lady Catherine that evening. Her ladyship received them civilly, but it was plain that their company was by no means so acceptable as when she could get nobody else. She was, in fact, almost engrossed by her two nephews, speaking to them, especially to Darcy, much more than to any other person in the room.

Colonel Fitzwilliam seated himself by Elizabeth, and they conversed with so much spirit as to draw the attention of Lady Catherine herself, as well as of Darcy, whose eyes had been repeatedly turned toward them with a look of curiosity. Her ladyship seemed to share the feeling, but was more wont to acknowledge it, for she did not scruple to call out to her nephew, "What is it you are talking of? What are you telling Miss Bennet? Let me hear what it is."

"We are speaking of music, madam," said he.

"I must have my share in the conversation if you are speaking of music," replied Lady Catherine. "If I had ever learned, I should have been a great proficient. And so would Anne, if her health had allowed her to apply. I am confident that she would have performed delightfully. How does Georgiana get on, Darcy?"

As Darcy spoke with affectionate praise of his sister's proficiency, Elizabeth fidgeted in her chair, battling the urge to inquire as to Miss Darcy's proficiency in certain other arts. She glanced at Colonel Fitzwilliam, hoping to determine by his countenance whether he knew of his cousin's trade in the bodies of young women, but all she could discern was his growing regard for her, which manifested itself in his breeches as the flap expanded outward. She experienced a fluttering in her belly, which moved to the meeting place between her thighs, and she found herself wondering if Colonel Fitzwilliam's manhood compared in quality to that of the chorister or, indeed, Mr. Wickham.

"Georgiana cannot expect to excel if she does not practice a good deal," said Lady Catherine.

"I assure you, madam, that she does not need such advice," her nephew replied. "She practices very constantly."

On this point Elizabeth had no doubt, and she feared that she would not be able to hold her tongue for much longer. Fortunately, Colonel Fitzwilliam chose that moment to remind Elizabeth of her earlier promise to play, and she took her place at the pianoforte, her admirer drawing a chair very near to her, which afforded her a much improved vista of his lap, particularly when he leaned back in repose, as if seeking to recommend to her the contents of his breeches. Lady Catherine listened to half a song, and then talked, as before, to Darcy till he suddenly walked away from her, moving with steady deliberation toward the pianoforte, where he stationed himself so as to command a full view of the performer.

At the first convenient pause, Elizabeth turned to him with an arch smile and said, "You mean to frighten me, Mr. Darcy, by coming to hear me? There is a stubbornness about me that never can bear to be frightened at the will of others. My courage always rises at every attempt to intimidate me."

"I shall not say you are mistaken," he replied, "because you could not really believe me to entertain any design of alarming you. I have had the pleasure of your acquaintance long enough to know that you find great enjoyment in occasionally professing opinions that in fact are not your own."

Elizabeth could not mistake the challenge behind his words. Perhaps Darcy suspected that Wickham had imparted some intelligence to her, in which case there seemed little cause for her to continue to remain silent on the subject. To Colonel Fitzwilliam, she said, "Your cousin will give you a very pretty notion of me and teach you not to believe a word I say. I am particularly unlucky in meeting with a person so able to expose my real character in a part of the world where I had hoped to pass myself off with some degree of credit. It is provoking me to retaliate, and such things may come out as will shock your relations to hear."

"Pray, let me hear what you have to accuse him of!" cried Colonel Fitzwilliam.

"You shall hear then—but prepare yourself for something very dreadful."

Here they were interrupted by Lady Catherine, who demanded to know what they were talking of, and the time of disclosure was lost. Elizabeth resumed her playing. Lady Catherine approached and, after listening for a few minutes, said to Darcy, "Miss Bennet would not play at all amiss if she practiced more. She has a very good notion of fingering, though her taste is not equal to Anne's."

Elizabeth cast a glance at Darcy to see how cordially he assented to Miss de Bourgh's praise, but neither at that moment nor at any other could she discern any symptom of love. If he *were* betrothed to Lady Catherine's sickly daughter, he gave no indication of it.

The next morning, while writing to Jane, Elizabeth was startled by a ring at the door. Mr. and Mrs. Collins and Maria had gone on business into the village, leaving her to her letter. To her very great surprise, Mr. Darcy entered the room. He looked equally astonished on finding her alone, and apologized for his intrusion by letting her know that he had understood all the ladies were present. Elizabeth considered his reference to propriety the pinnacle of amusement, and she tried to reconcile in her mind how he could be a procurer of women and yet so successfully present the exterior of a gentleman.

After polite inquiries were made, the conversation seemed in danger of sinking into total silence. Mr. Darcy appeared quite ill at ease in Miss Bennet's company, fidgeting in his chair, crossing and uncrossing his legs, and finding much of interest in his fingernails. Elizabeth became exceedingly puzzled as to his motive for coming, and she wondered why he kept leaning so far forward in his chair, as if endeavoring to conceal something on his person. At times he was very nearly bent double, as if offering her the top of his head to converse with. Despite the opportunity to do so, she found herself unable to rekindle her desire to demand he own Wickham's assertions. A short dialogue ensued on the subject of the country, followed by a curious line of inquiry as to Elizabeth's attachment to Hertfordshire and her family, which was soon put to an end by the entrance of Charlotte. Mr. Darcy related the mistake that had occasioned his intruding on Miss Bennet and, after sitting a few minutes longer without saying much to anybody, took his leave.

"What can be the meaning of this?" said Charlotte. "My dear Eliza, he must be in love with you, or he would never have called in this familiar way." She grasped Elizabeth's arm for emphasis, her fingers brushing repeatedly against her bosom. As her fingers moved idly over the curve of Elizabeth's bodice, Charlotte's expression was suddenly melancholy, as if she were struggling with a sad memory.

Elizabeth, distracted by the appearance of Mr. Darcy, failed to take note of her friend's overtures or the fact that they had advanced to far more than light touches and had instead become a series of gentle squeezes that had begun to extricate her bosom from her gown, the tips of which now protruded. As Elizabeth gave Charlotte a report of Darcy's silence, the prospect of his affection no longer appeared very likely, and both women could only suppose that his visit proceeded from the difficulty of finding anything to interest him at Rosings.

Mrs. Collins, seeming neither relieved nor disappointed, leaned forward to place a kiss on the exposed expanse of Elizabeth's bosom, her tongue licking the tip nearest her until it became erect, at which point she attended the other, her lips coaxing it into a matching state, her activities rendering them a most beguiling shade of pink that inspired a painful longing to take place in her loins. Her friend's sharp intake of breath startled Charlotte, and she rescued herself from the situation by leading Elizabeth to a mirror and remarking to her that she would look most prepossessing were she to adopt the décolletage of Lady Caroline Bingley. As Elizabeth observed her reflection with a doubtful expression, Charlotte, who had gone for too long without the taste of womanly flesh on her tongue, began to question the wisdom of having invited her friend to visit, and now looked forward with eagerness to the time of her departure.

Both Mr. Darcy and his cousin continued to call with regularity at the parsonage, sometimes together, sometimes separately, and occasionally accompanied by their aunt. It was evident Colonel Fitzwilliam came because he had pleasure in their society, and Elizabeth was reminded, by her own satisfaction in being with him as well as by his evident admiration of her by the straining flap of his breeches, of her former favorite George Wickham. But why Mr. Darcy came so often was more difficult to understand. It could not be for the society, as he frequently sat for some while without opening his lips, and when he did speak, it seemed more the effect of necessity rather than desire.

Elizabeth spent much of her time at Hunsford taking pleasant rambles within the park, for the weather had been very fine. Although she did not have occasion to repeat an observation of the curious events she had witnessed with Lady Catherine and her horsewhip, screams continued to be heard from various corners of Rosings, returning to her mind the handsome chorister, the image of whom continued to provide her with many nights of private pleasure. That she should encounter Mr. Darcy on her walks was of some surprise. Elizabeth felt all the perverseness of the mischance of the meeting and, to prevent a recurrence, took care to inform him that it was a favorite haunt of hers. How it could happen again and again was therefore quite inexplicable, particularly when Darcy began to think it necessary to walk with her. He never said a great deal, but it struck her that he was asking some very odd questions as to her feelings toward Rosings, which seemed to indicate his expectation that she would be staying there during future visits to Kent. Elizabeth supposed he had Colonel Fitzwilliam in his thoughts and was alluding to what might arise in that quarter.

Elizabeth was out walking one day and perusing Jane's last letter, much of which indicated that her sister had not written in good spirits, when, instead of being again surprised by Mr. Darcy, she saw on looking up the approach of Colonel Fitzwilliam. He seemed delighted to see her, the flap of his breeches distending in agreement, and she felt immediately cheered. Seeing that she had a letter from home, the two fell to talking of Hertfordshire, the conversation turning inevitably to that of Netherfield. Though Colonel Fitzwilliam was acquainted but a little with Miss Bingley and Mrs. Hurst, he knew that their brother was a great friend of Mr. Darcy's. "I have reason to think Bingley very much indebted to Darcy," said he. "But I ought to beg his pardon, for I have no right to suppose that Mr. Bingley was the person meant."

"What is it you mean?" asked Elizabeth, unable to imagine anyone being indebted to Darcy unless it was for something highly disreputable. Her thoughts began to fly about in all directions, inspired in part by her sister's letter and the sadness it relayed, most of which related to matters of the heart. Perhaps Bingley had accumulated a large debt from frequenting his friend's bawdy house and Darcy had released him from it, which might go some way toward explaining Bingley's sudden loss of interest in Jane, who was innocent of the fleshly arts as, indeed, were *all* her dear sisters.

Colonel Fitzwilliam hesitated before extracting from Elizabeth a promise never to reveal what he was about to say. "It is a circumstance Darcy could not wish to be generally known. What he told me was merely this: that he congratulated himself on having lately saved a friend from the inconveniences of a most imprudent marriage, though without mentioning names or any other particulars. I only suspected it to be Bingley from believing him the kind of young man to get into a scrape of that sort, and from knowing them to have been together the whole of last summer."

There could not exist in the world *two* men over whom Darcy could have such boundless influence. That he had been involved in the measures taken to separate Bingley and her sister Elizabeth had never doubted, but she had always attributed to Miss Bingley the principal design and arrangement of them. Darcy's pride was the cause of all that Jane had suffered and still continued to suffer; he had ruined her hope of happiness. Feeling quite suddenly ill, Elizabeth grasped Colonel Fitzwilliam's arm for support, using it to help lower herself to the grass, whereupon he sat down beside her. "Did Mr. Darcy give you reasons for this interference?" asked she.

"I understood that there were some very strong objections against the lady."

Elizabeth's heart swelled with indignation, though she made no answer. Her eyes were bright, and her complexion had taken on a high color. To anyone unaware of the implication of what had just been relayed to her, she looked every bit a young woman much invigorated by the presence of her male companion.

This was what Colonel Fitzwilliam concluded as well, when, without ceremony, he pushed her back onto the grass and rolled on top of her. Before Elizabeth could protest, his tongue was driving past her lips and into her mouth, searching out her own, the protrusion she had spied in his breeches urging itself with increasing force against the cleft of her womanhood. Colonel Fitzwilliam began to move against it with a steady motion, as if his manhood were actually entering her rather than merely abrading her skirts. Despite the distress brought about by their conversation, Elizabeth felt a furious pulsing much like that which she had experienced in the company of Mr. Wickham before he set his sights on Miss King. Indeed, Colonel Fitzwilliam had much to recommend him, even if, as she now determined, his manhood was not quite so generous in proportion as Wickham's.

Colonel Fitzwilliam continued to apply a most pleasing pressure against the place to which Elizabeth took her fingers in order to trigger a sensation of soaring, and she ceased all attempts at objection, allowing him to carry on. She felt very near to achieving this very same state and saw no harm in a brief lapse of decorum, particularly when neither of them had brought any portion of themselves into exposure.

During all this time Colonel Fitzwilliam had laid not even a finger on her, no doubt highly aware of the impropriety of doing so, and his gentlemanly consideration of her sensibilities and reputation served to elevate her good opinion of him, though she would not have minded the added enjoyment of a hand seeking out her bosom. With some discretion, Elizabeth parted her thighs so that his movements could be more favorably employed. She raised up her pelvis ever so slightly to gain the most benefit as Colonel Fitzwilliam urged his hardness against her folds, aiming directly at the sensitive ridge of flesh between them, which her thin garments did little to protect. She wondered how she could feel every nuance of his manhood so clearly through the fabric of his breeches, and it was only later she realized that he had unbuttoned the flap and released it.

Elizabeth closed her eyes, waiting anxiously for her moment of flight to be granted, when suddenly Colonel Fitzwilliam cried out, falling on her as if dead, the length of flesh that had been freed from his breeches diminishing with such rapidity that it seemed as if it had never existed at all.

Quickly recovering himself, Colonel Fitzwilliam stood up from the ground, an expression of supreme satisfaction suffusing his features. Elizabeth, brushing away the blades of grass that had attached themselves to her gown, waited for him to assist her, rather vexed that there had not been sufficient time for her to experience the pleasure she had been expecting. With a hasty bow, Colonel Fitzwilliam took his leave, walking away in the direction from whence he had come, leaving Elizabeth to raise herself off the grass on her own. It was then she noticed the puddle of moisture that had been deposited on the front of her gown. It began to drip downward, threatening to soil her slippers. She tried to wipe it off, her fingers creating yet more untidiness until she was at last forced to abandon the enterprise.

The upset that the day occasioned brought on a headache,

and it grew so much worse by the evening that it determined Elizabeth not to attend Mr. and Mrs. Collins and Maria to Rosings, where they were engaged to drink tea and where both Mr. Darcy and Colonel Fitzwilliam would most assuredly be present. Elizabeth had no desire to see the former, and had been left with a sense of having been ill used by the latter. The fact that her gown was ruined beyond repair did little to soften her feelings toward Colonel Fitzwilliam.

When everyone had gone, Elizabeth chose for her employment the examination of all the letters that Jane had written to her. Mr. Darcy's shameful boast to Colonel Fitzwilliam of the misery he had been able to inflict gave her a keener sense of her sister's sufferings, though it was some consolation to think that his visit to Rosings was soon to end, as would that of his cousin, who was to depart with him. Despite his attentions in her direction, Colonel Fitzwilliam had made it clear that a match between them was impossible. Elizabeth reflected on an earlier statement he had made to her and to which she now wished she had paid greater regard. "There are too many in my rank of life who can afford to marry without some attention to money." Indeed, it would appear that in her many comparisons of him to Wickham, she had failed to note the most significant one of all.

Elizabeth was suddenly roused by the sound of the doorbell, and her spirits were a little anxious that it might be Colonel Fitzwilliam. Perhaps by having compromised herself in his company, he had concluded that she was a woman of reckless morals and had come to take from her what he felt was his due. After the events of the afternoon, that he should behave in so ungentlemanly a manner would not have surprised her at all. As she readied herself to fend off his advances, to her utter amazement Mr. Darcy walked into the room.

In a hurried manner he began an inquiry after her health, imputing his visit to a wish of hearing that she was much improved. When Elizabeth acknowledged that she was, Darcy sat down for a few moments and then, getting up, walked about the room. His demeanor was most agitated as he came toward her and said, "In vain I have struggled. It will not do. My feelings will not be repressed. You must allow me to tell you how ardently I admire and love you."

Elizabeth's astonishment was beyond expression, and for some time she could not speak. Her silence Darcy seemed to take as encouragement, and he went on to speak eloquently of his warmth and ardor for her, though there were feelings besides those of the heart to be detailed as well. He chronicled his sense of her inferiority and that of her family, concluding his speech by representing to her the strength of his attachment, which, despite all his endeavors, he had found impossible to conquer. In expressing to her his hope that it would be rewarded by her acceptance of his hand, he reached toward the flap of his breeches and began to unbutton it.

Till now Elizabeth had been in such a state of disbelief at his declaration, followed by anger at his review of her circumstances, that she had not taken note of his condition. Before she could put forth a reply, Darcy released his manhood from the confines of his breeches, displaying it fully to her. As she watched, he proceeded to stroke it, his fingers moving with practiced fondness along the sleek surface, traveling from base to tip, and then back again. His member was of considerable length and girth, making it a worthy rival to that which belonged to the chorister, if indeed, not its superior, and Elizabeth very much suspected that it far surpassed even Wickham's impressive specimen. The nest of curls at the place from which it sprang were darker than those on Darcy's head and looked nearly as silken, and for a moment she imagined herself passing some very pleasant moments twining them around her fingers.

Since Elizabeth had never before been offered a proposal

of marriage, she was uncertain if this manner of courtship was at all customary. Her friend Charlotte had never spoken of Mr. Collins's application to herself; therefore she had little basis for comparison, though she could most assuredly comprehend the practical nature of a gentleman's wish to make known his every asset to a young lady on whom he had set his sights. Darcy squeezed and pulled at the length of himself with his fingers, as if compelling it to grow still longer in what appeared to be a heartfelt attempt to impress her, paying particular attention to the roll of flesh near the tip, drawing it repeatedly down to reveal to her what lay beneath. Elizabeth detected a tiny bead of moisture that had gathered there like a drop of dew on a rose petal, and she fought a curious desire to lick it away with her tongue. The image of her so doing set off such a powerful reaction in the place of her womanhood that she was required to bite down on her lip as distraction lest she took a hand to herself—or worse still, her tongue to Darcy.

In spite of her deeply rooted dislike, Elizabeth could not be entirely insensible to the compliment of such a man's affection, nor to the appeal of what promised to be a most excellent representative of manly pleasure-giving, though her intentions did not vary for an instant. "In such cases as this, it is, I believe, the established mode to express a sense of obligation for the sentiments avowed, however unequally they may be returned," she began. "It is natural that obligation should be felt, and if I could *feel* gratitude, I would now thank you. But I have never desired your good opinion, and you have certainly bestowed it most unwillingly. I am sorry to have occasioned pain to anyone."

Darcy's complexion reddened with anger, his noble offering suddenly shrinking to a size that brought to Elizabeth's mind the miserable version belonging to the dough-like gentleman she had seen receiving his punishment from Lady Catherine's horsewhip. "And this is all the reply I am to have the honor of expecting!" cried he. "I might, perhaps, wish to be informed why I am thus rejected."

"I might as well inquire," replied she, "why with so evident a desire of offending and insulting me, you chose to tell me that you liked me against your will, against your reason, and even against your character? But I have other provocations. Had not my feelings decided against you, do you think that any consideration would tempt me to accept the man who has ruined, perhaps forever, the happiness of a most beloved sister? You cannot deny that you have been the means of dividing her from Mr. Bingley."

"I have no wish of denying that I did everything in my power to separate my friend from your sister, or that I rejoice in my success. Toward *him* I have been kinder than toward myself." With dignity, Darcy returned his manhood to his breeches, the procedure far more effortless than it had been to remove it.

"But it is not merely this affair," Elizabeth continued, "on which my dislike is founded. Long before it had taken place my opinion of you was decided. Your character was unfolded in the recital that I received many months ago from Mr. Wickham."

The mention of that gentleman's name caused something akin to rage to flash in Darcy's eyes, and Elizabeth's desire to confront him with every accusation that had been leveled against him abruptly died. She could well believe that such a man was responsible for dispatching his own sister to a life of ill repute.

"You put great credence in the opinions of Mr. Wickham," replied Darcy. "Perhaps, Miss Bennet, you might be more inclined to accept such an offer from *him*, since you clearly believe his character to be wholly unblemished."

The comment angered and embarrassed Elizabeth in equal measure, and she wondered if word had reached him as to Wickham's defection to Miss King. "Indeed, Mr. Darcy, I do believe it so, but we are speaking of *your* offer to me. You are mistaken if you suppose that the mode of your declaration affected me in any other way than sparing the concern I might have felt in refusing you, had you behaved in a more gentlemanlike manner," she retorted. She experienced then a moment of doubt as she brought to mind the proud majesty of his manhood and that it could have been hers, merely for the asking. That her tongue should again hunger to taste the drop of moisture she had spied at the crown was a source of much vexation to her, as were the resulting flutters at her womanhood such thoughts inspired.

"Could you expect me to rejoice in the inferiority of your connections?—to congratulate myself on the hope of relations whose condition in life is so decidedly beneath my own? You have said quite enough, madam. I perfectly comprehend your feelings, and have now only to be ashamed of what my own have been. Forgive me for having taken up so much of your time, and accept my best wishes for your health and happiness." With a bow, Darcy swiftly removed himself from Miss Bennet's presence.

Chapter Fifteen

ELIZABETH AWOKE THE NEXT MORNING TO THE SAME meditations that had at length closed her eyes, her astonishment no less overwhelming than it had been the evening before. Though it was gratifying to have inspired so strong an affection, Darcy's shameless avowal of what he had done with respect to Jane, and his unpardonable evasion of acknowledging the crimes Mr. Wickham had accused him of, stole away any chance that she could ever consent to be his. Her doubts, however, continued to linger, and she decided to indulge herself in fresh air and exercise, hoping it might clear away the image of Darcy's manhood from her mind. It disturbed her greatly that she should now find her thoughts so frequently reflecting on the handsomeness of it. Even her sleep was haunted, for she had woken more than once in the night, experiencing that sensation of soaring without having even touched herself. That this should have transpired while she dreamed that she had taken the entirety of Darcy's manhood into her mouth was, to Elizabeth, a disgrace of the highest order, as would be the fact that she had very much enjoyed it. The particulars continued to return to her as, all throughout breakfast, she kept envisioning herself on her knees before him, his manhood having reached to such depths in her mouth that the dark curls at the base tickled her nose. The fact that she seemed to have worshipped the object astonished her. Elizabeth, feeling its phantom presence in her throat, could barely manage to swallow a bite of her breakfast, necessitating Charlotte to inquire if she was unwell and, if such were the case, whether she wished to cut short her stay and return home to Hertfordshire. Elizabeth assured her that all was as it should be and she had merely been the victim of a restless sleep, the reply seeming to dishearten her friend rather than cheer her.

Not long after setting out on her walk, Elizabeth glimpsed a gentleman moving her way. Fearful of it being either of Lady Catherine's nephews, she began to retreat. The person who advanced was near enough to have seen her, however, and stepped forward. On seeing that it was Darcy, Elizabeth felt her face color and refused to meet his eye. She wondered if he could see into her mind and know the nature of her imaginings—see the length of himself filling her mouth, which he would have undoubtedly perceived as the greatest victory. Perhaps he already believed her to have taken part in such activities with Mr. Wickham, if not, indeed, Colonel Fitzwilliam, who might have alerted his cousin with much augmentation as to the manner of depravity engaged in by her on the previous day. Were anyone to discover the stains on her gown, her fate would most assuredly have been sealed.

Elizabeth found her gaze drawn repeatedly to Darcy's breeches, which continued to indicate his interest, and she knew not whether to curse him or drop to her knees before him.

Darcy held a letter out to her. "Miss Bennet, will you do me the honor of reading this?" With a slight bow, he turned back, and was soon out of sight.

The encounter, though brief, had left Elizabeth shaken, and she lowered herself onto the felled trunk of a tree, where she opened the letter and began to read:

> *Be not alarmed, madam, on receiving this letter, by the apprehension of its containing any repetition of those sentiments or renewal of those offers that were last night so disgusting to you. I write without any intention of paining you, or humbling myself, by dwelling on wishes which, for the happiness of both, cannot be too soon forgotten. However, my character requires that I address the offenses you last night laid to my charge, the first of which concerns your sister and Mr. Bingley, the second Mr. Wickham, the particulars of which we did not address.*
>
> *I had not been long in Hertfordshire before I saw that Bingley preferred your elder sister to any other young woman in the country. But it was not till the evening of the dance at Netherfield that I had any apprehension of his feeling a serious attachment, to which various members of your family indicated a general expectation of marriage. As regards your sister, though she received his attentions with pleasure, I observed that she did not invite them by any participation of sentiment. That I was desirous of believing her indifferent is certain, but I will venture to say that my investigation and decisions are not usually influenced by my hopes or fears. There were other causes of repugnance in my objections to the marriage. The situation of your mother's family, though objectionable, was nothing in comparison to that total want of propriety so frequently and so uniformly betrayed by your mother herself,*

your three younger sisters, and occasionally even your father. Pardon me, it pains me to offend you. I will only say further that my opinion of all parties was confirmed, and every inducement heightened that could have led me to preserve my friend from what I esteemed a most unhappy connection.

Mr. Bingley's sisters' uneasiness with the matter had been equally excited with my own, and we shortly resolved on joining him directly in London. There I readily engaged in the office of pointing out to him the certain evils of such a choice. I do not suppose that my advice would ultimately have prevented the marriage, had it not been seconded by the assurance of your sister's indifference, which I hesitated not in giving. Bingley has great natural modesty, with a stronger dependence on my judgment than on his own. To convince him was no very difficult point. There is but one part of my conduct in the whole affair on which I do not reflect with satisfaction; it is that I condescended to adopt the measures of art to conceal from him your sister's being in town. On this subject I have nothing more to say, no other apology to offer. If I have wounded your sister's feelings, it was unknowingly done, and though the motives that governed me may to you very naturally appear insufficient, I have not yet learned to condemn them.

With respect to Mr. Wickham, of what he has particularly accused me I am ignorant; but of the truth of what I shall relate, I can summon more than one witness of undoubted veracity. Mr. Wickham is the son of a very respectable man who had for many years the management of all *the Pemberley estates, and whose good conduct in the discharge of his trust naturally inclined my father to be of service to him; and on George Wickham, who was his godson, his kindness was therefore liberally bestowed. My father was not only fond of this young man's society, he had also the highest opinion of him, and hoping the church would be his profession, intended to provide for him in it.*

My excellent father died about five years ago, and his attachment to Mr. Wickham was to the last so steady that in his will he particularly recommended it to me to promote his advancement in the best manner that his profession might allow—and if he took orders, desired that a valuable family living might be his. There was also a legacy of one thousand pounds. His own father did not long survive mine, and shortly afterward Mr. Wickham wrote to inform me that, having resolved against the clergy, he hoped I should not think it unreasonable for him to expect a more immediate pecuniary advantage. He had some intention, he added, of studying law. The business was therefore most generously settled, and all connection between us seemed now dissolved. Wickham's studying the law was a mere pretense, however. I heard little of him, until he applied to me again by letter. He had found the law a most unprofitable study, and was now absolutely resolved on being ordained, if I would present to him the living in question. When I refused, he became violent in his abuse of me to others.

I must now mention a circumstance I would wish to forget, myself, and which no obligation less than the present one should induce me to unfold to anyone. It concerns my sister and Mr. Wickham, who took it upon himself to arrange meetings with her unbeknownst to myself. He so far recommended himself to Georgiana, whose affectionate heart retained a strong impression of his kindness to her as a child, that she was persuaded to believe herself in love, and to consent to an elopement. There would be no marriage, however. The legacy my father bequeathed, and the stately sum I added to it, went toward the purchase of a property in town, which Wickham established as a bawdy house. As regards my sister, he recruited her to his trade, stealing her innocence and causing her ruin. I shall spare you further details, though be assured they are vile indeed. Although she is now safely returned to my guardianship, I fear her future chances are at an end. For indeed, who would have her now? I cannot help supposing that the desire of revenging himself on me was a strong inducement in Wickham's choice of Georgiana, as was his desire to appropriate her legacy.

This, madam, is a faithful narrative of every event in which we have been concerned together, and if you do not absolutely reject it as false, you will, I hope, acquit me henceforth of injustice toward Mr. Wickham. I know not what form of falsehood he had imposed on you, but ignorant as you previously were of everything concerning both myself and Wickham, detection could not be in your power, and suspicion certainly not in your inclination.

Yours,
Fitzwilliam Darcy

Elizabeth read and reread the letter, absolute in her determination to believe none of it. Darcy's belief of her sister's insensibility to Bingley she instantly resolved to be false, and his account of the worst objections to the match made her too angry to have any wish of doing him justice. When this subject was succeeded by his account of Mr. Wickham, she wished to discredit it entirely. Yet her thoughts could not rest, and Elizabeth proceeded to examine every sentence that related to him. The account of Wickham's connection with the Pemberley family was exactly what he himself had related to her, as were nearly all the particulars, but for the fact that Wickham had accused Darcy of what he himself was guilty of, if Darcy was to be believed. Every line proved more clearly that the affair, in which she had believed Darcy's conduct less than infamous, was capable of a turn that must make him entirely blameless.

The profligacy that he laid at Wickham's charge exceedingly shocked her. Of his former way of life nothing had been known in Hertfordshire excepting what he had told himself. As to his real character, his countenance, charm, and manner had established him in the possession of every virtue. As Elizabeth tried to recollect some trait of integrity or munificence that might rescue him from the attacks of Darcy, she could remember nothing more substantial than the general approbation of the neighborhood. As for his being the cause of Miss Darcy's ruin, her brother would never have hazarded such a story if he had not been well assured of its corroboration.

She was now struck with the impropriety of Wickham's communications to her, a stranger, and wondered that it had escaped her before. Indeed, the more Elizabeth considered the history of her dealings with Wickham, the more convinced she became that Darcy spoke the truth. She had, to her extreme folly, allowed his charm and flattery to persuade her of his good character and, to a considerable degree, the promise of what was contained in his breeches. To think that she had enjoyed the most rapturous pleasures as she imagined his manhood availing itself of her womanhood, or worse still, her backside! Neither could she deny the justice of Darcy's description of Jane. Her sister's feelings, though fervent, were little displayed, and there was a complacency in her manner not often united with great sensibility. In Darcy's reproach of her family, Elizabeth's sense of shame was severe. The justice of the charge struck her too forcibly for denial as she recalled her mother's frenzied behavior and improper remarks and Lydia's reckless cavorting with officers, innocent though it was.

Elizabeth spent some while in wandering the lane, reflecting on events and chastising herself for her part in them. At length she returned to the parsonage, where she was informed that both Mr. Darcy and Colonel Fitzwilliam had called separately of each other, hoping to offer her their farewells, for they were departing on the morrow. She felt much relief for having missed them.

Chapter Sixteen

ON THE MORNING THE TWO GENTLEMEN LEFT KENT, MR. Collins hastened to Rosings to console Lady Catherine and her daughter, returning with a message from her ladyship, who reported that she felt herself so dull as to make her desirous of having them all to dine with her that evening.

Elizabeth could not see Lady Catherine without thinking that, had she chosen to accept Mr. Darcy's affections, she might now have been presented to her as her future niece, and she could but dare to imagine what her ladyship's indignation would have been. That her sickly daughter had been the one intended for him Elizabeth could no longer take amusement from. Both mother and daughter appeared equally out of spirits, with Miss de Bourgh speaking not at all, and Lady Catherine's temper sharper than usual. Elizabeth attributed it to the departure of Mr. Darcy and Colonel Fitzwilliam, for there was no doubt that her ladyship maintained a genuine fondness for them both.

As she recalled the scene with Lady Catherine and the four unclothed figures over which she wielded her horsewhip, Elizabeth wondered if her manner of discipline extended to her nephews. The image of Colonel Fitzwilliam bound to a timber post did not seem so remote a prospect, and considering how remarkably ill he had treated her, she would not have minded being the one to administer his sentence. As regards his cousin, she could not envisage the prideful Mr. Darcy acquiescing to such a humiliating punishment by allowing himself to be stripped to his boots, his backside bared to the repeated lash of the leather. Nor could she imagine his noble manhood growing greater and greater until it finally burst forth with its juices in the same manner as that which had transpired with the chorister as he underwent his own punishment at the hands of her ladyship. Elizabeth was certain Darcy had been very near to reaching such a state on the occasion of his proposal to her and, had she not made so patent her rejection of it, might have witnessed it for herself. She felt certain his offerings would have been far more agreeable than those which his cousin had deposited on her gown, and she entertained herself briefly with the idea of sampling it with her tongue, surprised by the wickedness of her thoughts.

Lady Catherine had been observing that Miss Bennet seemed unusually reticent, and accounted for it by supposing that she did not wish to return home so soon. "You must write to your mother and beg that you may stay a little longer," she replied, her tone indicating that she did not expect her will to be denied. "Then you may have the benefit of our pianoforte so that you can improve in those areas which are, at present, so lacking."

It took a moment for Elizabeth to realize that she had just been insulted, and she endeavored to respond with as much civility as possible. "I am very obliged to your ladyship for your kind invitation, but it is not in my power to accept it. My father expects me back at Longbourn." This was not expressly true, however, as her younger sisters had reported more than once in their letters that Mr. Bennet rarely left his library, and was only seen to open the door to Hill, the housekeeper.

Lady Catherine continued to pursue the matter, insisting that Elizabeth's family could certainly spare her for another fortnight, but Elizabeth refused to be persuaded, and began to think it most odd that her ladyship was so insistent on her remaining for a while longer at Hunsford. She could not fathom why, as neither of them appeared to have any particular regard for each other. The subject of riding was proposed as further inducement, the stables at Rosings being, without question, one of the finest in the country. To this Mr. Collins eagerly concurred, his gap-toothed countenance beaming, until a sharp look from his patroness silenced him. It was only when Lady Catherine suggested to Elizabeth that she might wish to sample her excellent supply of equestrian accoutrements that she became anxious to return to the parsonage, and it was to her great relief when the coach was ordered.

That night Elizabeth was awakened by the sound of screams in the near distance. She moved directly to the window, at first seeing only the moonlit grounds of the parsonage and Rosings beyond. As she was about to turn back to her bed, she glimpsed several figures emerging from a grove of trees by the park. They appeared to be running away from something. She counted five in all, and they were none of them dressed, save for their boots. From what Elizabeth could discern from her vantage point, all were men, and as they drew progressively closer, she was provided with happy affirmation of it. Their manly parts displayed themselves in varying states of restlessness, and it was a wonder to her that those of the party who had reached to their fullest stature even possessed the ability to run, they looked so weighted down by their burdens. Elizabeth tried to determine if the chorister whom she had seen twice before was among them, and thought for a moment that she recognized him until he turned away, removing from her observation the agreeable characteristic that would have most distinguished him. That their distress was authentic she had no doubt, and she considered going down to offer assistance when her attention was distracted by yet another figure coming into view behind them. Unlike the others, this one was clothed from head to toe. Elizabeth knew who it was immediately; there could be no mistaking that tall stature, or the horsewhip. The five men ran off in the direction of the road, with Lady Catherine in close pursuit, her whip snapping through the air.

It came with some relief when the day arrived for Elizabeth to return home to the comparative dullness of her family. Her stay in Kent had provided more excitement than she was accustomed to, and she looked forward to being reunited with her sisters. She and Maria departed Hunsford with a good deal of fanfare, particularly from Mr. Collins, who appeared genuinely pleased and humbled to have had the enjoyment of Elizabeth's company. "It gives me great pleasure to hear that you have passed your time not disagreeably," said he. "Our situation with regard to Lady Catherine's family is indeed the sort of extraordinary advantage and blessing that few can boast. You may, in fact, carry a very favorable report of us into Hertfordshire." Elizabeth was generous with her thanks and assurances of happiness, to which Mr. Collins offered these words in parting: "My dear Charlotte and I have but one mind and one way of thinking. We seem to have been designed for each other. My dear Miss Elizabeth, I can from my heart most cordially wish you equal felicity in marriage."

Elizabeth felt for a moment quite ashamed at having made such impolitic use of her cousin's pipe during her stay at Hunsford; indeed, she had done so only hours before, the contents of Mr. Darcy's letter having put him in an entirely different light from the one in which she had initially placed him, and she could not deny that her opinion of him had been much altered as a result. The details of his proposal were still fresh in her mind, as were those of his manhood, which inspired in her a state of considerable agitation as she recalled its every contour and ridge. She had gone to bed imagining her fingertips caressing its length, her ears hearing the quickening of his breaths just as they had done on the evening he made his heart known to her. That it was, in fact, Elizabeth's own flesh beneath her fingertips and not Darcy's was momentarily lost to her as she pulled down the covering at the crown of his manhood, the force of her desire so great that she could feel it beneath her tongue.

After a while Elizabeth's touches could no longer satisfy the increasing demands of her body, and she was compelled to go downstairs to seek out Mr. Collins's pipe, applying it to both her front and her rear openings before the relief she required was finally granted—and even then she was left with a sense of not being entirely fulfilled. That Darcy was to blame she had no doubt, and she wondered if he would forever haunt her thoughts and dreams. She took her fingers to herself yet again, employing every device and trick she could think of, concentrating her efforts on the segment of flesh in her cleft, spinning it about, shaking it from side to side, even pinching it between her fingertips until at last she received her reward. She had spent a most frustrating night and was thankful when the morning of her departure arrived.

Elizabeth and Maria's carriage was at last allowed to drive away, and Mr. Collins, smiling his gap-toothed smile, stood waving them off, flanked by his wife, whose expression appeared to indicate a great sense of relief. A few minutes into their journey, Maria said to Elizabeth, "How many things have happened! We have dined nine times at Rosings, besides drinking tea there twice. How much I shall have to tell!"

And how much I shall have to conceal! Elizabeth added privately, experiencing a renewal of those sensations that were best kept in the bedchamber.

They arrived back at Gracechurch Street, where they were to stay with the Gardiners before returning with Jane to Hertfordshire. Elizabeth told her sister of Mr. Darcy's proposal, though, not wishing to cause further grief, she refrained from revealing his interference in Mr. Bingley's potential future happiness with Jane. She also omitted the particulars of Darcy's extraordinary method of courtship in the display of his manhood, or her feelings on the subject, believing her sister's sensibilities too delicate. Elizabeth made no mention of Wickham or his dealings with Darcy's sister, her uncertainty as to how much of the specifics she should disclose occasioning her reticence on the matter. As for Lady Catherine and her horsewhip, were she to relate the tale, Jane would probably conclude that Elizabeth had been availing herself of her mother's potions obtained from the gypsies.

The three young ladies set off for Hertfordshire a few days later, stopping at the appointed inn where Mr. Bennet's carriage was to meet them and carry them the rest of the way. To their very great surprise, both Kitty and Lydia were waiting for them, and after welcoming their sisters, they triumphantly displayed a table set out with such cold meat as an inn larder usually affords. "Is not this an agreeable surprise?" asked Lydia. "And we mean to treat you all, but you must lend us the money, for we have just spent ours at the milliner's shop." The subject of bonnets was then entered into with much enthusiasm by the two youngest Bennet sisters, after which the conversation turned to the militia, which was shortly due to leave for Brighton. News of the departure did much to ease Elizabeth's mind, though Lydia indicated an expectation that the Bennet family would soon be following. "It would be such a delicious scheme!" she cried. "Mamma would like to go, too, of all things!"

Lydia's eyes glowed with excitement, the rapidity of her breaths prompting her generously proportioned bosom to expand further outward from the bodice of her gown. With much eagerness she began to eat. She had not, however, finished relaying all her news, and after swallowing a rather large chunk of meat, she gleefully informed Elizabeth and Jane that Mr. Wickham was no longer in danger of marrying Miss King, who had left Hertfordshire and given no indication of any plan to return. The circumstances of her departure were a source of much speculation to the residents of the county, some saying that she had gone to stay with her uncle in Liverpool, while others claimed to have caught sight of her in London. There had even been talk that Miss King had fallen on hard times and turned to vice; this report was obtained by Lydia from one of the groundskeepers at Longbourn, who had overheard some of the regiment talking in the tavern one night. "Miss King, a lady of ill repute!" she cried. "Can you imagine?"

"Lydia, I do hope you are not adding fuel to such rumors, for surely the talk of drunken men cannot be paid much heed," scolded Jane. "I only hope there is no strong attachment on the side of either Miss King *or* Mr. Wickham."

"Oh, Wickham never cared three straws about her. Who could care about such a nasty little freckled thing?" replied Lydia, seizing the remains of a joint of gammon.

The carriage was soon ordered, and after much contrivance, the whole party with all their boxes and parcels was placed inside it. As they rode back to Longbourn, Lydia continued to talk of bonnets, parties, and officers, making frequent mention of Colonel and Mrs. Forster, with whom she had been spending a good deal of time. Elizabeth listened as little as she could, but there was no escaping the frequent mention of Wickham's name. She could not help wondering if this story Lydia had obtained from the groundskeeper had any worth. Knowing what she now did about Wickham, if Miss King had, in fact, lost her way, he might well have had a hand in it.

The sisters had not been many hours at home before Lydia and Kitty set off to Meryton in pursuit of the officers. Elizabeth declined to go; she dreaded seeing Wickham again and was resolved to avoid it for as long as possible. She discovered that the Brighton scheme, of which Lydia had hinted earlier, was under frequent discussion between her parents, most of it taking place at the library door, which remained locked against Mrs. Bennet. Mr. Bennet gave not the slightest indication of yielding, though his responses were at the same time so vague that his wife had not yet despaired of succeeding.

By the next morning, Elizabeth's impatience to acquaint Jane with what she had learned about Wickham could no longer be borne. Upon hearing her sister's account, Jane cried, "I do not know when I have been more shocked! Wickham so very bad, it is almost past belief! And poor Mr. Darcy!"

"Mr. Darcy has not authorized me to make his communication public. On the contrary, every particular relative to his sister was meant to be kept as much as possible to myself. Wickham will soon be gone; therefore at present I will say nothing about it."

"You are quite right. To have his errors made public might ruin him forever," replied Jane. "He is now, perhaps, sorry for what he has done and anxious to re-establish his character. Surely he is not so villainous as he has been portrayed."

Elizabeth, who continued to marvel at her sister's child-like insistence to always see the goodness in all, was unable to imagine Mr. Wickham in so positive a light as to be suddenly desirous of fostering his good name. The recent departure of Miss King had caused her to envision the worst: poor

Miss King being kept prisoner in Wickham's bawdy house in London, then being cast out into the streets when there was little left for him to steal of her body and fortune. As Elizabeth pondered the depravity to which she was being subjected, she found her thoughts returning yet again to Darcy's manhood and the admiration she had experienced in his eyes when he had presented it to her. That such a tender heart had been made accessible to her spoke equally well of its wealth of feeling for a sister. Unlike Miss Darcy, perhaps Miss King did not have the benevolence of a brother willing to take her in, regardless of the cost to his own reputation, were events to be made known.

The tumult of Elizabeth's mind was momentarily allayed by having unburdened these secrets to Jane, though the biggest secret of all she could not impart. She saw that her sister was unhappy and still cherished a very tender affection for Bingley, yet she dared not make an unfortunate situation even more grievous by disclosing the facts related to their separation.

"I am sure Jane will die of a broken heart, and then Mr. Bingley will be sorry for what he has done," said Mrs. Bennet one day, her eyes so wide and staring that none of the family could bear to look at her. She had grown quite gaunt since Elizabeth had gone to Kent, the protruding eyes and loss of weight giving her a skeletal appearance. She seemed to barely touch food, choosing only to drink her special tea, which she did in abundance. Elizabeth did not know which was more unpleasant—the sight of her mother or that of her sister Mary, whose moustache had now been joined by a beard. The distractions of Hunsford parish now felt many years distant, and at times she wondered if she had ever been there at all.

Chapter Seventeen

A DEEP GLOOM ONCE MORE DESCENDED ON LONGBOURN House. Lamentations resounded perpetually at the imminent departure of the officers, most coming from Kitty and Lydia, though their mother shared in their grief, recalling her own such separation during her youth. "I cried for two days together when Colonel Miller's regiment went away. I thought it should have broken my heart," said she, her apoplectic eyes moistening at the memory of the handsome young redcoat who had got her with child. She glanced in the direction of the library inside which Mr. Bennet had sequestered himself, wondering how she had ever married him. When she thought of her militiaman and how his every touch sent a shimmering through her like that of a thousand stars, and compared it to Mr. Bennet's clumsy overtures, she experienced an urge to take a knife to her husband's back. "If one could but go to Brighton!" pronounced Mrs. Bennet loudly enough for her words to penetrate the locked door of the library. "A little sea bathing would so help with my nerves!"

"Oh, yes, if one could but go to Brighton! But papa is so

disagreeable!" cried Lydia, her voice equaling in volume her mother's.

Although Elizabeth tried to find amusement in the exchange, all sense of pleasure was lost in shame. She felt anew the justice of Darcy's objections to her family and, in observing Lydia, never had she been so much disposed to pardon his interference in the views of his friend. With neither her father's guiding force nor her mother as commendable example, there seemed little hope for any of her sisters to make a good match. Indeed, Mr. Darcy was in all likelihood congratulating himself on his fortuity in her refusal of his hand.

Lydia's gloom was shortly cleared away when she received an invitation from Mrs. Forster, the wife of the colonel of the regiment, to accompany her to Brighton. Mrs. Forster was a very young woman, and only lately married. While Elizabeth and Jane had been gone, she and Lydia had become particular friends, sharing the same high spirits, which gave Elizabeth further cause for concern. As Lydia flew about the house, calling for everyone's congratulations and laughing and talking with more violence than ever, the luckless Kitty bemoaned the unfairness of it all; having seniority in years to her sister, she believed that she, too, should have been invited.

Elizabeth resolved to speak privately on the matter to her father at the first available opportunity. Although Mr. Bennet had instructed his family never to disturb him when he was in the library, she had no recourse; in these last months it had become increasingly rare to find him anywhere else. Her knock on the door received no reply, however. She was certain her father was there, as she had seen him go in shortly after the delivery of a special post that morning.

Mr. Bennet was seated at his writing desk, his attention engaged by the latest addition to his collection of drawings and the buxom presence of Hill, whose hands were busily working the length of his manhood; therefore he did not hear his caller at the door. He leaned back in his chair with his legs parted wide, the housekeeper having with some difficulty folded her ample form into the small space beneath the escritoire at his feet. A drawing depicting two young ladies attired only in their short stays was propped against the account books he had abandoned when the post arrived. One reclined on her back, with the other facing her on her hands and knees, but positioned contrariwise, their faces most happily situated between each other's thighs, where they had found much to amuse themselves. Mr. Bennet considered the vista most inspirational, as was evidenced by the size and rigidity of his manhood as it projected out from his breeches. Hill held it contained in both hands, moving them swiftly up and down, the loose flap of skin at the tip continually bringing into exposure the shiny pink flesh beneath and prompting Mr. Bennet to groan with delight, particularly when Hill teased this place with her tongue.

Elizabeth, hearing sounds from within, rapped with greater firmness against the door, eventually trying the handle. The door was locked against her. "Papa?" she called. "Are you there?"

Mr. Bennet could not at once determine the identity of his intruder from the noise of the blood pounding in his ears, though he imagined it to be Mrs. Bennet, who made it her life's employment to ruin his pleasure at every turn. He hissed at Hill to make haste, determined for matters to reach a conclusion before the intruder endeavoring to break down the door decided instead to climb in through the window. Reclaiming one of her hands, Hill placed it on the swollen pouch beneath his manhood, cupping it with such firmness that Mr. Bennet's eyes filled with tears, though he made no complaint. The housekeeper then applied herself in earnest, squeezing and pulling her employer's testes with considerable force while she did likewise with his member until at last he gave out a sharp cry, releasing his pleasure onto the bodice of her gown and the floor.

Hill would not have occasion to tidy herself or, for that matter, quit her station beneath Mr. Bennet's desk, for by this time Elizabeth was all but pounding on the door with the urgency of her need to speak to her father about Lydia; indeed, she could not for the life of her imagine what he was doing that necessitated him keeping her waiting so long. At last she heard a turn of the lock, which was followed by the opening of the door. Mr. Bennet stood there in confusion, his features suffused with color as if he had just returned from a long ride. For a moment he appeared not to recognize her, then at once recovered himself and allowed her entry, though he kept well away from his desk and did not invite his daughter to sit down.

Elizabeth noted Hill on her knees beneath the escritoire and concluded that her father had been writing a letter and spilled some ink, which the housekeeper was endeavoring to clean. With as much forcefulness as her position allowed, Elizabeth represented to him all the improprieties of Lydia's behavior, the little advantage she could derive from the friendship of Mrs. Forster, and the probability of her being yet more imprudent in the company of such a woman at Brighton, where the temptations were likely to far outweigh those at Meryton. To her astonishment, Mr. Bennet no longer held an objection and appeared resigned to the situation. "If you were aware," added Elizabeth, "of the very great disadvantage to us all from the public notice of Lydia's unguarded and imprudent manner, I am sure you would judge differently in the affair."

"Has she frightened away some of your lovers?" Mr. Bennet inquired. "Such squeamish youths as cannot bear to be connected with a little absurdity are not worth a regret. Come, let me see the list of pitiful fellows who have been kept aloof by Lydia's folly."

Elizabeth saw Mr. Darcy in her mind's eye and felt overcome by shame. "Indeed, I have no such injuries to resent. But our respectability in the world must be affected by the wild volatility and disdain of all restraint that mark Lydia's character. If you, my dear father, will not take the trouble of checking her exuberant spirits, and of teaching her that her present pursuits are not to be the business of her life, she will soon be beyond the reach of amendment. She will be the most determined flirt that ever made herself or her family ridiculous!"

Mr. Bennet would have liked to be rid of Lydia, and he harbored the hope that in Brighton she might perhaps find a young man, or perhaps even an old one, foolish enough to take her. One less daughter to feed and clothe at a time when the family's finances were dwindling considerably from his private expenditures held much appeal, though he had lately noticed other depletions in funds for which he could not account. As he led Elizabeth to the door, he replied, "We shall have no peace at Longbourn if Lydia does not go to Brighton. She is luckily too poor to be an object of prey to anybody. At any rate, she cannot grow many degrees worse, without authorizing us to lock her up for the rest of her life." With those words, he shut the door in Elizabeth's face.

With this answer his daughter was forced to be content, though her opinion on the subject did not waver, and she left her father feeling disappointed and sorry for the future.

On the final day of the regiment's remaining at Meryton, Mr. Wickham dined with the other officers at Longbourn. Having lost all regard for him, Elizabeth felt her objections toward that quarter increase when she found herself selected by him as the object of idle and frivolous gallantry. That he believed her preference could be secured at any time by the renewal of his attentions was beyond provocation. As she observed the straining flap of his breeches, she could not but wonder if it had been similarly so when he had been courting Miss King. Elizabeth's excitement at securing such approval from Wickham was at an end; had he unbuttoned his breeches and displayed his manhood to her, she would quite likely have yawned.

When he inquired as to the nature in which her time had passed at Hunsford, Elizabeth immediately mentioned Mr. Darcy's stay at Rosings, giving emphasis to the fact that they had seen each other daily, which elicited the expected astonishment. Wickham listened with an apprehensive attention, then, with a forced gaiety of tone, commented as to that gentleman's lack of civility in manner.

To this Elizabeth replied, "I think Mr. Darcy improves upon acquaintance."

"Indeed?!" cried Wickham. "You, who so well know my feeling toward Mr. Darcy, will readily comprehend how sincerely I must rejoice that he is wise enough to assume even the appearance of what is right. I only fear that the sort of improvement to which you are alluding is merely adopted on his visits to his aunt, and his wish of forwarding the match with Miss de Bourgh."

"Oh, I did not mean that his mind or his manners were in a state of improvement, but that, from knowing him so much more intimately as I now may claim to, his disposition was better understood."

Wickham's alarm at the reply was manifest by a heightened complexion and agitated look, and Elizabeth could not repress a smile as she noted that the swelling in his breeches was no longer evident. They parted at last with mutual civility, and possibly a mutual desire of never meeting again.

The regiment departed from Meryton, and shortly thereafter Lydia, who had promised to write very often to her mother and Kitty, though her letters were always long expected and very brief. The time fixed for Elizabeth's tour of the Lakes with Mr. and Mrs. Gardiner was fast approaching, and this gave her some consolation for the dullness of life at

Longbourn. No longer did she take to pleasuring herself in her bed at night, for there was little in the way of inspiration to be found. Though she tried to bring to mind the handsome manhood belonging to the chorister in Hunsford, or, to her shame, even that of Mr. Darcy, a general lassitude had taken over her body, and no amount of manipulation by her fingers could conjure up the required response. Indeed, her parts had not felt so distressed since Mr. Collins's proposal of marriage to her!

A letter shortly arrived from Mrs. Gardiner, informing Elizabeth that Mr. Gardiner had business in London, and they were therefore obliged to give up the Lakes; they would instead undertake a more contracted tour, going no farther northward than Derbyshire. In that county there was enough to occupy them, and to Mrs. Gardiner it held a particularly strong attraction, for now they could include a visit to the town in which she had formerly passed some years of her life. It was impossible for Elizabeth to think of Derbyshire without thinking of Pemberley and its owner. She did not expect, however, to encounter Mr. Darcy, nor did she wish to. The taint her family had placed on her had made such a prospect most undesired and best avoided.

The weeks passed with great anticipation until the Gardiners finally arrived at Longbourn, and the party soon set off on their journey, eager for amusement. After seeing all the principal wonders of the county, they settled themselves in the little town of Lambton, the place of Mrs. Gardiner's former residence. Elizabeth found from her aunt that Pemberley was situated not five miles from there, and Mrs. Gardiner expressed an inclination to see the place again, to which Mr. Gardiner was in accord. Elizabeth, made anxious by this addition to their route, felt that she had no business at Pemberley and was obliged to assume a disinclination for seeing it. The possibility of meeting Mr. Darcy while viewing the place instantly occurred, and rather than run such a risk, she decided to speak openly to her aunt. Before so doing, however, she made inquiries of the chambermaid at the inn about Pemberley and whether the family was down for the summer. A most welcome negative followed the last question and, her alarm now removed, she felt at leisure to see the house herself.

That night for the first time in many weeks Elizabeth experienced that wondrous sensation of soaring that had so eluded her since leaving Kent. Though she did not endeavor to coax it into being, her flesh was in a heightened state of awareness at the prospect of seeing Pemberley. She could no longer deny that it held a great curiosity for her, or that its attraction was very much a result of its proprietor. As she lay in her bed, the image of Mr. Darcy's manhood displayed itself against the closed lids of her eyes, its every detail magnified—from the dark curls at the root to the tiny eye at the crown, which had wept with tears as he confessed to her his love. They had reminded Elizabeth of droplets of honey, and her desire to taste them proved as powerful now as it had been then. As she felt her tongue licking away these remembered tears, a familiar pulsing made itself known in the place of her womanhood, beating in harmony with her heart until she found that she was holding her breath.

Elizabeth threw off the bedcovers and raised up the hem of her nightdress, feeling bolder than she ever had as she parted her thighs, imagining that Darcy was there gazing upon her—nay, *studying* her. The thought of his eyes on these parts prompted a rush of moisture to flood her opening, and it moved down between the cleft of her backside like the tickling of a finger. The thought of it being Darcy's fingertip teasing her here spurred Elizabeth to even greater abandon and she opened her folds, displaying to him the secrets therein. Her fingers barely had time to alight on the place that gave her so much pleasure before she was flying high into the nighttime sky, its stars sparks of white light bursting within her loins.

"You must allow me to tell you how ardently I admire and love you."

Elizabeth's eyes flew open and she sat up in bed, a furious pounding in her chest. But there was no one in the room, and all was just as it had been when she had retired for the evening.

When the subject of Pemberley was revived by the Gardiners the next morning, and their niece was again applied to, Elizabeth, though still shaken from the previous night, readily answered that she had no objection to the scheme. To Pemberley, therefore, they were to go.

Chapter Eighteen

NOT EVEN ALL THE HIGH COMMENDATION OF HER AUNT could have prepared Elizabeth for the sight of Pemberley. Her spirits were in a flutter as Pemberley Woods first came into view, followed by the great expanse of a park, until at last her eye was caught by Pemberley House situated on the opposite side of a valley. It was a large, handsome building backed by a ridge of high woody hills and fronted by a river. They were all three of them warm in their admiration, and at that moment Elizabeth felt that to be mistress of Pemberley might truly be something!

As they crossed the bridge to the door, her apprehension of meeting its owner returned, for it was not impossible that the chambermaid had been mistaken as to the family's being away. The party was admitted into the hall, where they were joined by the housekeeper, a Mrs. Reynolds, who led them around, her manner all civility. From every window there were beauties to be seen, and the rooms and furnishings were both handsome and suitable to the fortune of its proprietor, with less splendor, yet more real elegance, than Rosings.

Elizabeth longed to inquire of the housekeeper whether her master was really absent. At length the question was asked by her uncle, and Mrs. Reynolds replied that Mr. Darcy was expected to arrive the next day with a large party of friends. Elizabeth felt only relief that their own journey had not been delayed by a day.

Mrs. Gardiner drew her niece's attention to a picture suspended with several other miniatures over the mantelpiece. Elizabeth recognized Mr. Wickham immediately and felt dismay at having even this small representation to remind her of her folly at being taken in by him. The housekeeper told them that he was the son of her late master's steward, who had been brought up by her late master at his own expense. "He is now gone into the army," she added, "but I am afraid he has turned out very wild." It required a considerable effort for Elizabeth to refrain from commenting as to the specific nature of Wickham's wildness.

Mrs. Reynolds, her admiration conspicuous in her voice and expression, pointed out another miniature, which was of Mr. Darcy. Upon learning from Mrs. Gardiner that Miss Bennet was already acquainted with the gentleman, her surprise was evident, and much mention was made by both Mrs. Gardiner and the housekeeper as to his handsomeness, to which Elizabeth's agreement was likewise solicited. Mrs. Reynolds then directed their attention to a miniature of Miss Darcy, informing them that she was also due on the morrow. "The handsomest young lady that ever was seen, and so accomplished!" said she, her countenance beaming. "In the next room is a new instrument just come down for her—a present from my master. Whatever can give his sister any pleasure is sure to be done in a moment. There is nothing he would not do for her."

"Is your master much at Pemberley in the course of the year?" asked Mr. Gardiner.

"Not so much as I could wish, sir, but Miss Darcy is

always down for the summer months."

Except, Elizabeth thought with sadness, *when she is working in Mr. Wickham's bawdy house*. Indeed, she could not but wonder in what state Miss Darcy would be arriving, particularly if she still suffered with her opium dependence.

Mrs. Reynolds next took them to the gallery, all the while continuing to offer praise of her master, whom she had known since boyhood. "He is the best landlord and the best master that ever lived. Some people call him proud, but I am sure I never saw anything of it." The remark elicited not the first in a number of questioning glances directed toward Elizabeth from her aunt, who, ignorant of the circumstances to which her niece had been made privy, was clearly puzzled by these most excellent reports of Darcy's character.

The gallery contained several family portraits, one of which was of Mr. Darcy, who stood staring down at Elizabeth with a smile she remembered to have seen sometimes when he looked at her. The approbation bestowed on him by Mrs. Reynolds was of no trifling nature, and as she stood before the canvas on which he was represented, Elizabeth thought of his regard with a deeper sentiment than had ever arisen before. As the others continued into another room, she remained where she was, transfixed by his painted image. Though she had never disputed Darcy's handsomeness, it was only now that she felt her eyes truly opened as to the full extent of it. Her gaze was nearly level with the flap of his breeches, and she experienced a renewal of the sensations from the night before as she recalled yet again the manner in which he had offered up his manhood for her inspection. There had been a nobility in his movements, as if he were bestowing on her a great honor. Had she only known then what she knew now!

Elizabeth's hand moved toward the meeting place between her thighs, the desire for relief so overwhelming as to render her faint. The voices of the others had faded sufficiently to inform her that they were no longer close, and she took the interlude to slip a hand beneath her skirts, her eyes meeting Darcy's as she began to manipulate herself toward release. Her fingers moved with surprising ease, and she even slipped one inside herself, imagining that it was Darcy's manhood. That it bore so little resemblance to the real object nearly made her laugh, and she tried two, finding the illusion slightly improved, at which point she proceeded to apply them in the same manner he might have done, thrusting them in and out until all that could be heard in the room was the sound of her wetness. The moment of rapture was sudden, and its intensity compelled Elizabeth to press the whole of her hand against her folds until the tumult had calmed, her eyes never once wavering from Darcy's painted versions. At last recovering herself, she rejoined her uncle and aunt, whose tour of the house had concluded.

Elizabeth was grateful to quit the house and return to the grounds, where temptation might perhaps be less likely to be found. As the party walked toward the river, Mr. and Mrs. Gardiner, distracted by the beauties before them, moved away from their niece, who had come to an abrupt standstill, for coming from the direction of the stables was the owner of Pemberley himself. Mr. Darcy was within a few yards of her, and so abrupt was his appearance that it was impossible for Elizabeth to avoid his sight. As he gave his horse over to the stableman, the men's eyes instantly met, the cheeks of both suffusing with the deepest blush.

Darcy for a moment seemed unable to move, but, at last recovering himself, he advanced toward Elizabeth, speaking to her in terms if not of perfect composure, at least of perfect civility. With each inquiry after her health and that of her family, she replied in kind, though she scarcely dared to lift her eyes to his face, her embarrassment was so profound. Had he been privy to her activities in the gallery, she could not have been more humiliated by the impropriety of her being discovered here. Her gaze flew about in all directions, eventually lingering on the flap of his breeches, which, to her astonishment, projected outward to an alarming degree. The strain being placed on the garment eventually prompted a button to come loose, and it flew away into the grass, where it remained ignored by both parties. At length every form of conversation failed them. As Elizabeth turned to go, she momentarily lost her footing. Darcy reached out to catch her hand; that it was the one she had just used to pleasure herself with forced a cry of despair from her throat. After standing a few moments more without saying a word, Darcy hurriedly took his leave.

Having witnessed the exchange and recognizing the gentleman from the portrait, Elizabeth's uncle and aunt came toward her, their words filled with admiration of Mr. Darcy's fine figure. She heard not a word, blushing again and again over the perverseness of the meeting and the embarrassment of her illicitly gained pleasure in the gallery. Her coming to Pemberley was the most ill-judged thing in the world, for it might seem as if she had purposely thrown herself in his way again. That he should even speak to her was amazing, and to speak with such civility, to inquire after her family—never had she seen his manners so lacking in vanity or heard his words spoken with such gentleness. She longed to know in what manner he now thought of her and whether, in defiance of everything, she was still dear to him.

While Elizabeth rejoined the Gardiners on their tour of the grounds, Darcy was in his room changing into fresh garments, as he wished to see her before she departed. His task would not be undertaken without some difficulty, however, for no matter how he struggled to contain his manhood, which had taken on a stature that astounded even himself, it refused to stay concealed. The few times he managed to force the unruly flesh into submission, he was unable to fasten the buttons of his breeches, and it pushed its way back out all over again. Indeed, he could not meet Miss Bennet in such a condition in the presence of others!

Darcy observed in the mirror his robust member standing out from his breeches. There appeared to be no recourse but for him to take his hand to it and empty from it its fluids. He moved to the window to check the progress of Miss Bennet's party; they were now some ways down the river, though he noted with optimism that their carriage was parked in the opposite direction. The bowl of water and soap he had used to wash with had not yet been taken away by the maid. Darcy generously soaped his hand and, enclosing it around his manhood, began to employ upon it a series of rapid pulling motions. Though he did not expect the process to take long, he was most anxious to rejoin his guests; therefore, to expedite matters, he closed his eyes and envisioned Miss Bennet lying unclothed on his bed, her womanly charms on full display as she parted her legs to him. He found the mysterious folds very pleasing, and was seized by a curious desire to put his tongue to them. For it to seem that his eyes had already been made privy to these visual delights was inexplicable, yet when Darcy imagined her unlocking her folds and revealing a vista of secret pink, it was as if it had taken place before. As he felt his tongue breaching the tiny opening her positioning had revealed to him, the release he required sprang forth, his anguished cry of "Oh, Miss Bennet!" resounding in the room.

Darcy returned his depleted member to his breeches and hastened out to where he had last spied Miss Bennet. He found her by the river with a lady and gentleman, the latter in conversation with the groundskeeper. Darcy stopped momentarily to calm himself, his breathing still quite labored from his exertions. Miss Bennet faced away from him, and he stood for some time observing the agreeable way in which her gown draped itself over the curve of her backside. That these parts were equally pleasing to the eye as were those of his earlier imaginings was without question, and Darcy found himself musing on engagements of a most impolitic nature involving Miss Bennet bent forward with her skirts raised high as she presented her hind cheeks to him.

She possessed a very fine figure, which was both slender and shapely at the same time. Of all the ladies of Darcy's acquaintance, Miss Bennet's was perhaps only excelled by that of Miss Bingley, who preferred to exhibit her charms in a more explicit fashion. Her perseverance was admirable, even if undesired, for she had very recently invited him to seek his pleasure by installing his manhood within the cleft of her bosom, assuring him that it would be a most amusing enterprise. Although he was at times embarrassed for his friend Bingley to have claim to such a sister, he could hardly cast stones when he considered the circumstances of his own. Darcy, checking his breeches for any suggestion of his previous condition and finding that all was well, set off down the hill.

At the sight of Mr. Darcy's approach, Elizabeth's astonishment was equal to what it had been earlier, and it increased when he asked if she would do him the honor of introducing him to her friends. This was a stroke of civility for which she was unprepared, and she could hardly suppress a smile at his seeking the acquaintance of some of those very people against whom his pride had revolted in his offer of marriage. That he was surprised by her connection to the Gardiners was evident, though he sustained it with fortitude, even inviting Mr. Gardiner, who had expressed an interest in fishing, to do so at Pemberley as often as he chose. For Darcy to know that she had *some* relations who did not cause embarrassment was a source of much consolation to Elizabeth. Indeed, she could not at all account for the change in his manner.

The party began to make its way back to the carriage, with Mrs. Gardiner taking the arm of her husband, leaving her niece and Mr. Darcy to walk together. Elizabeth, wishing him to know that she had been assured of his absence before she came to Pemberley, replied that his arrival had been very unexpected, as had been borne out by the housekeeper. To this Darcy explained that business with his steward had occasioned his coming before the others. "Among them are some who will claim an acquaintance with you—Mr. Bingley and his sisters," he added. Elizabeth's thoughts returned to the last occasion in which Bingley's name had been mentioned between them, and she waited for Darcy to end the moment of awkwardness that had now developed, as he no doubt remembered similarly. "There is also one other person in the party," he continued after a pause, "who more particularly wishes to be known to you. Will you allow me to introduce my sister to your acquaintance during your stay at Lambton?"

The surprise of such an application was great. Though Elizabeth was perfectly aware that Darcy's wish of introducing his sister to her was a compliment of the highest kind, she continued to wonder in what condition she would find the poor girl, for it seemed most unlikely that Miss Darcy bore no evidence of her time spent in service at Wickham's bawdy house. Elizabeth could but hope that she, on meeting Miss Darcy, possessed the good grace to bear it.

They parted on each side with the utmost politeness, and Mr. Darcy handed the ladies into the carriage. When it drove off, Elizabeth saw him watching her departure with great solemnity, his breeches once more a place of much activity, and she felt again a pulse in the cleft of her womanhood at the feel of his eyes on her. It required some restraint of spirit to refrain from acting on it. Elizabeth fully expected to spend her nighttime hours in solitary pursuit of pleasure, as there seemed little chance that sleep would be hers with all that had occurred on this day.

The observations of her uncle and aunt now began in

earnest. "From what we have seen of him," said Mrs. Gardiner, "I really should not have thought that he could have behaved in so cruel a way to poor Wickham. There is something of dignity in his countenance that would not give one an unfavorable idea of his heart."

Elizabeth felt called on to say something in vindication of his behavior, and, in as guarded a manner as possible, she gave them to understand that by what she had heard from his relations in Kent, Mr. Darcy's actions were capable of a very different construction. His character was by no means so faulty, nor Wickham's so amiable, as they had been considered in Hertfordshire. Mrs. Gardiner appeared quite disturbed by this revelation, though Elizabeth would speak no further on the subject. She could do nothing but think with wonderment of Darcy's civility and, above all, of his wishing her to be acquainted with his sister.

That night Elizabeth soared into flight no fewer than four times, and would have done so for a fifth before exhaustion finally took hold of her. The fingers of her hand had sent her into raptures with a swiftness she would never have imagined possible, and she was forced to bite her lip to suppress the cries that threatened to erupt from her and awaken the other guests at the inn. Had she not done so, she felt certain they would have been heard all the way to Pemberley.

The following morning Mr. Darcy called at the inn with his sister. Elizabeth's uncle and aunt were all amazement, at once suspecting that such attentions indicated a partiality for their niece, the embarrassment of Elizabeth's manner joining to the circumstance. She was quite amazed at her own discomposure and could scarcely meet Darcy's eye. Her pleasures from the night before had left her complexion with a heightened color, and she felt with certainty that he knew of the manner in which she had touched herself—and that *he* had been foremost in her thoughts as she did so.

Expecting to find Darcy's sister little more than a crazed

animal, Elizabeth was pleasantly surprised that she did not display a significant deterioration in appearance. Though there was a rather wan look to Miss Darcy's countenance and a general lassitude, there was also good humor in her face, and her manners were perfectly unassuming and gentle. Elizabeth welcomed the distraction of her society, and endeavored to engage her in conversation as much as possible, though the girl displayed a tendency toward shyness that made any extended discourse difficult.

They had not long been together before Mr. Darcy replied that Bingley was also coming to call, and within moments that gentleman entered the room. He inquired in a friendly way after Elizabeth's family, and looked and spoke with the same agreeable ease as he had ever done, though his attentions seemed to be fixed continually on Darcy, as if seeking his approbation. That Bingley's friend was overflowing with admiration for Miss Bennet was evident to all those present, and he wondered for how much longer he could claim his close companionship.

Passing the winter months with Darcy in London had provided Bingley with the utmost joy, and there was scarcely a time when they were not together. The two would sit up late into the night conversing on a variety of subjects, Bingley arranging it so that there was plenty to be had of strong spirits, weakening his own allocations with water while generously replenishing Darcy's. When it finally came time to retire, he frequently had to assist his friend to his room, where he undressed him and got him comfortably settled into his bed. Darcy was quite often asleep before his head touched the pillow, leaving Bingley to seek out his illicit pleasures while the rest of the household likewise slept, and he often spent considerable time in admiration of Darcy's handsome form, his heart swelling with emotion at the pleasing way in which his hair curled at his ears. With great tenderness, Bingley would lean forward to kiss his lips, tasting the spirits that had been left there, drawing out the moment till he would at last be tasting his friend's manhood.

Not even a few nights had passed since Bingley's hands were moving with stealth over the bare landscape beneath Darcy's nightshirt, his fingers stroking and prodding in places in which it was most impolitic to do so. He felt as though he had been given more riches than he could ever have dreamed of possessing, particularly when Darcy's manhood reacted to his touch, rising up thick and strong from his loins, as if boasting of its superior quality. Bingley placed a series of gentle kisses on the crown till the moisture being deposited on his lips indicated that it was time for more, at which point he opened his mouth to take him inside. Darcy emitted a small gasp and, though he gave no sign of awakening, Bingley knew that he needed to make haste lest he be discovered. Therefore he applied himself with rather less delicacy, the violent rising and falling of Darcy's chest each time Bingley accepted his length into his throat providing evidence that his friend's release was drawing near. Bingley, whose heart felt ready to burst from both fear and excitement, insinuated a finger into the opening at Darcy's backside, its intrusion resulting in a powerful stream of that gentleman's pleasure being deposited into his mouth. Indeed, that he had even thought to do such a thing astonished him!

Although he wished for more leisure in his activities, Bingley knew that each moment spent in this manner was a gift to him. It was his greatest fear that Darcy might one night awaken to find them both in a situation of considerable compromise—one that would, should it become public, make of them both outcasts in society. By the time his friend had entered full wakefulness, Bingley was already returned to his room, where he could at leisure replay the events in his mind, bringing forth his own release as the taste of Darcy's still lingered on his tongue. The thought of being forever deprived of these pleasures struck fear into Bingley's heart, and the presence of Miss Elizabeth Bennet added much to his sense of unease.

The three callers remained at the inn with Elizabeth and the Gardiners for the good part of an hour. Toward Bingley, Elizabeth's anger had been long done away with, and, in seeing him again, her thoughts naturally flew to her sister. As she monitored his behavior toward Miss Darcy, who had been set up as a rival to Jane, no look appeared on either side that spoke of any particular regard, and she concluded that the match had been a fabrication of Caroline Bingley. As regards Darcy, from that quarter she observed an expression of complaisance very far removed from his previous hauteur and disdain. The change in him was so great that she could scarcely keep back her amazement. Never had she seen him so desirous to please and so free from reserve. Indeed, the thought of becoming Mrs. Fitzwilliam Darcy was no longer a situation of repugnance to her.

When the visitors at last rose to depart, Darcy called on his sister to join him in expressing their wish of seeing Mr. and Mrs. Gardiner and Miss Bennet for dinner at Pemberley before they left, and the day after the next was fixed upon.

Chapter Nineteen

THAT EVENING ELIZABETH BEGGED AN EARLY LEAVE FROM
her uncle and aunt, wishing for some time alone to reflect
on all that had happened. As she thought of the letter Darcy
had written her, she realized that her original assessment of
his character had been made with foolish haste, despite his
earlier unremorseful admission as to his interference in the
romantic affairs of her sister and Bingley. To have actually
spoken such words to her face, intimating that Jane was not
of sufficient position or breeding to be a prudent match for
his friend! Why, Jane was the dearest and sweetest girl in all
of Hertfordshire, if not all of England!

"I have no wish of denying that I did everything in my
power to separate my friend from your sister, or that I rejoice
in my success," he had said, only to declare his love then as
if it were a thing to be abhorred. His arrogance as regards
Jane was without pardon; however, Elizabeth could no
longer hold this to her heart as sufficient cause for his condemnation, especially now that the full truth had been
revealed of his association with Mr. Wickham. Poor Darcy,

to have carried this secret around with him for so long, all the while being forced to watch Wickham parading about as a gentleman whose every action was beyond reproach. It had been all she could do not to take to the streets, alerting the whole of Meryton to his abominable character. Wickham was nay but a fortune hunter and profligate, not only bringing ruination on Darcy's sister, Georgiana, but masquerading as a friend to the Bennet family and, in particular, Elizabeth, who had foolishly allowed herself to be charmed by his words and his deep dislike of Darcy. At the time of their meeting, she had already cultivated an ill opinion of the man, and it required little reinforcement on the part of Wickham, from whose vicious tongue the lies tumbled forth in abundance. Elizabeth feared for any young lady on whom he set his sights, and was extremely grateful for her own escape.

When the day arrived for their dinner engagement at Pemberley, Mr. Gardiner was taken to join the gentlemen elsewhere, leaving Elizabeth and her aunt to be received by Miss Darcy, who was sitting with Mrs. Hurst and Miss Bingley. Georgiana's reception of them was very civil, though attended with all the embarrassment proceeding from shyness. Mrs. Hurst and Miss Bingley acknowledged the two ladies only by a curtsey and little in the way of conversation. Elizabeth was once again struck by how unaffected by her various ordeals Miss Darcy appeared to be, and she felt a renewal of anger toward Wickham. She wondered how much Bingley's sisters knew about her downfall, though she suspected that if they were acquainted with the entire story, any demonstration of kindness and sympathy toward Darcy's sister would not be untainted by motive.

Elizabeth soon noticed that she was being very closely observed by Miss Bingley, who had yet again chosen to wear a gown of a most immodest drape, leaving the full of her bosom on display, the rouged tips of which now appeared to be connected by a thin gold chain. Not for the first time did she wonder why no one dared to check her on her ill sense of fashion—particularly her own sister, such matters being too delicate for a brother to broach. The absence of conversation was replaced by the arrival of cold meat, cake, and a variety of the finest fruits, to which the ladies all availed themselves. Elizabeth, who found that she could scarcely eat from her excitement, was uncertain whether she welcomed the appearance of Mr. Darcy to the room or dreaded it.

When the gentlemen at last joined the ladies, Elizabeth felt a heat suffusing her flesh, beginning at her face and moving downward to her loins. Darcy seemed to suffer from it as well; his features immediately colored when he saw her, and a stirring began in his breeches, taking on the shape of his manhood as it pressed against the fabric. Elizabeth noted that this had escaped neither Miss Bingley's notice nor that of her brother. Mr. Bingley appeared most anxious as his sister stared openly and without reserve at the swelling in Darcy's breeches, her tongue licking with great deliberation over her lips. If the gesture had been contrived for Darcy's benefit, Elizabeth took pleasure from the fact that he paid not the slightest heed to her intrigues or, for that matter, the rouged tips of her bosom, which appeared to have grown as hard as the flesh in his breeches. There was now a desperation to her actions as Elizabeth observed Lady Caroline moving her chair nearer and nearer to Darcy's.

The gentlemen had scarcely settled themselves before Miss Bingley said with sneering civility, "Pray, Miss Eliza, are not the militia removed from Meryton? They must be a very great loss to your family."

Though Wickham's name had not been mentioned, it hovered in the room, as the speaker had undoubtedly intended. As Elizabeth endeavored to answer with a detached tone, an involuntary glance showed her Darcy, with an expression of great unease, looking at her, and his sister overcome with distress, unable to lift up her eyes. The pain in both brother and sister was manifest, and Elizabeth had to refrain from issuing a retort that would only have brought them further anguish, her already low opinion of Miss Bingley sinking still lower. Elizabeth's collected behavior soon quieted Darcy's emotion, and Miss Bingley, vexed and disappointed, dared not approach nearer to the subject of Wickham. Georgiana also recovered, in time, but was unable to speak or look at any of the guests for the remainder of the evening.

"How very ill Miss Eliza Bennet looks, Mr. Darcy," said Miss Bingley after Elizabeth and the Gardiners had gone. "I never in my life saw anyone so much altered as she is since the winter. She has grown so brown and coarse!" As she leaned purposefully toward Darcy, the rouged peaks of her bosom projected out like offerings of sweets, the gold chain connecting them glittering in the light, seeming to invite him to pull on it. "For my own part," she rejoined, "I must confess that I never could see any beauty in her. Her complexion has no brilliancy, and her features are not at all handsome. Her nose wants character—there is nothing marked in its lines. Her teeth are tolerable, I suppose. As for her eyes, which have sometimes been called *fine*, I could never see anything extraordinary in them. They have a sharp, shrewish look."

Lady Caroline paused, as if to allow her review of Miss Bennet to be fully comprehended by her audience. When Darcy failed to comment, she pressed her bosom against him, lowering her voice to a whisper. "I doubt she possesses any talent with the birch. Indeed, I cannot imagine her marking your backside quite so handsomely or skillfully as I. Pray, Mr. Darcy, allow me to provide some release for that fine specimen in your breeches, for only a woman such as myself can truly offer it the most sublime of pleasures!" Accepting Darcy's silence as encouragement, Miss Bingley continued. "I remember when we first knew Miss Bennet in Hertfordshire how amazed we all were to find that she was a reputed beauty. I particularly recollect your saying, '*She,* a beauty!—I should sooner call her mother a wit.' But afterward she seemed to improve on you, and I believe you thought her rather pretty at one time."

"Yes," replied Darcy, whose manhood had now shrunken to an unrecognizable size, "but that was only when I first saw her, for it is many months since I have considered her as one of the handsomest women of my acquaintance." He rose abruptly from his chair and quit the room, leaving Miss Bingley to pull at the gold chain at her bosom as she stared after him in astonishment.

That night Mr. Hurst would be made the delighted recipient of Miss Bingley's birch, though, to his folly, he had mistaken her ill temper for eagerness, which left him unable to sit properly for a week and elicited much scolding from his wife as regards his ceaseless fidgeting. Lady Caroline went through several lengths of birch, leaving an erratic patchwork of red in her wake, her vexation at Darcy's rebuff so great that she afterward spent the best part of two hours with a large wooden member strapped to her loins, imagining that it was Darcy's finely formed backside being presented to her rather than the flaccid version belonging to her brother-in-law. Indeed, the thought of Darcy's unsullied opening being at her complete mercy was more than she could bear, and she took a finger to herself, manipulating the agitated flesh housed within the cleft of her womanhood until she cried out from the force of her pleasure, all the while not missing a single stroke with the wooden member. Darcy's imaginary backside seemed to mock her, inspiring her to do her worst, for by now Miss Bingley had quite forgotten the true identity of the gentleman beneath her and saw only the one who continually refused her. Her finger resumed its movement at her folds, and as she felt yet another release building in her loins she pulled hard on the chain at her bosom. Her pelvis reacted with violence, the object attached to it moving with such speed and vigor that it would not have been surprising to see Mr. Hurst swallow up an entire chair the next time he sat down.

When Lady Caroline had at last finished with him, Mr. Hurst was weeping from the exertion of his releases, having experienced more than one, and the fierceness with which they had been conferred. Had it not been for his sister-in-law's continual cries of "Your backside is mine, Darcy!" he might have enjoyed the encounter a good deal more.

Darcy and Elizabeth retired to their respective beds with a pleasing contentment that night, the tender looks that had passed between them earlier that day doing much to further soften their hearts toward each other. As Elizabeth lay in her bed in Lambton touching herself, so too did Darcy in Pemberley, their hands moving in unison at their loins. Indeed, had either been aware of what the other was doing, they would have been quite rightly seized with embarrassment. That their thoughts should be so closely united would have astonished them both, for as Elizabeth imagined that the fingers within the folds of her womanhood were those of Mr. Darcy, he imagined that those encircling his manhood belonged to her.

As Darcy proceeded to direct himself toward an inevitable conclusion, he noted how the length of flesh in his hand had increased in size since the winter, though how this could be possible he was unable to account for. He had not been in the close society of young ladies save for Bingley's sisters, neither of whom he had engaged with in any illicit form of activity, despite Lady Caroline's repeated attempts to court him with the birch and the occasional misfortune of her hand in his breeches. He had, however, been subjected to a number of stimulating dreams, all of which involved his being pleasured by a mysterious figure who came to him in the night. They had felt so very real, as had the ecstasy of release, for each time Darcy returned to consciousness he would discover his manhood lying spent against his belly, as if in a condition of having been recently depleted of its fluids. One moment he was in conversation with Bingley, the next awakening in his bed in this curious state. It was most perplexing!

The culmination of both parties' efforts would at last manifest itself in cries of delight, one originating from Lambton, the other Pemberley, leaving Miss Bennet and Mr. Darcy eager for the next occasion in which they would see each other.

Chapter Twenty

ELIZABETH HAD BEEN A GOOD DEAL DISAPPOINTED IN NOT finding a letter from Jane on their first arrival at Lambton, and this disappointment had been renewed on each of the mornings since. But on the third her repining was over by the receipt of two letters at once, one of which was marked that it had been sent elsewhere. She was not surprised by it, as Jane had written the address remarkably ill. Elizabeth had just been preparing to walk out with the Gardiners when the letters came in, and noting their niece's distraction, her uncle and aunt set off by themselves, leaving her in the parlor to read them in quiet.

She picked up the letter that had been written first, expecting it to contain a report of the family's engagements and such news as the country afforded. Though such reports were present, it soon became evident that these lighthearted accounts were intended to soften the news of what was to come.

Dearest Lizzy, wrote Jane, *something has occurred of a most unexpected and serious nature. What I have to say relates to poor Lydia. An express came at twelve last night from Colonel Forster, providing a report that he was informed by his wife that Lydia eloped to Scotland with one of his officers; to own the truth, with Wickham! Imagine our surprise! But I am willing to hope the best, and that his character has been misunderstood. Thoughtless and indiscreet I can easily believe him, but this step (and let us rejoice over it) marks nothing bad at heart.*

"Misunderstood indeed!" cried Elizabeth, hurriedly seizing the other letter Jane had written.

Dearest Lizzy, I hardly know what to write, but I have bad news for you, and it cannot be delayed. Imprudent as the marriage between Mr. Wickham and our poor Lydia would be, we are now anxious to be assured it has taken place, for there is too much reason to fear they are not gone to Scotland. Though Lydia's short letter to Mrs. Forster gave them to understand that they were going to Gretna Green, something was dropped by Denny expressing his belief that Wickham never intended to go there, or to marry Lydia at all.

Further mention was made of the couple's having been seen traveling the London road, which Jane, who still refused to believe entirely ill of Wickham, took to indicate that they intended to be married in town. To Elizabeth, who knew the truth of his disreputable activities in London, this could mean but one thing—that her poor innocent sister was being recruited to work in Wickham's bawdy house.

Elizabeth's eyes filled with tears. Stupid, stupid Lydia! It was evident from Jane's report that her youngest sister, in her eagerness to be the first of the Bennet girls to marry, had unwittingly chosen a path that would make her Wickham's latest victim. If only she had not gone to Brighton with Mrs. Forster! Now it had fallen to Elizabeth to set Lydia's folly to rights. Her father was too occupied with his own affairs, preferring to distance himself from his daughters' dramas; her mother, who should by rights bear in equal measure such a burden, was of too highly strung a nature to do so. As regards Jane, she preferred to see only the good in people, which had led to a certain lack of prudence that would not be of advantage when matched against the wickedness of a man the likes of George Wickham. How terribly Elizabeth had misjudged him and, indeed, misjudged Darcy!

She had wished for nothing more but to spend the day reflecting on the recent developments between herself and Mr. Darcy, and for a moment she closed her eyes, taking comfort from the image of his handsome face before her as it was on the occasion of his proposal in Kent. When he had professed to her his love, he had looked at her with such entreaty. The added attendance of his manhood was, she felt certain, intended as a further means of inducement, and he had undoubtedly expected her to admire it. As Elizabeth remembered all this again, an extraordinary heat spread over her cheeks and neck, and it moved lower and lower till she thought she might faint, very nearly doing so when it culminated in the place of her womanhood. It felt as if she were floating on a cloud and bathing in fire at the same time.

Elizabeth had to acknowledge that Darcy's strong reservations as regards a marriage between Bingley and Jane, and those directed toward themselves, would be proved correct once Lydia's disgrace and ruination became public. That this should be the final deed to compel him toward the feminine charms of the disagreeable Lady Caroline Bingley weighed on her with surprising despair. Even the sickly Miss de Bourgh might now seem preferable to a gentleman of Darcy's standing. Elizabeth had no recourse but to resign herself to life as an old maid, for not even Mr. Collins, had he not married Charlotte, would have her now.

She was wild to be at home to share in her woes with Jane and, in her anguish, knew not whether to sit or stand, weep or scream. At that moment the door was opened by a servant, and, to Elizabeth's astonishment, Mr. Darcy entered the room. His face immediately displayed concern when he saw her pale countenance. "Good god, Miss Bennet, whatever is the matter?" cried he.

"I must find my uncle at once!" Elizabeth rose from her chair. "It cannot be delayed!"

Darcy moved toward her, seeming not to know what to do. With some degree of awkwardness, he placed a hand on her shoulder as a means of calming her. "Let me or the servant go after Mr. and Mrs. Gardiner. You are not well enough to go by yourself."

Elizabeth hesitated, but her knees trembled beneath her, and she felt how little would be gained by her attempting to pursue them. Darcy's hand continued to rest on her shoulder, bringing about a renewal of the feelings she had experienced earlier. From the instant of his touch, a tingling had begun at the points of her bosom, as if they had been brushed by a cold gust of air, and she felt them hardening beneath her garments. That her first thought should be for Darcy to take them between his lips so overwhelmed her that she nearly cried out. She knew to experience these things was very wrong, particularly in circumstances of such calamity as this.

"Let me call your maid. Is there nothing you could take to give you relief? You are very ill!" Darcy appeared as distraught as Elizabeth; his usual composure was gone, replaced by an anxious hovering.

Noting his state of wretched suspense, Elizabeth at length composed herself enough to speak. "I have just had a letter from Jane, with such dreadful news. My younger sister has eloped—has thrown herself into the power of Mr. Wickham. They have gone off together from Brighton. *You* know him too well to doubt the rest. She has no money, no connections, nothing that can tempt him. She is lost forever."

Darcy was fixed in astonishment. "I am grieved indeed. But is it absolutely certain? What has been attempted to recover her?"

"I know very well that nothing can be done. How is such a man to be worked on? I have not the smallest hope. It is every way horrible!"

As Elizabeth revealed the details of Jane's letter, Darcy walked up and down the room, his brow contracted, his air gloomy. With each word she relayed, she knew the likelihood for a union between them was fast fading; her chance at happiness had been destroyed by the weakness of her family. Darcy would imagine that he had made a lucky escape, as would Mr. Bingley, once word of Lydia's "elopement" with the wretched Mr. Wickham became public. Never had Elizabeth so honestly felt that she could have loved Darcy as now, when all love must be in vain. Lydia's disgrace had tarnished any prospects for either herself or her sisters to make a good marriage, or perhaps any marriage at all. Her poor father, to be burdened to his dying day with so many unmarried daughters!

Darcy at last came to a stop before her. "Rest assured, Miss Bennet, that this matter shall remain with me in confidence."

"When my eyes were finally opened to his real character!" she cried. "But I was afraid of doing too much. Wretched, wretched mistake!" Elizabeth concealed her face with her hands, too aggrieved and humiliated to look him in the eye.

Darcy placed both of his hands on her shoulders, and she lowered her own. Their faces were by this time within inches of each other, and she saw that his earlier gloom had been replaced by an emotion more characteristic of the gentleman she had met at Pemberley; indeed, he looked very much on the verge of kissing her. There was an intimacy to his touch that exceeded even that of the pleasuring of her own hand, and Elizabeth cast her eyes downward, fearful that he read her thoughts.

At length Darcy spoke, his words prefaced by an anxious

clearing of the throat. "I, more than anyone, know the true nature of Mr. Wickham."

Elizabeth, whose distress was already manifest, found it being still furthered by the nearness of his presence, which had prompted a fluttering to take place within the folds of her womanhood. Her legs had become most unsteady beneath her, and she felt on the brink of collapse, the recovery of which was not improved when Darcy's hands began to deliver a determined pressure against her shoulders, urging her downward until she had fallen to her knees before him. There she was met by a familiar sight—that of the distending flap of his breeches.

Darcy looked down at her, his face blooming with color. His hands left her shoulders and moved to her head, where he released the ornaments from her hair, allowing it to flow loose so that he could draw his fingers through it. Elizabeth found the sensations highly agreeable, much as the act of pulling a brush through the hair affords a similar satisfaction, and she closed her eyes, giving herself over to the delight of his touch. She became so entranced by the actions of his fingers that she failed to notice when one of his hands no longer occupied itself in her hair, but instead occupied itself elsewhere.

Elizabeth felt something warm and moist touching her lips in a gentle kiss, and suddenly her eyes flew open. The hand that had been in her hair now contained something long and fleshy, and it was being offered to her mouth. She recognized it instantly; it had been the inspiration for many nights of solitary pleasure ever since the moment of its introduction. "Mr. Darcy!" she cried, all astonishment. Her face burned with heat, and she knew not whether to be embarrassed or pleased that he had once more seen fit to honor her with the presentation of his manhood. As she licked away the moisture it had left on her lips, she tasted a tangy sweetness that was not at all displeasing.

Darcy gazed down at her with a dreamlike countenance, his other hand moving to the back of her head, cradling it tenderly before urging it forward to his loins. Before Elizabeth could open her mouth to speak, he filled it. "Oh, Miss Bennet . . . ," he said, sounding very unlike his usual composed self.

Though she believed some reply was required, Elizabeth found herself unable to offer one. The great mass of Darcy's manhood had crushed the words forming within her, as well as the breaths, and she feared she might be smothered as it grew still larger inside her mouth, lying heavily against her tongue and pushing upward and outward against her teeth. Perhaps to die in this manner would not be so very disagreeable at all!

Despite her fantasies of engaging in just such a scenario as the one in which she now found herself, Elizabeth was ill prepared for the primitive reality of it, and she wondered why she did not simply rise up from the floor and quit the room or, better still, call out for assistance. Surely this was not the sort of act a gentleman forced on a lady or, indeed, a lady applied to a gentleman. Perhaps certain women might do such things, but they were women of extremely unwholesome character—the sort men such as Wickham consorted with. The fact that one of these women was now her youngest sister did not fail to give Elizabeth pain. At the moment, however, she could not find time in her thoughts for Lydia, for she was too bewildered by what was transpiring, and when she glanced up to gauge Darcy's reaction, noted that he appeared equally so. They had both found themselves in a strange land, with a strange language and customs. Truly she did not know what was expected of her!

Darcy cupped Elizabeth's ears with his hands, as if seeking to offer guidance, indicating that her own hands were not required, and she allowed them to rest in her lap. A rhythm soon began between them, a slow rocking motion that increased in speed as her head moved forward and back in harmony with a corresponding motion from his loins. The fluttering at Elizabeth's womanhood had now been replaced by a powerful throbbing, and she pressed her thighs together, hoping for relief lest she go mad with the need to attend to herself with her fingers. That she should make such a display of herself before Mr. Darcy was something Elizabeth was ill prepared for. And although she realized she should cease from the activity, she could not, and she was soon squeezing her thighs together in time with his movements, pleased to have found such a clandestine alternative to the application of her hand. Whereas before she had desired only the swift return of her uncle and aunt, she now prayed for their delay so that she might experience again that astonishing sensation of flight, which promised to be made even more so by Darcy's participation in it.

Elizabeth felt a tension building in her loins and, unable to ignore it any longer, stuffed her fist inside her skirts and bore down on it. By this time Darcy was calling out her name repeatedly in a voice of anguish, his manhood filling her mouth just as it had in her dream at Hunsford. The silken curls at the base tickled her nose, and she breathed deeply of his scent, which reminded her of leather and the countryside. She allowed Darcy to do with her as he wished, taking a forbidden pleasure in her wickedness. Why, a servant could walk in on them at this very moment! Elizabeth, thrilling at the prospect of such a dishonorable discovery, suddenly drew back her head until all that remained in her mouth was the crown of Darcy's manhood, then just as suddenly drove her face forward, absorbing the full length of him with a wantonness that astonished even herself. A convulsing took place in her mouth, followed by the dispensation of a hot liquid, the arrival of which was met by her own convulsions as her release joined his in a manner most extraordinary.

Neither party stirred nor spoke for several moments until

Darcy at last removed himself from her mouth and, with some embarrassment, returned his waning manhood to his breeches. Elizabeth took the interlude to dab the froth from her lips with the hem of her petticoat, having by this time swallowed the rest. She had not known what else to do, fearing that spitting it out might be crass and unladylike. She could not look at Darcy, or he at her, though the features of both were equally suffused with color. As Elizabeth made as if to stand, he reached for her hand, assisting her from the floor, the awkwardness between them far worse than it had been in all the time of their acquaintance.

At length Darcy spoke, his manner giving her to believe that he wished for nothing more than to remove himself from her company. "I am afraid you have been long desiring my absence. This unfortunate affair will, I fear, prevent my sister's having the pleasure of seeing you at Pemberley today."

"Please be so kind as to apologize for us to Miss Darcy," replied Elizabeth, surprised she could speak at all. "Say that urgent business calls us home immediately. Conceal the unhappy truth as long as it is possible."

Assuring her of his secrecy and leaving his compliments for her relations, Mr. Darcy quit the room, leaving Elizabeth to wonder whether they would ever again see each other. Her eyes filled with tears as she believed he was lost to her forever, with all that remained of his love the taste of him on her tongue.

Chapter Twenty-One

ELIZABETH RETURNED WITH THE GARDINERS TO LONGBOURN, her thoughts fixed by self-reproach and anguish, which was shared in equal measure between her encounter with Darcy and her role in not having alerted her family to the evils of Mr. Wickham. Though it was generally believed that Lydia had eloped with Wickham in a romantic flight of fancy, she knew better, and she feared greatly for her sister's well-being. The nature of Wickham's illicit trade in London was known only to herself and Jane, who continued to maintain that some form of mistake had been made. The fact remained, however, that Lydia had gone off with a man of questionable character to engage in a marriage that was likely never to take place, which was disgrace enough in itself.

Elizabeth found the household in a turmoil. Mr. Bennet refused to come out of his library and only opened the door long enough either to take in the meals that had been left for him or allow Hill entry to perform various domestic tasks. He displayed little in the way of concern for Mrs. Bennet, whose nerves had become so compromised that she had to be bound with chains to her bed lest she do herself, or any-one else, a mischief. Hill had already been made the recipient of a particularly grievous bite, followed by a number of foul accusations involving both herself and Mr. Bennet. Kitty, for the most part, appeared unmoved. She seemed to take a secret satisfaction in the scandal, having still not forgiven Lydia for going off to Brighton without her. As for Mary, her condemnation of Lydia's behavior was conspicuous in her words and countenance. Her beard had by this time grown quite long, giving her a rabbinical appearance very suited to her manner, and she offered her opinions freely and without any inclination toward their amendment. Jane remained much the same; her sanguine hope of good, which the benevolence of her heart suggested, had not yet deserted her. She still expected that it would all end well and that every morning would bring a letter from either Lydia or Wickham to announce their marriage.

Mrs. Bennet, to whose apartment they all repaired, received them exactly as might be expected—with tears and lamentations of regret, invectives against the villainous conduct of Mr. Wickham, and complaints of her own sufferings and ill-usage. She blamed everybody but the person to whose ill-judging indulgence the errors of her daughter must principally be owing. Her eyes bulged alarmingly, as if they had been loosened from their sockets, and she pulled against the chains keeping her bound, spitting and hissing at her callers. "If I had been able to go to Brighton with all my family, this would not have happened!" she cried. "But poor dear Lydia had nobody to take care of her. She is not the kind of girl to do such a thing if she had been well looked after. Where is Mr. Bennet? Oh, my nerves!"

Mr. Gardiner, who looked frightened out of his wits at the sight of his sister, told her that he meant to be in London the very next day and would put forth every endeavor for recovering Lydia. "Though it is right to be prepared for the worst, there is no occasion to look on it as certain. Till we know that they are not married, and have no design of marrying, do not let us give the matter over as lost."

"Oh, brother, how kind you are!" cried Mrs. Bennet. "Find them out, wherever they may be, and if they are not married already, *make* them marry. As for wedding clothes, tell Lydia she shall have as much money as she chooses to buy them, after they are married, but to wait till she has seen me, for she does not know which are the best warehouses. Tell them what a dreadful state I am in, that I have such tremblings, such flutterings, all over me—such spasms in my side and pains in my head, that I can get no rest by night nor by day!"

With much relief, the visitors quit the room, later rejoining in the dining parlor. Mary took Mrs. Bennet's chair with a seniority most unbefitting her position, addressing her sisters with a grave countenance. "This is a most unfortunate affair and will probably be much talked of. But we must stem the tide of malice, and pour into the wounded bosoms of each other the balm of sisterly consolation." She paused to allow her words to be absorbed and to dry her beard, the ends of which had dipped into her bowl of soup. "Unhappy as the event must be for Lydia, we may draw from it this useful lesson: that loss of virtue in a female is irretrievable; that one false step involves her in endless ruin; and that she cannot be too much guarded in her behavior toward the undeserving of the other sex." Elizabeth stared in amazement, but was too much oppressed to make any reply. Mary continued to console herself with the moral extractions from the evil before them until, at last, the meal was concluded.

In the afternoon, when the two elder Miss Bennets were for a brief time by themselves, Elizabeth asked for further particulars. Jane reported that she had found no fault in the conduct of either Colonel Forster or his wife, both of whom had sounded the alarm. Nor had she found any fault as to Mr. Denny's sudden refutation of his previous assertion that

Wickham had no intention of marrying Lydia.

"Denny denied knowing anything of their plans and made no further mention of Wickham's unwillingness to marry our sister," replied Jane, "and from *that*, I am inclined to hope, he might have been misunderstood before." She appeared ready as ever to absolve all parties of any wrongdoing. Elizabeth, however, maintained a slightly different opinion on the matter, as she began to suspect that Denny, too, might have had an involvement. That Lydia had been partial to Denny was without question. It seemed doubtful that Wickham could have kept his unsavory dealings a secret from the entire regiment, particularly those with whom he most closely associated. Considering the lively nature of the flirtation between himself and Lydia, Elizabeth had to conclude that it was quite likely Denny was a regular patron of Wickham's bawdy house—and might at this very moment be further corrupting her sister's innocence by forcing on her any number of vile acts.

"And what of Colonel Forster? Did his distress over the matter appear genuine?" asked Elizabeth, her suspicions further aroused. Her mind was so busily engaged in drawing yet more connections between the officers in Wickham's regiment and Lydia's disgrace that she did not even hear the reply. For Colonel Forster to remain completely unaware of the activities of the officers who served under him was impossible. Until this moment Elizabeth had never given any thought to the propriety of his marriage to a woman far too young both in age and in demeanor for a gentleman at his time of life—especially a woman who had chosen Lydia to be her particular friend. Now she viewed the union as highly suspect and, indeed, unseemly. "And what of Lydia's note to his wife? Could Colonel Forster repeat the particulars of it?"

"He brought it with him for us to see." Jane removed it from her pocketbook and gave it to Elizabeth, who took it away to a window to read.

My Dear Harriet,

You will laugh when you know where I have gone, and I cannot help laughing myself at your surprise tomorrow morning, as soon as I am missed. I am going to Gretna Green, and if you cannot guess with whom, I shall think you a simpleton, for there is but one man in the world I love, and he is an angel. I should never be happy without him, for he has a prick the size of a horse! Oh, Harriet, I can hear you scolding me for saying such wicked things, but you know how much I adore a good romp with a gentleman whose manly bounties render me unable to walk for a fortnight! You need not send them word at Longbourn of my going, if you do not like it, for it will make the surprise the greater when I write to them and sign my name "Lydia Wickham." What a good joke it will be! I can hardly write for laughing. But oh, I must go now, dear Harriet, for my darling Wickham is right at this very moment drawing up my skirts so that he can possess me for the sixth time today! Indeed, my backside received several visits from him yesterday, and now I can scarcely sit! Give my love to Colonel Forster. I hope you will drink to our good journey.

Your affectionate friend,
Lydia Bennet

"Oh! thoughtless, thoughtless Lydia!" cried Elizabeth when she had finished reading. "What a letter to write at such a moment! But at least it shows that she was serious on the subject of their journey. Whatever Wickham might afterward persuade her to do, it was not on her side a scheme of infamy."

Elizabeth left Jane to seek out her father. The door to the library was locked, as expected, and she at first knocked lightly, then with increasing soundness until she was pounding on the door. Mr. Bennet neither opened it to his daughter nor issued any form of greeting, and in time she went away, leaving her father to lament in private over this latest business with Lydia.

In truth, Mr. Bennet had given little thought to his youngest daughter in recent days. He was far too occupied now with the delights of Hill, who, rather than content him with the pleasure of her hand, was at this moment bent forward over the escritoire with her skirts to her waist, the ample landscape of her rear cheeks on full display. Mr. Bennet's breeches were down about his ankles, his manhood lodged well up the forbidden passage of the housekeeper's backside, his own less generous version moving frantically to and fro as he sought to bring about his release. He could still taste the pleasing tang of her womanhood, which he had earlier sampled with his tongue, having been inspired toward such proceedings by one of his treasured drawings. He had found it a most agreeable encounter, as had Hill, who thrashed about in a manner indicating that she derived considerable enjoyment from the proceedings, her copious folds nearly swallowing his lips. Mr. Bennet had been required to strike her backside with his hand a number of times to silence her squeals while his tongue was thus employed, the bite mark on her hand offering testimony that certain members of the household had already been made privy to their activities. His actions appeared to inflame her further, however, for with each strike of his palm, Hill's cries grew louder until she gave out one final cry and went limp. At this point Mr. Bennet realized that she had achieved a release very much like that which he himself enjoyed, though never in his many years of marriage to Mrs. Bennet had he observed such a reaction from his wife. On the contrary, whenever he completed his matrimonial duties, his wife often looked at him as if she wished to kill him.

Hill's backside proved most commodious, and as he continued to avail himself of it, Mr. Bennet began to think that she had quite likely entertained other gentlemen in this fashion, for indeed, it was this very commodiousness that was causing him difficulty. He suspected Sir William Lucas as being the principal caller to these parts and was, for a moment, seized by jealousy. He had caught a number of looks passing between them during that gentleman's visits and now wondered at the occasions when Sir William left the room, only to return with a severely flushed countenance. Mr. Bennet took hold of Hill's stout waist and, planting his feet solidly on the floor, applied himself in earnest, his testes swinging like a sack of grain between his thighs, his sole desire being to bring matters to a swift conclusion so that he could eat the meal that had been brought for him. He feared the slices of beef had by now grown cold, and a glance toward the tray on which the plate had been set indicated that it was situated within a pool of congealed gravy.

Mr. Bennet's frantically moving backside posed quite a sight, should anyone passing by the library window have seen him; and, in fact, Mrs. Gardiner chose that very moment to walk out in the garden. Her head pained her grievously since visiting with Mrs. Bennet earlier that day, and she hoped that taking some refreshment out of doors might be of benefit. Though she had agreed to remain behind in Hertfordshire and share in the attendance of Mrs. Bennet while her husband went to London to seek out the fugitives, it was a prospect she no longer relished, for her sister-in-law appeared quite demented and, at times, menacing, and Mrs. Gardiner had begun to fear for her own safety, as well as that of her nieces. As she strolled past the library window, a movement behind the glass caught her eye, and she turned her head, expecting to see Mr. Bennet waving her off. What she saw instead caused her to start, and she ran quickly away from the house, not returning till nightfall.

Mrs. Gardiner knew not whether to offer a report to Mr. Gardiner of what she had witnessed or say nothing, her embarrassment such that she was uncertain if she could even give voice to its description. Her husband departed for London early the next morning, and all opportunity for disclosure was lost.

Chapter Twenty-Two

ALL OF MERYTON WAS NOW DETERMINED TO BLACKEN the man who, but three months before, had been beyond reproach. Mr. Wickham was declared to be in debt to every tradesman, and his intrigues, all honored with the title of seduction, had been extended into every tradesman's family. The recent increase in births in the town seemed to indicate more than coincidence, particularly when so many of the infants shared similar features, despite being unrelated. Everybody declared that Wickham was the wickedest young man in the world, and numerous declarations were put forth that they had always distrusted the appearance of his goodness. Elizabeth believed enough of what was being said to confirm her assurance of her sister's ruin.

Mrs. Gardiner received a letter from her husband within days of his departure, reporting that he had been to all the locations where there had been sightings of the couple and inquired at all the principal hotels, but had not gained any satisfactory information. He had also written to Colonel Forster, asking him to find out from Wickham's intimates in the regiment whether he had any relations or connections who would be likely to know in what part of town he had concealed himself, and Mr. Gardiner was at this moment following these leads. Mr. Gardiner added that he was wholly disinclined to leave London at this time, and not to expect him back in Hertfordshire for some while. He promised to write again when time allowed, though he indicated with some conviction that he did not expect it to.

The family was grateful for the news, but Mrs. Gardiner thought her husband's tone rather odd and not at all in character. Why such a change should come over him in a matter of days was something she could not fathom, and she attributed it to his resolve to locate Lydia and Wickham.

Anxiety increased in the household as morning after morning went past without further word from Mr. Gardiner. Though small parcels occasionally arrived in the early morning by special post for Mr. Bennet, no form of correspondence was forthcoming from Gracechurch Street. Mrs. Bennet, who continued to remain chained to her bed for her own safety and that of others, began to fear for her brother, believing that he would enter into a dual with Wickham. "Who will make him marry Lydia if my dear brother is killed?" she cried, heedless to the distress her words caused her sister-in-law. Mrs. Gardiner became so alarmed that she immediately wrote her husband, expressing her desire to join him at Gracechurch Street as quickly as possible. She received no reply.

Before they were to hear again from Mr. Gardiner, a letter arrived from an entirely different quarter. Since Mr. Bennet refused to leave the library, Mary, on learning that the writer was Mr. Collins, insisted on reading it to the family, her manner somber and befitting her greatly altered appearance; only the presence of a skullcap would have made her transformation complete. The letter began with condolences for the grievous affliction now being suffered by Mr. Bennet and his family, to which Mr. and Mrs. Collins offered their sincerest sympathies.

"*The death of your daughter would have been a blessing in comparison of this*," read Mary. "*And it is the more to be lamented, because there is reason to suppose, as my dear Charlotte informs me, that this licentiousness of behavior in your daughter has proceeded from a faulty degree of indulgence; though, at the same time, I am inclined to think that her own disposition must be naturally bad, or she could not be guilty of such an enormity. You are grievously to be pitied; in which opinion I am not only joined by Mrs. Collins, but likewise by Lady Catherine and her daughter, to whom I have related the affair. They agree with me in apprehending that this false step in one daughter will be injurious to the fortunes of all the others; for who, as Lady Catherine herself condescendingly says, will connect themselves with such a family?*" Here Mary paused to check the reactions of her sisters and, appearing to be satisfied, concluded the reading. "*Let me advise you, dear sir, to throw off your unworthy child from your affection forever, and leave her to reap the fruits of her own heinous offense.*"

Elizabeth, more than her sisters, felt the full meaning of her cousin's words as she recalled her last encounter with Mr. Darcy, who, in all probability, now considered her a woman of loose morals and one not worthy of his affection. She had allowed her fantasies and desires to cloud her judgment, and the price to be paid was dear. That her tongue should even at this very moment long for a taste of his manhood was confirmation of her depravity, and she felt all the shame it was ever possible to feel, which was further deepened by Lydia's disgrace.

The upset caused by Mr. Collins's letter was shortly alleviated by the arrival of another from Mr. Gardiner, though this time it was addressed to Mr. Bennet rather than his wife. With so many days of silence having passed, the family was eager for any news at all, and therefore could not wait for Mr. Bennet to quit his self-imposed exile in the library. The sisters and Mrs. Gardiner went directly to Mrs. Bennet's bedside, where Elizabeth read aloud her uncle's letter. "*At last I am able to send you some tidings of my niece. They are not married, nor can I find there was any intention of being so; but if you are willing to perform the engagements that I shall venture to make on your side, I hope it will not be long before they are.*"

"There, you see?" cried Mrs. Bennet from the prison of her bed. "My dear brother has put everything to rights. Lydia will soon be married to Wickham! Will someone please remove these silly chains? I have so much to prepare for! I must purchase a new bonnet for the wedding, and—"

"But wait, there is more," interrupted Elizabeth, wondering why no one had thought to bind her mother's tongue as well as her limbs. "*I fear that matters are considerably worse than you have imagined, my dear brother. Wickham's business in town is of a most unsavory nature, as have been his intentions toward my niece. There is no delicate way in which to report this—Mr. Wickham is operating a bawdy house, and Lydia has been engaged there in employment. I have undertaken the sacrifice of momentarily quitting Gracechurch Street and taking a room in Wickham's establishment so that I may, with greater success, act on your behalf as regards the securing of a marriage between them. Pray, dear brother, do not thank me as yet, for there is so very much more to do!*"

At once Mrs. Bennet began to scream, the sound so piercing that a crack appeared in one of the window panes, and it required several blows to her face from her sister-in-law's hand before she was finally quieted. Mrs. Gardiner could not fathom why her husband had felt compelled to move himself into such a place and hoped his business there would be completed with the utmost haste.

Mr. Gardiner concluded his letter with salutations for all, and a promise to write again when he had further news. Yet it would be some while before another letter arrived at Longbourn House, for in the course of his negotiations on behalf of his brother-in-law, Mr. Gardiner had arranged to be provided with the very best rooms in the house and given free reign of Wickham's most prepossessing ladies, some of whom were procured to pose in positions of great compromise for an artist who occasionally came to draw them. Among these many soiled doves, Mr. Gardiner believed he glimpsed Miss King going into one of the rooms with an officer of some rank, though he could not be certain, having only been acquainted with her briefly.

Companionship in Wickham's establishment was plenteous, and Mr. Gardiner spent his hours reclining quite happily among silk cushions and the silken bodies of ladies of all ages, shapes, and shades. He found himself particularly taken with a damsel from the desert, who later confessed to him in words seasoned with the spices of faraway lands that she had fallen on hard times when her husband had turned her out of his harem, deeming her too old to be of use. She had eyes like the darkest almonds and the lips of rose petals, and Mr. Gardiner would have been content to live out the remainder of his days in her arms, had he not a duty to his family. She possessed the scent of the desert sand, and in her eyes he beheld a moonlit sky over Araby. As he lay back like a sultan on his bed, his exotic temptress fed him berries that she had thoughtfully peeled for him, flavoring them generously with the juices from her womanhood and even installing a few inside herself so that Mr. Gardiner's tongue could remove them. He became quite skilled in the endeavor, which required little more than placing his lips at her opening and applying a gentle suctioning, followed by the insertion of his tongue, until he had at last secured his prize. Afterward she performed a dance, the snakelike

214

movements of her body inspiring in him a fervor he had never experienced with Mrs. Gardiner. Her shapely form was cloaked in silk scarves, which she removed one by one, drawing them over Mr. Gardiner's head before dropping them to the floor. While her hips and bosom swayed before him, he prepared his manhood with his hand, pulling upon it to make it longer, as he wished it to be at its most impressive stature before embarking on the fulfillment of his desires. Mr. Gardiner's lady would not even be given time to complete her dance before he was seeking his pleasure inside her womanhood, which squeezed him in an embrace that sent him to the heavens, his captivation by now so complete that he did not pause to reflect on the authenticity of her wretched tale.

Mr. Gardiner spent the remainder of his time at Wickham's establishment in this way engaged, his pleasures made poignant by the realization that they would soon be ended. His business with Wickham had been concluded in a most surprising manner, with negotiations agreed to by all parties concerned. He had no recourse but to remove himself to Gracechurch Street; Mrs. Gardiner had written a number of letters, the last of which contained the declaration that she was making arrangements to be returned to him. His time with his beloved desert temptress was nearing an end, and it was incumbent on him to make the most of it. Although his credit had by this time run out, Mr. Gardiner continued to make considerable use of his favorite's delightful attributes, unconcerned that Wickham was adding to the debt whenever his manhood entered the moist opening between his adored one's thighs. Each time she wrapped her legs around his neck to accept him into herself, Mr. Gardiner experienced all the vigor of his youth returning to him and believed she felt similarly, for she was long past her own. That the dark tips of her bosom no longer pointed heavenward mattered not to him, nor that the landscape of flesh on her thighs and backside resembled the dimpled flesh of an orange. Her interior felt as if it had been heated by the desert sun, gripping his length with all the tightness of a girl who had not yet lost her maidenhood, and Mr. Gardiner frequently found himself discharging his pleasure into her a second time without having even withdrawn himself from the first. With their every coupling, his countenance beamed with pride as they achieved the moment of release at the same time. That this too went unchecked by Mr. Gardiner was yet further evidence of his happily besotted state, and he looked forward with dread to his return to Gracechurch Street.

The much-awaited letter from Mr. Gardiner finally arrived at Longbourn with instructions for Mr. Bennet as to the financial settlement that had been arranged between himself and Wickham, offering added assurances of a swift wedding in town, which the family was not expected to attend. Elizabeth once again read out the contents in her father's stead, comprehending that urgent action from Mr. Bennet was required. "*You will easily comprehend, from these particulars, that Mr. Wickham's circumstances are not so hopeless as they are generally believed to be. I am happy to say there will be some little money, even when all his debts are discharged, to settle on my niece. Send back your answer as fast as you can.*"

"Oh, where is my father?" cried Jane. "Lizzy, whatever shall we do?"

With her uncle's letter still in hand, Elizabeth hastened outside to the stables, where she recalled seeing a disused anvil from the time the family had employed a smithy. It was quite cumbersome in weight and shape, but the urgency of the matter endowed her with a strength she never knew she possessed. She carried the burden back into the house and directly to the locked library door. If there was any hope to salvage what little remained of Lydia's reputation, it was now. She hurled the anvil at the handle, breaking it off.

The door opened from the force of the blow, revealing Mr. Bennet slumped at his writing desk, looking extremely disheveled and fatigued. His face was marked by several days' growth of beard that did much to emphasize the family resemblance between himself and Mary. The room itself was in a pitiable state, with books pulled from their shelves and curious drawings propped hither and thither, not to mention the rotting remains of what might once have been a butternut squash lying in one corner. Various items of what appeared to be ladies' undergarments were strewn about, as if suddenly discarded by their wearers. Elizabeth, however, did not have time to reflect on the reasons for the latter, for there were matters of far more consequence to attend to. "Dear father," she cried, "you must write immediately to our uncle. There is no time to lose!"

Mr. Bennet took the letter from his daughter's outstretched hand, his grizzled countenance becoming increasingly puzzled as he read the contents. "Yes, they must marry; there is nothing else to be done," said he. "But there are two things that I want very much to know—how much money your uncle has laid down to bring it about, and how I am ever to pay him? For no man in his senses would marry Lydia on so slight a temptation as what has been offered here."

"That is very true," replied Elizabeth. "His debts to be discharged, and something still to remain! It must be my uncle's doings! Generous, good man, I am afraid he has distressed himself. A small sum could not do all this."

Elizabeth, leaving him to write his reply, sought out Jane. After much discussion of the matter, they concluded that Mr. Gardiner had taken on the financial burden himself, though they dared not even guess as to the amount. Indeed, it would be impossible for their father to ever repay him. The sisters went to relay the news to their mother, who was being attended by Mary and Kitty. Mrs. Gardiner had earlier taken to her room with pains in her head, which had been brought on by too many hours of administering to her sister-in-law and concern for her husband, whom she was now most anxious to join.

Mrs. Bennet's joy burst forth as violent from delight as she had ever been fidgety from alarm and vexation. "My dear, dear Lydia!" she cried, her chains rattling and jangling with her frenzied movements. "She will be married! My good, kind brother! I knew he would manage everything! How I long to see her, and to see dear Wickham too! But the clothes, the wedding clothes! Lizzy, run down to your father and ask him how much he will give her. Oh, to think that in a short time I shall have a daughter married. Mrs. Wickham! How well it sounds!"

A fortnight had passed since Mrs. Bennet had been out of her bed, but on this happy day the family deemed it safe to remove her from her chains and allow her to resume a normal life. She again took her seat at the head of her table, her spirits oppressively high. No sentiment of shame could dampen her triumph. The marriage of a daughter was now on the point of accomplishment, and her thoughts and words ran only to elegant nuptials, fine muslins, new carriages, and which of the grander houses in the neighborhood would make a proper situation for her daughter, without either knowing or considering what the couple's income might be.

Despite her mother's delight, Elizabeth could find little joy in the situation. In looking forward, neither happiness nor worldly prosperity could be expected for her sister by marrying Wickham. As regards herself, she knew Darcy was lost to her forever by Lydia's disgrace, and by her own. Her behavior on that final morning in Lambton had been nothing short of dishonorable. To take a man into her mouth as she had done, why, it did not bear thinking about, despite the enjoyment it gave them both. She had received no word from Darcy since leaving Derbyshire; neither concern nor censure was to be hers. It appeared that he considered her behavior so base that he could not even bear to engage with her by post. Indeed, it would not be the first time a gentleman had withdrawn from her his attentions. Elizabeth knew too well the unpredictable nature of the other sex. Now, when she was convinced that she could have been happy with Darcy, it was no longer likely they should meet. He had cast her from his mind and heart, and the happiness she had felt at Pemberley now seemed many years distant. No longer did she take to pleasuring herself in her bed, for there was little inspiration to be had save for that which only furthered her pain.

Chapter Twenty-Three

MR. AND MRS. WICKHAM WERE WELCOMED AT LONGBOURN House with much delight by Mrs. Bennet, and after embracing her youngest, she gave her hand, with an affectionate smile, to Wickham, who now could do no wrong. Their reception from Mr. Bennet, to whom they then turned, was not quite so cordial, and he scarcely opened his lips. The easy assurance of the young couple was enough to provoke him, though he was also quite angered over the matter of the library door, which, thanks to his second daughter, could no longer be locked.

Elizabeth herself was disgusted by the couple's behavior, and even Jane was shocked. Lydia was still Lydia—untamed, unabashed, noisy, and fearless, as she turned from sister to sister, demanding their congratulations. Wickham was not at all distressed; his manners remained always pleasing, as if his character and his marriage were exactly as they should be, and when he turned to greet Elizabeth, she detected a familiar activity in his breeches and found herself astonished that he could be so utterly incapable of shame.

"Only three months since I went away!" cried Lydia. "I am sure I had no idea of being married when I came back again. Oh, I have had such very good fun!"

The room fell silent; that Lydia should publicly admit to having enjoyed her time in Wickham's bawdy house was beyond comprehension. Only Mrs. Bennet appeared unaffected by the declaration, and much of this was owing to her resumed intake of her special nerve medicine. Elizabeth at last could bear it no longer. She quit the room and returned no more till she heard the family assembling in the dining parlor, joining them in time to hear Lydia say to her eldest sister as she claimed her chair, "Jane, I take your place now, and you must go lower, because I am a married woman."

Mrs. Bennet's good cheer once more turned to distress when the conversation turned to the couple's forthcoming departure for parts north, and when she spoke, her voice rose in its customary shrillness. "My dear Lydia, I don't at all like your going such a way off. Must it be so?"

"Oh, but you and papa and my sisters must come to see us! We shall be at Newcastle all the winter, and I am certain there will be some balls. And then, when you go, you may leave one or two of my sisters behind, and I daresay I shall get husbands for them before the winter is over!"

"I thank you for my share of the favor," replied Elizabeth. "But I do not particularly like your way of getting husbands."

The visitors were not to remain above ten days with them, which, for everyone but Mrs. Bennet, was ten days too many. Wickham had received his commission before he left London and was to join his regiment in the north after he left Longbourn. It appeared that the days of his trade in the bodies of young women were finally at an end, though Elizabeth could not help wondering if he might establish a similar operation in Newcastle, and she feared for the innocents who might fall prey to him. Although Lydia remained, for the most part, the same Lydia as ever, Elizabeth noted changes in her appearance, such as a darkening around the eyes, which she suspected might indicate an opium addiction. She had detected the very same feature in Miss Darcy, but only now did she make the link. Before a moment arose to question her sister in private, Lydia launched into a lengthy and breathless account of every detail of her wedding—from what was eaten for breakfast to the drape of Wickham's blue coat. Jane yawned all throughout, and Elizabeth was nearly overcome by sleep until she heard a name that set her heart and loins on fire.

"My uncle was called away on business," continued Lydia. "Well, I was so frightened I did not know what to do, for he was to give me away! Luckily he came back in time. However, I recollected afterward that if he had been prevented going, the wedding need not be put off, for Mr. Darcy might have done as well."

"Mr. Darcy!" repeated Elizabeth, all astonishment.

"Oh, yes! He was to come there with Wickham, you know. But gracious me, I quite forgot! I ought not to have said a word about it. I promised them so faithfully! It was to be such a secret!"

Both Elizabeth and Jane assured her they would say nothing, but they each burned with curiosity, particularly Elizabeth, who felt she could scarcely breathe at the mere mention of the man. A wild pulsing made itself known at her womanhood as she recalled the taste of him from when he had completed his pleasure in her mouth, and she nearly cried out with longing. That she would never again desire such a thing from any other man she had no doubt, and she wished more than ever that she could be once more on her knees before him, welcoming the length of his manhood onto the bed of her tongue. How she longed to breathe in his scent as his release coursed down her throat. Within moments Elizabeth was writing a letter to Mrs. Gardiner, who had since been returned to London, insisting on knowing the meaning of Darcy's presence at her sister's wedding.

It required several days before Mrs. Gardiner could properly reply to her niece's letter. Since arriving at Gracechurch Street, she had been in a turmoil on discovering the presence of another woman in the household. Mr. Gardiner remained extremely vague as to the details of how this dark-eyed houri from the desert had come to be there, though Mrs. Gardiner suspected it bore some connection to Mr. Wickham's bawdy house. The woman spoke but a little, yet was generally pleasing in manner and countenance, and Mrs. Gardiner could not truly find fault with her daily presence. It was only in the night, however, that matters took on a slightly different tenor, for Mrs. Gardiner would hear the most curious moans, followed by an eerie singing, coming from her husband's bedchamber. It sounded as if it were in a foreign tongue and was often quite high-pitched in tone. Still more curious was the voice of Mr. Gardiner as it joined in with this singing. Her husband could claim knowledge of no other language save for that belonging to the king, and his wife considered this recent turn of events most perplexing.

Night after night Mrs. Gardiner found her ears being subjected to these oddities until at last she felt called upon to investigate. By the time she reached her husband's room, the singing had taken on a wailing note, reminding her of the cats that roamed the neighborhood at night. The door was ajar, and she pushed it farther open to better investigate what manner of activity was transpiring therein. From her vantage point, she could survey the entirety of the room and, in particular, the bed, upon which she recognized the unremarkable figure of Mr. Gardiner clad only in his nightshirt, which had ridden up to his waist. His bare backside faced toward her, and it appeared to be engaged in some form of strenuous activity, urging itself forward and back in a series of repetitive motions that were as ridiculous as they were graceless. Mrs. Gardiner soon ascertained the figure of Gracechurch Street's newest inhabitant lying beneath him with her legs held high in the air, her feet poised at an angle of such extreme width it would have rendered its observer incapable of walking had she endeavored to emulate it.

Mrs. Gardiner continued to monitor the activities of her husband's backside, the sight of which reminded her as to why she preferred to forgo her matrimonial duties whenever possible. To her horror, the opening between his hind cheeks actually appeared to be winking at her each time they rose upward, at which point his manhood came into view, displaying a vigor she could not recall having been made the recipient of since their wedding night. She caught occasional glimpses of the place in which her husband was depositing himself, and it was as dark and red as a ruby. It seemed to swallow him up with ease, leaving nothing remaining but the sagging pouch of flesh swaying between his thighs as he endeavored to apply himself with such speed that his wife feared he might suffer a mischief. The couple's singing had by this time grown quite anguished and, indeed, most disagreeable to listen to, and just as Mrs. Gardiner believed she could bear it no longer, Mr. Gardiner collapsed onto his companion, their final notes equaling in spiritedness what they possessed in unpleasantness.

Mrs. Gardiner returned to her room, far less troubled by the nature of her discovery than she might have believed possible. She and Mr. Gardiner had accumulated many years of marriage between them; therefore being released from this particular wifely duty provided her with little distress. On the contrary, she now looked forward with eagerness to enjoying her nights in peace, with the agreeable companionship of novels to amuse her. She had on previous visits to Longbourn borrowed from Mr. Bennet's library a number of books, and she very much wished to begin reading *A*

Strumpet's Pleasure at the first opportunity.

Mrs. Gardiner at last replied to Elizabeth, the length of her letter making up for its tardiness as she chronicled in detail how Mr. Darcy had called on her husband with news of the fugitive couple's whereabouts, then put forth his plan to set matters to rights. *The motive he professed was his conviction of its being owing to himself that Wickham's worthlessness had not been so well known as to make it impossible for any young woman of character to love or confide in him*, wrote Mrs. Gardiner. *He called it, therefore, his duty to step forward and endeavor to remedy an evil that had been brought on by himself. If he had another motive, I am sure it would never disgrace him.*

Mrs. Gardiner then described how Darcy had been to see Wickham, and insisted on seeing Lydia to persuade her to quit her present disgraceful situation, but found her absolutely resolved on remaining where she was. Wickham was equally so resolved, for business at his bawdy house had increased considerably since her arrival. It only remained for Darcy to secure and expedite a marriage, which he learned had never been Wickham's design. *Wickham of course wanted more than he could get, but at length was induced to be reasonable,* explained Mrs. Gardiner. *Mr. Darcy's next step was to make your uncle acquainted with the terms. They battled it together for a long time, which was more than either the gentleman or lady concerned in it deserved. But at last your uncle was forced to yield, and instead of being allowed to be of use to his niece, was forced to put up with only having the probable credit of it.*

Although it was agreed for Mr. Darcy to be in London when the wedding took place, and all money matters then to receive the last finish, Mr. Gardiner took it upon himself to take up temporary lodgings at Wickham's establishment so that he might better monitor the situation and make certain neither party reneged on the agreement. He remained there until Mr. Darcy's return, and, despite Mr. Gardiner's strong feeling that he should continue in residence a while longer, Darcy was quite insistent that his business was concluded and he should return to Gracechurch Street without delay. *Will you be very angry with me, my dear Lizzy, if I take this opportunity of saying how much I like him?* wrote Mrs. Gardiner. *His behavior to us has, in every respect, been as pleasing as when we were in Derbyshire. He wants nothing but a little more liveliness, and that, if he marries prudently, his wife may teach him. I thought him very sly; he hardly ever mentioned your name. Pray, forgive me if I have been very presuming, or at least do not punish me so far as to exclude me from Pemberley. I shall never be quite happy till I have been all round the park!*

The contents of her aunt's letter threw Elizabeth into a flurry of confusion. It was beyond comprehension that Darcy had done all this for a girl whom he could neither regard nor esteem, though her heart and loins did whisper that he had done it for *her*. How heartily did she grieve over every ungracious sentiment she had ever encouraged, every saucy speech she had ever directed toward him. She read over her aunt's commendation of him again and again, sensible of some pleasure, though mixed with regret, on finding how steadfastly the Gardiners had been persuaded that affection and confidence existed between Mr. Darcy and herself. If only it were so!

Elizabeth had been reading her letter in the garden when Mr. Wickham approached. He offered his apologies for having interrupted her solitude, whereupon the two fell into conversation. Wickham appeared all charm and ease, as if nothing untoward had passed. That his breeches had once more become a place of considerable activity did not escape her notice, and she wondered again at the impertinence of such a man whose very existence belied all sense of humility. He seemed particularly insistent that she notice his condition, urging his loins forward as he spoke, placing on display the shape of his manhood as it pressed against the fabric. Wickham made much fanfare of having to adjust it, offering Elizabeth a long-suffering smile as he reestablished its location so that it was now pointing skyward, only to have to do so again as it began to lean toward the right. Indeed, she would not have been at all surprised had he seen fit to remove his manhood from his breeches entirely. His eyes held the expectation that she would be inclined to make use of it, were he to do so, and he focused his attention on her lips, casting repeated glances down toward his breeches, as if suggesting she might wish to take the contents into her mouth.

Elizabeth could only experience relief that she now felt nothing, not even a slight flicker at her womanhood. At Wickham's mention of her recent visit to Pemberley, it immediately became clear that he wished to learn of her dealings with Darcy and, in the interim, uncover the extent of her knowledge on the subject of himself.

"Did you see him while you were at Lambton?" he asked.

"Yes," replied Elizabeth. "He introduced us to his sister."

"And do you like her?"

"Very much."

"I have heard that she is uncommonly improved of late, especially when one considers the disreputable circumstances in which she was engaged." At this, Wickham's manhood gave a violent twitch, prompting from him yet another readjustment. "I hope she will turn out well."

"I daresay she will, now that she has been removed from those individuals who engaged her in such circumstances and returned to the safety and protection of her brother."

Elizabeth's meaning provoked a heightening of Wickham's countenance; however, he appeared for the most part unaffected. The activity in his breeches continued to plague him, and, to her amazement, he did exactly what she imagined he would. Within moments he was clutching his manhood, his expression indicating that he was bestowing on Elizabeth a great prize, his pride turning to dismay when she made no move to accept it. She continued to remain unmoved as Wickham, wrapping his fingers around the crown, proceeded to squeeze it as if he were endeavoring to choke the breaths from it, his eyes rolling upward with an ecstasy known only to himself, the exposed flesh turning an angry red. He looked again to Elizabeth and, receiving no response, began to employ a series of short tugs that were concentrated in the same region, his actions generating a good deal of groaning from himself, but little in the way of interest from his observer. Elizabeth resumed the reading of her letter, leaving Wickham to return his now-deflated member to his breeches, whereupon he took his leave.

The day of Wickham and Lydia's departure soon arrived, to which everyone experienced great relief but Mrs. Bennet, who was tearful at what was to be a very long separation from her daughter. "Oh, my dear Lydia! How ever shall I bear it? Write to me very often, my dear."

"As often as I can," replied Lydia. "But you know married women have never much time for writing. My sisters may write to *me*. They will have nothing else to do."

Wickham's adieus were more amiable than his wife's. He smiled, looked handsome, and said as many agreeable things as could be managed, though his manhood remained conspicuously dormant when he offered his farewell to Elizabeth. "He is as fine a fellow," said Mr. Bennet when they were gone, "as ever I saw. He simpers and smirks and makes love to us all. I am prodigiously proud of him. I defy even Sir William Lucas himself to produce a more valuable son-in-law."

Chapter Twenty-Four

WHEN NEWS REACHED LONGBOURN THAT MR. BINGLEY WAS returning to Netherfield for a few weeks of shooting, Mrs. Bennet was quite in the fidgets, though she told anyone who would listen that she cared not in the least, since that particular gentleman was nothing to her family. Jane gave everyone to believe that she was unaffected by the news; however, her countenance and manner declared otherwise. Elizabeth did not know what to make of it. Had she not seen Bingley in Derbyshire, she might have supposed him capable of coming to Hertfordshire with no other view than what was acknowledged, but she still thought him partial to Jane.

"As soon as Mr. Bingley comes, you will wait on him of course," said Mrs. Bennet to her husband.

"You forced me into visiting him last year and promised, if I went to see him, he should marry one of my daughters. But it ended in nothing, and I will not be sent on a fool's errand again," Mr. Bennet replied sharply. His humor had been markedly ill of late, owing to his frustration in not having sufficient opportunity to attend to matters of the flesh, as well as the rather grievous bump to the head he sustained while attempting to seek a solution to this obstacle to pleasure. Owing to his daughter's breaking down the door, the library was no longer a place of sanctuary for him, and he had been forced to search out other locations, all of which had proved faulty. He should have realized that the generously proportioned Hill would not fit comfortably into a cupboard with himself.

Indeed, the housekeeper was in particularly boisterous spirits on the occasion of their appointment in the cupboard, for no sooner had they shut themselves inside than she raised up her skirts and, propping one foot on a shelf, presented her womanhood to Mr. Bennet. He dropped instantly to his knees, their close confines thwarting his tongue from taking a leisurely tour of her folds lest his back give out, and he managed but a few errant licks before he was forced to stand upright, replacing his tongue with his manhood, which sank easily into Hill's cavernous depths. The excitement of once again availing himself of the housekeeper's womanhood prompted Mr. Bennet to execute his movements with a good deal more fervor than was prudent, and the shelf beneath Hill's foot weakened with every stroke she received. She was at last forced to remove from it her foot, only to wrap her thigh around him in a heavy embrace, crushing her folds against him. Grasping hold of the generous cheeks of her backside, Mr. Bennet propelled his loins forward one last time, nearly shouting with glee when he felt his liquids surging up from his testes and through the length of his manhood, directly into Hill. Her interior quivered against his immersed flesh and she pulled him to her, crying her pleasure into his neck.

Neither party would even be given sufficient time to catch a breath before Mr. Bennet was turning the housekeeper around and attending to her other opening. His earlier release allowed him to carry on for some time, to which

Hill's delight was manifest as she cried out with ever-increasing volume, her arms thrashing about every which way and sending objects crashing to the floor. Moisture had broken out on Mr. Bennet's brow as he applied his manhood with greater force, wishing he had more room in which to move. He reached around to clutch the massive spheres of flesh that constituted the housekeeper's bosom, which he had let loose from her stays, squeezing them in time with his thrusts. This prompted yet more vocalizing from Hill, whose abundant backside seemed to swallow him so deeply he feared he might never find his way back out again. Mr. Bennet expected to be discovered at any moment and wondered at the reaction of the unsuspecting soul who happened upon him with his manhood planted well up the housekeeper's hind passage, taking a wicked delight that it should be his wife. The thought of Mrs. Bennet's mad shrieks did much to inspire Mr. Bennet's second release, and, taking firm hold of the sturdy expanse of Hill's waist, he put forth one final thrust, which was met in kind as Hill drove herself backward to meet it, whereupon they fell to their knees, locked together in rapture, the loose shelf above dropping onto their heads.

Mr. Bennet would be saved from a visit to Netherfield, for Mr. Bingley called at Longbourn on the third day after his arrival in Hertfordshire. Seeing his approach from a window, Mrs. Bennet quickly summoned her daughters. Jane resolutely kept her place, but Elizabeth, to satisfy her mother, went to the window, where she observed Mr. Darcy riding alongside Bingley. For a moment she felt quite ill, and she went to sit with Jane, hoping her face did not betray her emotions. Her astonishment at his coming to Longbourn and voluntarily seeking her society again was almost equal to what she had experienced on first witnessing his altered behavior in Derbyshire.

"Good gracious, it is Mr. Darcy!" cried Mrs. Bennet.

"Well, any friend of Mr. Bingley's will always be welcome here, but I must say that I hate the very sight of him." She continued with her condemnation of Darcy until he and his friend had joined the ladies in the parlor, where refreshments were offered.

Elizabeth said as little to either as civility would allow and at first ventured only one glance at Darcy, fearful of what she might find. He looked serious and, she thought, not at all like the man she had seen at Pemberley. Bingley appeared both pleased and embarrassed, and was received by Mrs. Bennet with a manic enthusiasm that made her two daughters ashamed, especially when contrasted with the cold and ceremonious politeness of her curtsey and address to his friend. Darcy, after inquiring of Elizabeth how Mr. and Mrs. Gardiner were, said scarcely anything, either speaking to Bingley or not at all. Unable to resist another glance, she raised her eyes to his face, finding him frequently looking at the floor. She lowered her gaze to his breeches, hoping for some indication that he might be pleased to see her, but detected no telltale signs of his affection. She was disappointed and angry with herself for being so.

Mrs. Bennet directed her conversation entirely toward Bingley and, after inquiring of his plans, went on to express her delight at having a daughter well married. Her words were shrill and ill chosen, particularly regarding her praise of Mr. Wickham—to whom she referred as a clever gentleman of commerce, which prompted Darcy to choke on his drink—and it quickly became apparent to Elizabeth that the gypsies had been to call. The gentlemen at last rose to leave, and Mrs. Bennet, momentarily mindful of her intended civility, invited them to dine at Longbourn in a few days' time. "When you have killed all your own birds, Mr. Bingley," said she as they parted, "I beg you will come here and shoot as many as you please on Mr. Bennet's manor. I am sure he will be vastly happy to oblige you!"

Elizabeth and Jane spent the remainder of the day convincing themselves of their impartiality toward the callers, continuing in this way until the gentlemen rejoined them some days later for dinner. Bingley was, as usual, all politeness, and Elizabeth thought his behavior toward her sister was such as showed an admiration of her, though more guarded than formerly. His eyes seemed frequently turned toward Darcy, though whether it was to seek his consent or disapprobation she could not be certain. As regards herself and Darcy, she was in hopes that the evening would afford some opportunity of bringing them together, for ill luck had placed them at opposite sides of the dinner table, rendering conversation impossible.

The gentlemen afterward joined the ladies in the drawing room for tea and coffee. Elizabeth followed Darcy's handsome figure with her eyes. Her heart felt ready to burst, and her hands trembled so that she could scarcely keep hold of her cup. She could think only of their last moments together at Lambton. How she longed to taste him again, no matter the unseemliness of the act. As Elizabeth wondered how it might be to have him filling the place of her womanhood rather than merely her mouth, she experienced a clutching in her loins, and when Darcy suddenly appeared at her side with his empty cup, she nearly cried out from the shock of it. Yet again she wondered if he could read her thoughts, for he seemed equally startled as herself, and she felt her face growing hot with embarrassment that he might know her desires.

After a few polite inquiries from both sides, they each fell silent, and Darcy eventually walked away to rejoin Mr. Bingley. Elizabeth hoped for another opportunity for conversation when the card tables were brought out, but they were confined for the evening at different tables, and she had nothing to encourage her but that his eyes were so often turned toward her side of the room as to make him play as unsuccessfully as herself. The evening concluded with everyone in good spirits, particularly Mrs. Bennet, who had taken Mr. Bingley's conduct toward her eldest daughter as an indication that he was intending to renew his attentions toward her. Jane, however, continued to assert her indifference toward the gentleman, insisting in private to Elizabeth, who appeared strangely distracted since the departure of their guests, that she found his company pleasing, but nothing more.

On their return to Netherfield, both Bingley and Darcy expressed satisfaction at the pleasant manner in which the evening had been passed, though the former engaged in most of the conversation, the latter behaving with more reticence than usual. Bingley, clearly in good humor, filled and refilled his friend's glass with spirits, experiencing many of the same emotions from Darcy's nearness as those which Elizabeth had borne earlier. He was ever mindful that time was no longer in his favor, as it was becoming apparent that Darcy's opinion of Miss Bennet had been considerably altered, and Bingley feared that he would be forever lost to him if he did not act swiftly to make his feelings known. That he loved Darcy was certain. Whether Darcy would welcome such love or flee in disgust from it was an entirely different matter.

"Bingley, why are you holding my hand?"

Bingley gave a start. He had been unaware of even doing so, and he coughed nervously by way of distraction, using the interval to refill Darcy's glass with more spirits, hoping they would shortly take effect. They had both eaten well at Longbourn, and the outcome he awaited was taking far longer than expected. He observed closely as the eyes of his friend became misted from drink, which was shortly followed by a slackening of the jaw and corresponding slump of the shoulders. When he attempted once again to engage Darcy in conversation, receiving only incomprehensible replies, he deemed it safe to carry on. Setting down his own glass of spirits, which he had diluted with water, he went to stand before his friend. When Darcy displayed no reaction, Bingley placed his hand at Darcy's chin and tipped his face gently upward to his own, his legs nearly giving out beneath him as their mouths met in a kiss. Darcy stirred, but made no protest.

The taste of spirits on his friend's lips caused Bingley to become light-headed, and his heart swelled with love, as did the flesh of his manhood, which desired far more from Darcy than merely a kiss. With each moment that passed Bingley's boldness increased, and he took much encouragement when his tongue located Darcy's, for the latter's was not withdrawn. On the contrary, he detected a pleasing return of affection that astonished him, and he slipped his hand down to Darcy's lap, nearly crying out at discovering a substantial presence in his breeches. As he continued to engage him in a kiss, Bingley unbuttoned the flap and slipped his hand inside, taking hold of his friend's manhood, its warmth tearing at his heart. It swelled to his touch, lengthening and thickening in a manner that was most agreeable, and he began to stroke it, hoping to promote Darcy's pleasure, the fruits of which he would receive in his mouth. The moisture at the tip collected on his fingers, and Bingley stole a few drops with his tongue, shivering with delight. Darcy began to moan, sounding as if he were trying to speak, and Bingley placed his ear to his lips to better hear, experiencing a sinking sensation in his belly on hearing the word "Elizabeth."

Bingley proceeded to make haste lest he be discovered before his mission was complete. Darcy's flesh was heartbreakingly silken, and Bingley trembled each time the shiny pink crown came into view. He had never seen anything so beautiful, and he pulled down on the loose flesh covering it again and again, tormenting himself with the vista until he could no longer refrain from placing his mouth upon it, prompting from Darcy a series of moans that spoke of some private anguish known only to himself. Perhaps when his friend realized to whom he owed so many nights of pleasure, he might do away with all thoughts of Miss Bennet, for there were some acts of the flesh that only Bingley could perform, and he very much desired to be given an opportunity to do so with his beloved Darcy. The mere thought of using his manhood to penetrate Darcy's backside had been sufficient to bring on his release as he lay in his bed at night, and he wondered for how much longer his patience could be sustained.

The torment in his mind led Bingley to apply his mouth with reckless vigor to Darcy's manhood, his lips drawing hard upon it, for he was determined to taste his friend's pleasure before the night was through. Darcy began to stir, and suddenly his eyes flew open.

"Bingley, what are you doing?!" he cried, jumping up from his chair. "Good god, man, have you gone mad?"

Bingley knew then that all hope was lost. He would never be triumphant in winning Darcy's love.

Chapter Twenty-Five

MR. BINGLEY CALLED AGAIN AT LONGBOURN A FEW DAYS later, this time alone. Darcy had left for London the morning after the failed seduction, but was to return to Hertfordshire within a week; whether he would keep to his word, however, Bingley knew not. He arrived at such an hour that the ladies were not dressed, and Mrs. Bennet, in her dressing gown and with her hair half finished, ran to her eldest daughter's room with the announcement, crying out for her to make haste, her tone bordering on hysteria.

Mr. Bennet was in the library, though his time for privacy was long since past. The broken door could not be mended, and he had not sufficient funds in the household accounts to replace it. He occupied himself with a fire in the hearth, to which he was feeding one by one his cherished drawings, watching with grief as each was eaten by the flames. Mary remained in her room, where she was engaged in the study of an ancient text belonging to the Semites, rocking curiously to and fro as she sang the words inscribed on the pages. Therefore it was left to Mrs. Bennet and the three remaining

Miss Bennets to entertain Mr. Bingley in the parlor.

Mrs. Bennet, who wished to remove all but Jane from Bingley's presence, sat looking and winking at Elizabeth and Kitty, her manner more demented than usual and making not the slightest impression on them. After some moments she called for Kitty to leave the room with her, returning again to request the same of Elizabeth. There was nothing for it but Jane to remain behind, and she did so with much anxiousness, which was shared by Bingley. The two spent some time staring at each other, both appearing on the verge of speaking, then just as quickly not. Bingley at last rose from his chair and went to Jane. He reached for her hand with great awkwardness, finding the words he required difficult to pronounce. The night in which his love had been rejected by Darcy had decided him; he would ask Miss Bennet to marry him.

Miss Jane Bennet was a pretty young woman with an agreeable manner and a gentleness of spirit, and Bingley believed it unlikely he would find anyone more suitable. It was a situation helped in good measure by the fact that her sister appeared to have attracted the interest of his friend, which would allow for further opportunities to unite him with Darcy, particularly if that gentleman chose to increase his attentions toward Miss Elizabeth Bennet. That Darcy might reject his friendship as well as his love weighed heavily on him. They had neither of them referred to the events that had taken place on the evening of the failed seduction, and he hoped it would remain so.

Bingley felt called on to kiss Miss Bennet, and he placed his lips to hers. They were not nearly so pleasing as Darcy's, and he experienced none of the excitement he had earlier felt with his friend. Concerned that Miss Bennet might consider him unskilled in matters of the heart, he closed his eyes and imagined that her lips were Darcy's. This provided him with rather more enthusiasm for the task than was sensible, and he pulled Miss Bennet from her chair until they were both entangled on the floor. Though she made no protest, Bingley sensed her confusion, which seemed to increase when he ceased from his kisses and turned her so that she was facing the floor. Persuading himself that it was Darcy's stalwart figure beneath him rather than the more yielding version belonging to Miss Bennet, Bingley unbuttoned his breeches and rolled on top of her, pressing his manhood into the cleft of her backside, the agreeable shape of which was conspicuous beneath her gown.

The only sound in the room was that of Bingley's labored breathing, for in his desire to possess Darcy, he had become so stimulated that, without realizing he had done so, he had lifted up the hems of Miss Bennet's garments to her waist. He felt himself entering the dark place he had spied briefly between her hind cheeks before shutting his eyes against the true identity of his desired object, the moisture from his manhood assisting him in his endeavors. He began to push farther inside her, at first with uncertainty, then with increasing confidence as a familiar sensation of pleasure built up in his loins. Miss Bennet continued to lie without complaint beneath him, Bingley's movements forcing the breaths from her chest in harmony with his own, until he believed it was only Darcy and himself on the floor.

Bingley began to weep, his love for his friend was so great. For this moment to ever be his to claim he had dared no longer hope for, and he would have happily died than to open his eyes to the reality. Each time he drove himself forward, it felt as if he were entering fire; Darcy's interior was as hot as it had been when he had covertly applied his finger to it. To his delight, his friend's backside had begun to raise itself up from the floor to meet his strokes, indicating that they were very much welcome. Bingley felt a heaviness in his testes as the moment of release threatened to approach, and he launched the full length of himself forward until he had gone as deep as he could go, then did so again and again, desperate to fill his adored one with his love. He reached around to grasp hold of Darcy's manhood, expecting to find it rising up with its usual pride and grandeur, only to find instead his fingers sinking into something soft and wet. Bingley's eyes flew open in shock, yet before he became fully aware of what he was touching, his loins gave forth their gift. "Darcy!" he sobbed, collapsing heavily onto Miss Bennet.

Elizabeth found the couple still on the floor, their breaths rapid, their complexions of heightened color, though by now both parties had righted their garments. Bingley appeared particularly moved, and there were tears on his cheeks. He suddenly rose, seeming not to know in which direction to look, then, remembering himself, he reached down to assist Jane from the floor. After whispering a few words to her, he ran from the room.

Jane could have no reserves from her sister. Instantly embracing her, she acknowledged with the liveliest emotion that she was the happiest creature in the world, though she omitted the particulars of what had just transpired between herself and Mr. Bingley. Indeed, she had found it most curious, yet not in the least distressing, and she looked forward with eagerness to its repetition, though she knew not for the life of her why he should choose to call out his friend's name. "Oh, Lizzy, to know that what I have to relate will give such pleasure to all my dear family! How shall I bear so much happiness?" cried Jane. She then hastened away to relay the news to her mother while Bingley was in conference with her father.

Mr. Bennet at once sanctioned the relationship, grateful for the burden of yet another daughter to be removed from him, especially on a household income that had been dwindling with alarming rapidity. He often amused himself with the thought that he might shortly be required to send Mrs.

Bennet to work at Wickham's bawdy house, providing they agreed to take her. He had believed finances would improve now that his special drawings were no longer a consideration; however, Hill had begun to demand a weekly sum from him in order to continue with their special arrangement. Mr. Bennet could ill afford to lose both a housekeeper *and* a source of pleasure to himself; therefore he felt obliged to meet her demands. Though Hill was no great beauty and her youth many years behind her, she possessed a robustness of spirit toward the fleshly pursuits that Mr. Bennet found inspiring. Her buxom form was a delight to embrace, and there was much of interest to grasp on to. He would sooner exchange spuds for meat at the dinner table than be deprived of her companionship.

From this time forward, Mr. Bingley was a daily visitor at Longbourn House, arriving frequently before breakfast and always remaining till after supper. Mr. Bennet began to count the days till the couple would be happily ensconced at Netherfield, for, like most young men, Bingley possessed an appetite to rival that of a horse, and Mr. Bennet could ill afford to keep feeding him. News of the engagement quickly spread all throughout Meryton, and the Bennets were pronounced to be the luckiest family in all the world, though only a few weeks before, when Lydia had first run off, they had been marked out for misfortune.

Chapter Twenty-Six

ONE MORNING ABOUT A WEEK AFTER BINGLEY'S ENGAGEMENT with Jane had been formed, the Bennets received an unexpected caller. The quality of the carriage indicated that it belonged not to anyone of their acquaintance. As the ladies sat waiting anxiously, the door was thrown open, followed by the entrance of a tall and imposing personage dressed in black. It was Lady Catherine de Bourgh.

Mrs. Bennet, all amazement, was flattered by having a guest of such high importance and received her with the utmost politeness, despite the inappropriateness of the hour. Refusing all offers of refreshment, Lady Catherine directed most of her conversation toward Elizabeth, finding much to criticize in the situation of the room and the size of the property, all but ignoring Mrs. Bennet and her other daughters. Elizabeth expected that she would produce a letter for her from Charlotte, as it seemed the only probable motive for her calling, but no letter appeared. After a silence, Lady Catherine requested Elizabeth to accompany her on a walk in the grounds, her manner indicating that she did not expect to be refused.

Lady Catherine continued to find fault with everything she saw until at last they quit the house. Elizabeth was determined to make no effort at conversation with a woman who was now more than usually insolent and disagreeable, and they walked for a way without speaking; however, as soon as they entered the copse, Lady Catherine began in an angry tone, "A report of a most alarming nature has reached me. I was told not only that your sister was on the point of being most advantageously married, but that you, Miss Elizabeth Bennet, would, in all likelihood, be soon afterward united to my nephew, Mr. Darcy. I know it must be a scandalous falsehood. Though I would not injure him so much as to suppose the truth of it possible, I instantly resolved on setting off for this place that I might make my sentiments known to you."

Elizabeth, coloring with amazement and disdain, replied, "If you believed it impossible to be true, I wonder you took the trouble of coming so far. What could your ladyship propose by it?"

"At once to insist upon having such a report universally contradicted."

"Your coming to Longbourn to see me and my family will be rather a confirmation of it, if, indeed, such a report is in existence."

Lady Catherine's unpleasant countenance turned menacing. "I am not to be trifled with, Miss Bennet. Let me be rightly understood; this match, to which you have the presumption to aspire, can never take place. Mr. Darcy is engaged to my daughter. Now what have you to say?"

"Only that if he is so engaged, you can have no reason to suppose he will make an offer to *me*."

Lady Catherine hesitated, then went on to outline the arrangement between Mr. Darcy and Miss de Bourgh, which had been in place since their infancy. "Do not expect to be noticed by his family or friends, if you willfully act against the inclinations of all," she added. "You will be censured, slighted, and despised by everyone connected with him. Your alliance will be a disgrace; your name will never be mentioned by any of us."

"These are heavy misfortunes," said Elizabeth, "but the wife of Mr. Darcy must have such extraordinary sources of happiness attached to her situation that she could, upon the whole, have no cause to repine."

"Obstinate, headstrong girl! Is this your gratitude for my attentions to you last spring?" cried Lady Catherine, shaking her fists in the air. "Do not defy me, Miss Bennet! Are you engaged to my nephew? And if not, do you promise not to enter into such an arrangement? I *must* have my answer!"

Each query put forth by Lady Catherine was met with a reply that provided less than satisfaction. In no uncertain terms, her ladyship accused Elizabeth of the basest forms of seduction and duplicity, her words so foul their recipient felt compelled to clap her hands to her ears. She found herself being charged with every conceivable crime of the flesh, including lying with her own kind and coupling with farm beasts. That Lady Catherine should believe her nephew to be of such low character as to make an offer of marriage to a woman of the sort she now accused Elizabeth of being was quite remarkable.

Yet more remarkable still was her ladyship's professing to know the full particulars of Lydia's elopement with Wickham. "Is such a girl to be my nephew's sister? Is her husband, the son of his late father's steward, to be his brother? Are the shades of Pemberley to be thus polluted?" screamed Lady Catherine, prompting a flock of ravens from a nearby tree to take flight. When she proceeded to impugn Mrs. Bennet for the faults of her daughters, Elizabeth could bear no more. She turned and walked off, leaving her ladyship to make her own way back to her carriage. "I am most seriously displeased!" Lady Catherine called after her.

The visit so angered Elizabeth that she could not at once

return to the house. Instead she set off on the road to Mery-ton, hoping the refreshment might calm her. Within moments Lady Catherine's carriage went charging past, spraying her with dust and stones. Despite the damage to her gown, Elizabeth carried on, her vexation such that she was unconcerned as to the state of her appearance. About a quarter of a mile before the town, she happened on an unoccupied gypsy caravan that had been left at the side of the road. She gave it no more thought until some time later, when rounding a bend in the road, she recognized her ladyship's carriage parked a short distance away. At first she wondered if there had been some mishap, which might explain the abandoned caravan; perhaps the gypsies had gone to offer their aid. Considering the speed with which the carriage had been traveling, Elizabeth would not have been surprised if some calamity had befallen either Lady Catherine or the horses. She feared for the horses.

Elizabeth remained at the opposite side of the road, where she stood in the shadow of a tree, not wishing to draw attention to herself. It was then she noticed two male figures crouching on their knees in the dirt alongside the road. Their dark features identified them as the gypsies from the caravan. Elizabeth thought she recognized the young stableman from Lucas Lodge, but could not be certain. A hand from each man was bound to the rear wheel of the carriage, which had apparently come askew in the journey, and their breeches, which had been drawn down to their ankles, left their bare backsides positioned high in the air in a most discourteous manner. The one facing her possessed a pleasing shape, as if muscled from a life spent in physical labor, and Elizabeth was not remiss in her admiration. It was marked by very little hair, and, unless she was mistaken, its opening was quite conspicuously displayed.

Lady Catherine suddenly came into view, a horsewhip raised high in her hand. "You dare to rob a defenseless woman?" she cried, striking first at one gypsy's upraised backside, then his companion's. Suddenly Elizabeth saw that they each had hold of the other's manhood and were busily working them with rapid up-and-down motions; that their purpose was to release the fluids of their pleasure was not lost on her, and she experienced a fluttering in the folds of her womanhood, which both shamed and excited her. Had she not been on such public display, she might have reached beneath her skirts to stimulate herself. Instead she moved farther to the left so that she could better view the proceedings, finding the vista much improved.

"I shall not leave go of you until your punishment is complete!" shouted her ladyship, bringing the horsewhip down again and again, inspiring the gypsies to move their hands with greater haste. They gazed out toward the road with faraway expressions, as if they knew not what they were engaged in, but only that they must follow it to a conclusion. Elizabeth was astonished that men should find enjoyment from touching those of their own sex, yet the evidence was right there before her, disputing all that she had ever known. As their hands continued to work the lengths of flesh projecting out from each other's loins, they began to groan, indicating that their release was fast approaching.

The gypsy who Elizabeth believed was from Lucas Lodge was the first to be successful. The two halves of his finely constructed backside began to clench and unclench in a most beguiling manner, as did the opening between them, his fluids arcing through the air and spraying the dirt, where it was joined by those of his companion. In observing all this, Elizabeth found her mouth hungering to taste Darcy's own offerings, and she nearly wept with the hopelessness of it all.

That Lady Catherine had taken the trouble of a journey from Rosings for the sole purpose of breaking off Elizabeth's supposed engagement with her nephew indicated her resolution to prevent their marriage by any means possible. This, to be sure, included making an application to him as to the evils attached to a connection with her. With Darcy's notions of dignity, he would probably feel that the arguments contained much good sense and solid reasoning. As for the origins of the report of their engagement, Elizabeth was at a loss to imagine—unless his being the intimate friend of Bingley and her being the sister of Jane was enough to supply the idea, for the expectation of one wedding might well have provoked thoughts of another.

The driver of Lady Catherine's carriage, who had till now not left his post, was ordered to free the two men, and it was during this interval that her ladyship spied Elizabeth. "Strumpet!" she screamed, bounding toward her from across the road, her horsewhip waving threateningly in the air. Elizabeth immediately took flight, her youth the chief advantage in allowing her to outrun her pursuer, who seemed determined to remove Elizabeth from existence.

Elizabeth, returned to the safety of home, managed to evade the queries from her family as to the reason for Lady Catherine's visit. The next morning, however, Mr. Bennet called her aside. "I have received a letter this morning that has astonished me exceedingly," said he. "I did not know that I had *two* daughters on the brink of matrimony. Let me congratulate you on a very important conquest."

The color immediately rose to Elizabeth's cheeks as she imagined the letter to be from Lady Catherine, offering an insulting commentary on her unsuitability as a wife for Mr. Darcy—or perhaps it was even from that gentleman himself disputing such an arrangement. But when her father stated that the writer was none other than Mr. Collins, Elizabeth was exceedingly puzzled.

He went on to read the contents, which indicated that his cousin believed congratulations might soon be in order for Mr. Bennet's success at having not only Jane but Elizabeth near to matrimony. "*The chosen partner of her fate may be reasonably looked up to as one of the most illustrious personages in this land*," read Mr. Bennet. "*This young gentleman is blessed with splendid property, noble kindred, and extensive patronage. Yet in spite of all these temptations, let me warn my cousin Elizabeth, and yourself, of what evils you may incur by a precipitate closure with this gentleman's proposals, which, of course, you will be inclined to take immediate advantage of.*" Here Mr. Bennet paused. "Have you any idea, Lizzy, who this gentleman is? But let me read on! *My motive for cautioning you is as follows. We have reason to imagine that his aunt, Lady Catherine de Bourgh, does not look on the match with a friendly eye.*"

"Mr. Darcy, you see, is the man!" cried Mr. Bennet. "Now, Lizzy, I think I have surprised you. Could my cousin, or the Lucases, have pitched on any man within the circle of our acquaintance whose name would be more unlikely? Mr. Darcy, who never looks at any woman but to see a blemish, and who probably never looked at you in his life!"

Though Elizabeth tried to join in her father's pleasantry, she could force only a reluctant smile. Never had his wit been directed in a manner so little agreeable to her. He read out the remainder of Mr. Collins's letter, which chronicled in detail Lady Catherine's severe displeasure at a union between her nephew and Miss Bennet. When he finished, he replied with heightened amusement, "Had they fixed on any other man it would have been nothing, but his perfect indifference and your pointed dislike make it so delightfully absurd!"

Elizabeth had never been more at a loss to make her feelings appear what they were not, and she was grateful when their meeting was interrupted by the arrival of Hill, whose functional gown had been replaced by an indecent confection that would have been more suited to a woman in service at Wickham's bawdy house. Hill's pendulous bosom overflowed from the top of the garment and was matched only in unsightliness by that of the bulky halves of her back-side overflowing from the bottom. Mr. Bennet indicated to Elizabeth that she was dismissed.

Chapter Twenty-Seven

DURING ONE OF HIS REGULAR MORNING VISITS TO Longbourn, Mr. Bingley arrived with Mr. Darcy. It was not long after Lady Catherine had called, and before Mrs. Bennet had time to tell Darcy of their having seen his aunt, of which Elizabeth sat in dread. Bingley, who wanted to be alone with Jane, proposed their all taking a walk. Mary, of course, remained behind, as did her mother and Mr. Bennet, leaving the remaining five to set off together.

Jane and Mr. Bingley lagged behind the party, and soon disappeared from view. Bingley, who had been suffering greatly since ceasing his covert visits to Darcy's room in the night, thought he might indulge himself with Miss Bennet in the same manner in which he had done when making an offer of marriage to her. She had not put forth any protest, and he concluded that she was unlikely to do so now. He found her docile temperament most pleasing and anticipated that their marriage would be a union filled with ease and contentment. He took her hand and led her into a small copse where they risked little chance of discovery. Bingley's manhood had by now reached to its full inspiration, for he had been observing Darcy's backside from the time they had first set out on their walk, noting the highly agreeable way in which it swayed from side to side, as if offering to him an invitation. The knowledge that he was never to gain possession of it was a cruelty beyond endurance, yet endure it he must.

Bingley reached for Miss Bennet and kissed her, hoping that one day he might not be required to close his eyes and imagine another when in an intimate engagement with her. That his love for Darcy would eventually fade he did not foresee, but that he might in time come to experience romantic feelings for Miss Bennet he believed possible. Within moments of their lips coming together, Bingley had her facedown on the grass and was slipping inside her, surprised by the relative ease of his journey. This was an unexpected piece of good fortune, and rather than exercising restraint for fear of causing her a grievance, he set himself to the task, his passions inflamed from his earlier study of his friend's backside. Indeed, he drove his manhood to such depths inside her that he nearly lost consciousness.

That Jane had remained unaware of Mr. Bingley's intentions to apply himself to her backside was not the case. Though she maintained no objections as to what appeared to be a most curious predilection on his part, and one which, despite its occasional discomfort, had afforded her with a certain amount of pleasure, she desired that he make an application to her womanhood as well, for they were to be husband and wife, after all! At the moment of their convergence, she had adjusted the position of her backside by ever so slightly raising it up, thereby directing Bingley's manhood to enter her more womanly place instead. She felt a little ashamed at the deception, but his cries of pleasure filled her heart with more love than she had ever believed it capable of holding, and her guilt quickly left her. With each of his thrusts, Jane found her pelvis being urged with increasing force against the ground, and a series of pleasing sensations began to build up, originating not from the place to which Mr. Bingley introduced his manhood, but instead from the cleft above. Jane again altered her stance so that she might derive the most benefit from it, coming to understand much of what Bingley himself was experiencing as her folds came into contact with an uneven portion of ground, her breath catching in her throat as they rubbed against the irregular surface. Bingley had by this time hastened his movements considerably, and Jane sensed that something momentous was about to transpire for them both. He had begun to emit a plaintive series of moans until suddenly Jane heard a sharp cry, at which point she felt a pulsing as he released his fluids inside her. Within moments, she, too, became overwhelmed by sensation, her fingers tearing at the grass as her loins burst forth with a multitude of sparks.

Elizabeth, Kitty, and Darcy had by this time reached Lucas Lodge, where the younger Miss Bennet wished to call on Maria. Elizabeth, momentarily reminded of the gypsy stableman whom she had seen at the roadside with Lady Catherine, experienced a disturbance at her womanhood as she recalled the image of his manhood and how the hand of his companion had forced from it his pleasure. Her desire for Darcy had never been so powerful as it was now, and Elizabeth hoped she could keep hold of her composure and resist the temptation to repeat what had been an unfortunate lapse of dignity for them both. That such overtures would even be welcomed gave her yet more reason for restraint.

When Kitty left them, Elizabeth walked on with Darcy alone. She believed an occasion to address the matter of Lydia and Wickham might never again be repeated, and she forced herself to speak. "Mr. Darcy, I can no longer help thanking you for your unexampled kindness to my poor sister," she began. "Ever since I have known of it, I have been most anxious to acknowledge to you how gratefully I feel it."

Darcy, clearly surprised, expressed his dismay that she had been informed of the particulars of what was to have been a confidential matter between himself and the Gardiners.

To this Elizabeth replied, "You must not blame my aunt. Lydia's thoughtlessness first betrayed to me that you had been concerned in the matter. Let me thank you again and again, in the name of all my family, for that generous compassion that induced you to take so much trouble, and bear so many mortifications, for the sake of discovering them."

"If you *will* thank me," said he, "let it be for yourself alone. That the wish of giving happiness to you might add force to the other inducements that led me on, I shall not attempt to deny. But your family owes me nothing. Much as I respect them, I believe I thought only of you."

Elizabeth was too much embarrassed to say a word. After a pause, he added, "You are too generous to trifle with me. If your feelings are still what they were last April, tell me so at once. *My* affections and wishes are unchanged, but one word from you will silence me on this subject forever."

To hear Darcy speak in this way gave Elizabeth a joy so great she believed she could not bear it, and she glanced down at his breeches, the flap of which protruded to such a degree that she thought the fabric might rip. When she at last responded, it was with the declaration that her sentiments had undergone so material a change since the period to which he alluded as to make her receive with gratitude and pleasure his present assurances.

The delight on Darcy's face was manifest, and he grasped hold of Elizabeth's shoulders and brought her forward in a kiss. "Oh, Miss Bennet!" he cried, pulling her to him in an embrace.

Elizabeth felt his manhood pressing against her loins and once again experienced an overwhelming need to take it into her mouth. That she now had the sanction of Darcy's love gave her a courage she never knew she possessed, and she dropped to her knees before him, reaching for the buttons on his breeches. Darcy looked down at her with great tenderness, and she saw that his eyes had filled with tears; indeed, her love for him had never been so strong as it was at this moment. His manhood sprang out to greet her, its state of excitement having already caused the flap of skin at the tip to retract. Elizabeth placed on it an affectionate kiss, her tongue licking shyly over the exposed crown, her actions encouraging a drop of moisture to escape from the tiny opening located there. As she licked it away, the flesh within her cleft pulsed in response, and she felt very much near the brink of release. Her first taste of him brought back to Elizabeth every moment of their encounter at Lambton, and she took hold of his length so that she could better direct its movements, no longer concerned about matters of propriety. It felt right and natural that she should be pleasuring him in this manner—and that she *was* pleasuring him there could be no doubt, for Darcy cried out her name again and again, his fingers grasping her hair with a fierceness born of desperation as her mouth drew hungrily upon him.

Darcy's satisfaction with her conduct made Elizabeth long to act with even greater daring, and, with her other hand, she cradled in her palm the pouch located beneath his manhood, squeezing it gently and in time with the movements of her mouth. That she had chosen, by instinct, an action that could bring still further delight was manifest as Darcy began to groan in earnest, thrusting his loins forward so that he could reach deep into her throat. His thighs began to tremble, as did the object in Elizabeth's mouth, and in one sudden movement he threw back his head, shouting her name to the sky as he filled her mouth with his sweetness, all of which she lovingly swallowed.

Not long afterward Elizabeth found herself lying back on the grass, the hems of her garments raised to an immodest height as Darcy knelt before her with his face between her thighs, his mouth moving with growing assuredness against the place of her womanhood. She had nearly wept with embarrassment when he parted her folds with his thumbs and spent some time in just studying her. For Darcy to find much to interest him here was a surprise to Elizabeth, though not an unpleasant one. The tip of his tongue had teased her in a most vexing fashion, concentrating on the ridge of flesh his thumbs had uncovered and even being so daring as to dip inside her, at which point she heard herself emit an unladylike squeal, corresponding with Darcy's ungentlemanly groans, which quivered agreeably against her womanly parts. That Elizabeth was in a heightened state of excitement was made evident by her flushed countenance and the amount of moisture she had deposited on Darcy's lips, and she fixed her fingers in his hair, urging his mouth against her. It was equally evident that Darcy was finding much to be enjoyed in the activity, for he had earlier neglected to recover his decorum by returning himself to his breeches, and when Elizabeth reached for his manhood, she discovered it in a renewed state of readiness. As she imagined it filling her, she experienced that astonishing sensation of being lifted high up into the sky, then just as suddenly dropped. "Oh, Mr. Darcy!" she cried, trapping his head with her thighs until her rapture had at last calmed.

They found at last, on examining their watches, that it was time to go, and they returned to Longbourn, their appearances in some disarray, as were those of Jane and Bingley, who had arrived some time before them. "Dear Lizzy, where can you have been walking to?" inquired Jane when they entered the house. She replied that they had wandered farther than they realized, and, though she colored as she spoke, neither this nor anything else awakened a suspicion of the truth. Elizabeth anticipated what would be felt in the family when her situation became known; she was quite aware that no one liked Darcy and feared that it was a dislike not even all his fortune and consequence might do away with.

That night she opened her heart to Jane, who looked all amazement. "You are joking, Lizzy. This cannot be— engaged to Mr. Darcy! No, you shall not deceive me. I know it to be impossible!"

"This is a wretched beginning indeed!" cried Elizabeth. "My sole dependence was on you, and I am sure nobody else will believe me, if you do not. I speak nothing but the truth. He still loves me, and we are engaged." Elizabeth's complexion radiated an appearance of good health from her earlier encounter with Darcy's tongue, and she felt as if her womanly folds had been kissed by the sun from his lips having been there. This, however, she could not relay to Jane; despite their closeness, there were some matters best kept from a sister, even a most beloved one.

The two continued to talk in earnest, Jane seeking every assurance that Elizabeth did, indeed, love Mr. Darcy. "Now I know that you will be as happy as myself," said Jane. "But Lizzy, you have been very sly. How little did you tell me of what passed at Pemberley and Lambton."

Elizabeth flushed, remembering not for the first time in so many hours how she had taken her first taste of Darcy when he had called on her at Lambton. It appeared that she could no longer conceal from Jane his share in Lydia's marriage, and she went on to supply the details and the motives of her secrecy, until there remained only the particulars of her intimacy with Darcy that were left unrevealed.

Chapter Twenty-Eight

"GOOD GRACIOUS!" CRIED MRS. BENNET AS SHE STOOD AT a window the next morning. "If that disagreeable Mr. Darcy is not coming here again with our dear Bingley! What can he mean by being so tiresome as to be always coming here? Lizzy, you must walk out with him again, that he may not be in Bingley's way."

Elizabeth could hardly keep from laughing at so convenient a proposal, yet was vexed that her mother should direct at him such an epithet. When no one else was of a mind to join the party, Elizabeth and Darcy set off on their own. During their walk, it was resolved that Mr. Bennet's consent should be sought in the course of the evening. Though Elizabeth did not fear so much for her father's disapprobation, it was her mother's that gave her cause for concern. So, too, did the disapproval of Darcy's aunt, whose determination to prevent their marriage bordered on the violent.

"You need not distress yourself. Lady Catherine's unjustifiable endeavors to separate us were the means of removing any doubts I might once have harbored," replied Darcy with a smile. He took Elizabeth into an embrace, and they once again found themselves on the grass with his head beneath her gown as she allowed her thighs to fall open in a most unseemly manner. For his tongue to have discovered yet more of interest there was of surprise to Elizabeth, though it provided her with no basis for complaint, not even when it sought out the opening to her backside, despite the profuseness of her embarrassment. The sensations it inspired were most agreeable, becoming even more so when he replaced his tongue with his finger, causing Elizabeth to react with a violence she did not know she possessed, her cries like those of some mad creature. That Darcy should think ill of her no longer distressed Elizabeth, as all had been settled between them. His desires had become hers, and as she urged her backside toward him to indicate her acceptance of his overtures, his finger forced from her a release, followed by a second from his tongue.

Within moments Darcy had laid himself upon her, and Elizabeth felt something hard pressing against the opening of her womanhood. How very much she had wished for this, yet now that it was happening, she worried that she might not be able to offer his manhood suitable accommodation. The thought of being a disappointment to him filled her with dread, but when she looked up into his eyes, she saw only love in them as he began to slowly push his way inside her. Elizabeth felt herself opening to him like a flower coming into bloom, and she gave herself over to enjoyment, her backside still burning with the remembered sensations of his finger, until the next thing she knew she had accepted his manhood in its entirety. Darcy, with great gentleness, began to move inside her, inquiring frequently as to her well-being, to which she offered her assurances. As their lips came together, Elizabeth tasted herself on his and was for a moment embarrassed until she remembered that he had exhibited no such sentiment when his mouth had been engaged with the source.

Darcy, overwhelmed with love for Miss Bennet, had never dared to hope this day would come. Her earlier reproof, so well applied, he would never forget: ". . . had you behaved in a more gentlemanlike manner." Indeed, was he behaving in a gentlemanlike manner now? Yet he had but to see the warmth in her eyes to know that she bore him no ill feeling. He would not for the world have caused her harm; therefore he kept back the more primitive aspects of his nature so as to render her experience as pleasant as possible, though he did suffer some shame from having breached the opening of her backside with his finger. He had been quite astonished by her reaction, and he took it as encouragement that she would at some point in the future accept him in this manner, which pleased him greatly. Darcy's manhood threatened to release his pleasure with every stroke, making his journey all the dearer, his restraint partly for himself in his desire to prolong it. That Miss Bennet had not been tampered with in this region was manifest; her womanhood fit him like the most elegant glove, and it required all his will not to lose himself before he had even begun. He now knew that Colonel Fitzwilliam's tale about his dealings with Miss Bennet was false. His cousin had offered him a most salacious report of having engaged with her in an intimate manner while at Rosings, and Darcy, as a matter of pride, wished to refute it. The tightness with which her interior held his manhood was all the proof he required.

Unable to fight the pressure building in his loins, Darcy, pulling Elizabeth to his chest, gave forth one great shudder, filling her secret core with the many long months of his need until he collapsed upon her. Elizabeth emitted a small cry from the force of his love, which grew into a more forceful cry as she, too, joined with his pleasure, its arrival causing her pelvis to thrust upward, taking him still deeper. Darcy remained locked within her, feeling the pulsing in her womanhood slowly recede. The couple lay in this way for some while, until at last his manhood lost its vigor and slipped out of her. He assisted her up from the ground and, noting her distress on discovering his liquids escaping out of her and down her thighs, offered his handkerchief so that she might wipe them away, quickly remembering himself to turn away as she did so.

After Elizabeth had regained her modesty, she took up again the teasing banter that had been one of the characteristics that had first drawn Darcy to her. She very much longed to know if his intention to resume his earlier courtship had existed from the start or was merely the result of impetuousness. "Pray, Mr. Darcy, what did you come down to Netherfield for? Was it merely to ride to Longbourn and be embarrassed, or had you intended any more serious consequence?"

"My real purpose was to see *you*, and to judge, if I could, whether I might ever hope to make you love me," he countered with great solemnity.

The couple returned to the house together, even happier than they had been on their departure.

In the evening, soon after Mr. Bennet withdrew to the library, Elizabeth saw Darcy rise and follow him, and her agitation was extreme. Though her father's opposition seemed unlikely, his unhappiness that his favorite child should distress him by her choice and fill him with fears and regrets in disposing of her was a wretched reflection on their union, and she sat in misery till Darcy appeared again with instructions for her to join Mr. Bennet in the library.

Elizabeth discovered her father walking about the room, looking grave and anxious. "Lizzy, are you out of your senses, to be accepting this man? Have you not always hated him? He is rich, to be sure, and you may have more fine clothes and fine carriages than Jane. But will they make you happy? We all know him to be a proud, unpleasant sort of man, but this would be nothing if you really liked him."

"I love him," she replied, with tears in her eyes. "Indeed, he has no improper pride. He is perfectly amiable. You do not know what he really is; pray, do not pain me by speaking of him in such terms."

"I have given him my consent. He is the kind of man to whom I should never dare refuse anything he condescended to ask. I now give it to *you*, if you are resolved on having him. But let me advise you to think better of it. I know that you could be neither happy nor respectable unless you truly esteemed your husband and looked up to him as a superior. Let me not have the grief of seeing you unable to respect your partner in life."

Elizabeth knew that he was referring to her mother, and the realization grieved her. She was earnest and solemn in her reply, and provided repeated assurances that Mr. Darcy was the object of her choice. To complete the favorable impression, she told her father what he had done for Lydia. Mr. Bennet heard her with astonishment.

Mr. Bennet's astonishment, however, would be trifling when compared to that of Mrs. Bennet, whose joy at the match was expressed in a hysterical manner the likes of which gave the family cause to reconsider a forced confinement to her bed. "Good gracious, dear me! Mr. Darcy! Who would have thought it! Oh, my sweetest Lizzy! How rich and how great you will be! What pin money, what jewels, what carriages you will have! Jane's is nothing to it. I am so pleased—so happy. Such a charming man!—so handsome, so tall! Three daughters married! Ten thousand a year! Oh, Lord! But my dearest love, tell me what dish Mr. Darcy is particularly fond of, that I may have it tomorrow."

It came to the relief of all when the evening drew to a close, and Elizabeth was at last able to retire to the peace of her bedchamber. Her flesh was in a heightened state of awareness from Darcy's earlier attentions and it required little effort to send herself into flight, not once, not twice, but *thrice*. That their marriage should be a happy one she had no doubt!

Chapter Twenty-Nine

JOYOUS WITH ALL HER MATERNAL FEELINGS WAS THE DAY ON which Mrs. Bennet got rid of her two most deserving daughters. Although she still suffered occasionally with her nerves, particularly when she looked at Mr. Bennet and compared him with the handsome redcoat of her youth, she was, for the most part, much improved. She no longer required the potions of the gypsies, which was just as well, for they had moved on, as travelers are wont to do. Even the gypsy stableman from Lucas Lodge had gone, having been required at Hunsford parish at the request of Mr. Collins.

Mr. Bennet missed his second daughter exceedingly and sought frequent solace in Hill's ample flesh. With three daughters married and his pursuit of drawings at an end, he now found that there were sufficient funds in the household accounts with which to meet the housekeeper's demands. Each party benefited, and it was an equitable arrangement for all.

Kitty, to her very material advantage, spent the chief of her time with her two elder sisters. In society so superior to what she had generally known, her improvement was great, as were the chances of her finding a husband. From the disadvantage of Lydia's society she was carefully kept, and though Mrs. Wickham frequently invited her to come and stay, Mr. Bennet would never consent to her going.

Mary, who now wore her long beard with pride, was no longer mortified by the comparisons between her sisters' beauty and her own. Rather she was drawn further toward the pursuit of her rabbinical studies, and had even convinced her father to allow her to follow a course of study in the holy city of Jerusalem, the expense of which would be borne in equal measure by her new brothers-in-law, Mr. Bingley and Mr. Darcy.

As for Wickham and Lydia, their characters suffered no alteration from the marriage of the two eldest Bennet sisters. Wickham, deciding the militia life was not for him, returned to London and the business of his bawdy house, with Lydia taking on the management of the ladies and occasionally stepping in when illness struck. And by these rather extraordinary means, the Wickhams came to discover marital bliss.

Miss Bingley, who was very deeply mortified by Darcy's marriage, continued her activities with the birch, engaging nearly every husband in the neighborhood with her unique talents. That she was never to mark the one backside she most desired to mark had struck a crueler blow than those she meted out, and her curious pastime was pursued with rather less zealousness than before. Even Mr. Hurst would note a shortage of enthusiasm, though he still offered himself with great regularity to his sister-in-law, hoping she might one day regain her fervor.

Lady Catherine was most indignant on the marriage of her nephew and abused both parties in her reply to the letter announcing its arrangement. The residents of Hunsford parish would be made to feel her wrath, as everyone from the butcher to the gravedigger found himself being punished for crimes ranging from too much fat on a cut of meat to the untidiness of a freshly filled grave. Miss de Bourgh was of too sickly a constitution to participate, and she spent most of her time indoors, listening to the screams.

Mr. Collins lived contentedly at Hunsford House with Mrs. Collins, continuing to enjoy the generous patronage and condescension of Lady Catherine in addition to the handsome delights of the gypsy stableman who looked after the parsonage's only horse. Despite his great satisfaction in life, he smiled less than ever, for he now exhibited not just the absence of one front tooth, but two, though its loss had been most agreeably suffered.

The Gardiners, along with Mr. Gardiner's desert damsel, made frequent visits to Pemberley. Darcy, as well as Elizabeth, loved the couple dearly, and they were both ever sensible of the warmest gratitude toward the two persons who, by bringing Elizabeth into Derbyshire, had been the means of uniting them.

The End

MITZI SZERETO is an author and anthology editor of erotic and multigenre fiction and nonfiction. She has her own blog, Errant Ramblings: Mitzi Szereto's Weblog (mitziszereto. com/blog), and a Web TV channel, Mitzi TV (mitziszereto. com/tv), which covers the "quirky" side of London. Her books include *In Sleeping Beauty's Bed: Erotic Fairy Tales*; *Getting Even: Revenge Stories*; *The New Black Lace Book of Women's Sexual Fantasies*; *Wicked: Sexy Tales of Legendary Lovers*; *Dying for It: Tales of Sex and Death*; and the *Erotic Travel Tales* anthologies. A popular social media personality and frequent interviewee, she has pioneered erotic writing workshops in the UK and Europe and has lectured in creative writing at several British universities. Originally from the US, she lives in Greater London, but can occasionally be spied taking tea with Miss Austen at her home in Hampshire.

More from Mitzi Szereto

Out of This World Romance

Steamlust
Steampunk Erotic Romance
Edited by Kristina Wright

Shiny brass and crushed velvet; mechanical inventions and romantic conventions; sexual fantasy and kinky fetish: this is a lush and fantastical world of women-centered stories and romantic scenarios, a first for steampunk fiction.
ISBN 978-1-57344-721-8 $14.95

The Sweetest Kiss
Ravishing Vampire Erotica
Edited by D.L. King

These sanguine tales give new meaning to the term "dead sexy" and feature beautiful bloodsuckers whose desires go far beyond blood.
ISBN 978-1-57344-371-5 $15.95

Dream Lover
Paranormal Tales of Erotic Romance
Edited by Kristina Wright

A potent potion of fun and sexy tales filled with male fairies and clairvoyant scientists, as well as darkly erotic tales of ghosts, shapeshifters and possession.
ISBN 978-1-57344-655-6 $14.95

Fairy Tale Lust
Erotic Fantasies for Women
Edited by Kristina Wright

Award-winning novelist and erotica writer Kristina Wright goes over the river and through the woods to find the sexiest fairy tales ever written.
ISBN 978-1-57344-397-5 $14.95

In Sleeping Beauty's Bed
Erotic Fairy Tales
By Mitzi Szereto

"Who can resist the erotic origins of fairy tales from Little Red to Rapunzel's long braid? Szereto knows her way around the mythic scholarship and the most outrageous sexual deviations in Pandora's Box." —Susie Bright
ISBN 978-1-57344-367-8 $16.95

Red Hot Erotic Romance

Obsessed
Erotic Romance for Women
Edited by Rachel Kramer Bussel

These stories sizzle with the kind of obsession that is fueled by our deepest desires, the ones that hold couples togeth-er, the ones that haunt us and don't let go. Whether just-blooming passions, rekindled sparks or reinvented relation-ships, these lovers put the object of their obsession first.
ISBN 978-1-57344-718-8 $14.95

Passion
Erotic Romance for Women
Edited by Rachel Kramer Bussel

Love and sex have always been intimately intertwined—and *Passion* shows just how delicious the possibilities are when they mingle in this sensual collection edited by award-winning author Rachel Kramer Bussel.
ISBN 978-1-57344-415-6 $14.95

Girls Who Bite
Lesbian Vampire Erotica
Edited by Delilah Devlin

Bestselling romance writer Delilah Devlin and her contributors add fresh girl-on-girl blood to the pantheon of the paranormal. The stories in *Girls Who Bite* are varied, un-expected, and soul-scorching.
ISBN 978-1-57344-715-7 $14.95

Carnal Machines
Steampunk Erotica
Edited by D. L. King

In this decadent fusing of technology and romance, outstanding contemporary erot-ica writers use the enthralling possibilities of the 19th-century steam age to tease and titillate.
ISBN 978-1-57344-654-9 $14.95

Heat Wave
Hot, Hot, Hot Erotica
Edited by Alison Tyler

What could be sexier or more seductive than bare, sun-warmed skin? Bestselling erotica author Alison Tyler gathers explicit stories of summer sex bursting with the sweet eroticism of swimsuits, sprinklers, and ripe strawberries.
ISBN 978-1-57344-710-2 $15.95

Best Erotica Series

"Gets racier every year."—*San Francisco Bay Guardian*

**Buy 4 books,
Get 1 FREE***

Best of Best Women's Erotica 2
Edited by Violet Blue
ISBN 978-1-57344-379-1 $15.95

Best Women's Erotica 2010
Edited by Violet Blue
ISBN 978-1-57344-373-9 $15.95

Best Women's Erotica 2009
Edited by Violet Blue
ISBN 978-1-57344-338-8 $15.95

Best Women's Erotica 2008
Edited by Violet Blue
ISBN 978-1-57344-299-2 $15.95

Best Bisexual Women's Erotica
Edited by Cara Bruce
ISBN 978-1-57344-320-3 $15.95

Best Fetish Erotica
Edited by Cara Bruce
ISBN 978-1-57344-355-5 $15.95

Best of Best Lesbian Erotica 2
Edited by Tristan Taormino
ISBN 978-1-57344-212-1 $17.95

Best Lesbian Erotica 2010
Edited by Kathleen Warnock. Selected and
introduced by BETTY.
ISBN 978-1-57344-375-3 $15.95

Best Gay Erotica 2010
Edited by Richard Labonté. Selected and
introduced by Blair Mastbaum.
ISBN 978-1-57344-374-6 $15.95

Best Gay Erotica 2009
Edited by Richard Labonté. Selected and
introduced by James Lear.
ISBN 978-1-57344-334-0 $15.95

Best Gay Erotica 2008
Edited by Richard Labonté. Selected and
introduced by Emanuel Xavier.
ISBN 978-1-57344-301-8 $14.95

In Sleeping Beauty's Bed
Erotic Fairy Tales
By Mitzi Szereto
ISBN 978-1-57344-367-8 $16.95

Can't Help the Way That I Feel
*Sultry Stories of African American Love,
Lust and Fantasy*
Edited by Lori Bryant-Woolridge
ISBN 978-1-57344-386-9 $14.95

Making the Hook-Up
Edgy Sex with Soul
Edited by Cole Riley
ISBN 1-57344-383-8 $14.95

---

* Free book of equal or lesser value. Shipping and applicable sales tax extra.
Cleis Press • (800) 780-2279 • orders@cleispress.com
www.cleispress.com

Ordering is easy! Call us toll free or fax us to place your MC/VISA order.
You can also mail the order form below with payment to:
Cleis Press, 2246 Sixth St., Berkeley, CA 94710.

ORDER FORM

QTY	TITLE	PRICE
———	————————————————————————	———
———	————————————————————————	———
———	————————————————————————	———
———	————————————————————————	———
———	————————————————————————	———
———	————————————————————————	———
———	————————————————————————	———

	SUBTOTAL	———
	SHIPPING	———
	SALES TAX	———
	TOTAL	———

Add $3.95 postage/handling for the first book ordered and $1.00 for each additional book. Outside North America, please contact us for shipping rates. California residents add 9.75% sales tax. Payment in U.S. dollars only.

* Free book of equal or lesser value. Shipping and applicable sales tax extra.

Cleis Press • Phone: (800) 780-2279 • Fax: (510) 845-8001
orders@cleispress.com • www.cleispress.com
You'll find more great books on our website

Follow us on Twitter @cleispress • Friend/fan us on Facebook